"ONE WICKED READ....

It seduces you...

teases and torments you...

then leaves you

screaming for more....

BRILLIANT."

—Larry Brooks

The power of attraction . . .

The art of seduction . . .

The thrill of surrender . . .

Jake & Mimi

A novel that takes you into the intoxicating private world of extreme pleasure — and into the mind of a secret player who wants to engage in the most dangerous game of all . . .

"A clever thriller and . . . [an] exploration of the outer reaches of pleasure and power . . . unusual and compelling." — *The Toronto Sun*

"Here's the first writer I've encountered in a long time whose prose can drink me under the table."
—Douglas Rushkoff, author of *Ecstasy Club*

JAKE & MIMI

FRANK BALDWIN

AN ONYX BOOK

ONYX
Published by New American Library, a division of
Penguin Putnam Inc., 375 Hudson Street,
New York, New York 10014, U.S.A.
Penguin Books Ltd, 80 Strand,
London WC2R 0RL, England
Penguin Books Australia Ltd, Ringwood,
Victoria, Australia
Penguin Books Canada Ltd, 10 Alcorn Avenue,
Toronto, Ontario, Canada M4V 3B2
Penguin Books (N.Z.) Ltd, 182–190 Wairau Road,
Auckland 10, New Zealand

Penguin Books Ltd, Registered Offices:
Harmonsworth, Middlesex, England

Published by Onyx, an imprint of New American Library, a division of
Penguin Putnam Inc. This edition is an authorized reprint of a Little,
Brown and Company hardcover. Reprinted by permission of Little, Brown
and Company.

First Printing, November 2002
10 9 8 7 6 5 4 3 2 1

Copyright © Frank Baldwin, 2002
All rights reserved

 REGISTERED TRADEMARK—MARCA REGISTRADA

Printed in the United States of America

PUBLISHER'S NOTE
This is a work of fiction. Names, characters, places, and incidents either are the
product of the author's imagination or are used fictitiously, and any resem-
blance to actual persons, living or dead, business establishments, events, or lo-
cales is entirely coincidental.

For Lora

PROLOGUE

Mimi Lessing stirs her hot cocoa with a spoon and then lifts the cup to her lips. She sits at a small table in Liaison, a café and consignment gallery in the West Village. She came from work, through the storm, and drops of rain still shine in her hair. But her table is near the fireplace, and the fire and the hot cocoa have warmed her. She wears a white silk wrap blouse, open at the neck to reveal a thin gold necklace with a single pearl at its center. When she is nervous, like now, she touches the pearl for comfort.

"You must have some questions, Mimi."

She looks into her cup and then lifts her eyes. "No, you've really thought of everything. Thank you."

The woman across from her is fifty, French, and elegant, with touches of silver in her cropped hair and a red scarf tied expertly at her neck.

"No questions?" she asks.

Mimi shakes her head, so the older woman starts

to gather up her papers from the table. She slides contracts and song lists and seating charts into a lavender binder, raises the binder to her chest, and then lays it down again on the table. She looks across at Mimi.

"I was your mother's idea, wasn't I?" she says.

Mimi puts down her cocoa. "It isn't that," she says quickly. "I'm grateful, really. You've done a wonderful job."

"What is it, then?"

Mimi's fingers find the pearl and press it into the soft well of her neck.

"It's just . . . I don't want the magic of the day to get lost . . . in all the details."

The woman reaches across the table and touches Mimi's cheek. "To be twenty-five," she says, smiling. "You'll have magic, Mimi, I promise." She rises from her chair, her long legs elegant in a black pantsuit. "Do you know the key to magic?" she asks, gathering a red shawl around her shoulders.

"No," says Mimi.

"Preparation," she says. "I'll call you next week."

Mimi watches her make her way through the quiet café, then sighs and finishes her cocoa. The ceiling lights are dim and far apart, but the glow of the fire plays over her pure complexion.

She looks out across the room, at the three paintings that hang on the far wall. Her eyes are soon drawn to the last of them, a Spanish hilltop wedding scene. It is beautiful in its simplicity. A single table for the wedding party and guests, with the bride and groom at its head. Their hands are clasped together, their eyes joyous. Mimi smiles wistfully. No seating charts or song lists, no wedding planner.

"Can I get you something else?"

The waiter's voice breaks her reverie. "No," she says. "Thank you." She looks again at the painting, then stands and puts on the beige fitted jacket of her work suit. She lifts her purse off the chair and walks to the front of the café, where she pauses for a moment in the doorway, looking out at the driving rain. She readies her umbrella and steps out the door.

The café is nearly empty now. Soft piano mixes with the murmur of the few scattered patrons and the occasional hiss of the steamer from behind the counter.

Through the streaked glass of the front window I can still see her. I take a sip of cappuccino and watch her red umbrella disappear into the night. I look into my cup and then back at the painting on the far wall. I study the eyes of the Spanish bride. The artist has captured them perfectly, captured the moment when a young woman passes from innocence. I take another sip and lay the porcelain cup on its saucer.

Soon Miss Lessing will pass from innocence. I take a dollar bill from my wallet and place it on the counter, and stand and pull my raincoat around me. It took me nearly fifty years to find her, and six weeks is all the time we have left alone together. Enough time, I hope, for her innocence to restore my own.

CHAPTER ONE

Some of us guys who put no stock in the next world like to lean pretty hard into this one. I lean hardest on the weekends.

Most Fridays I set aside for the gang, but thanks to Pardo, I'm on my own tonight. Pardo had pitched Sid's bachelor party as a "low-key affair." Nobody told that to the girls. They turned out to be a lot friendlier than anyone bargained for, and when Jeremy, wrecked from shots and still reeling from the show, staggered home to find Cindy waiting up for him in a teddy, offering a little late-night relief in exchange for some honest reporting, the guy stuck his neck right in the noose.

By eight the next morning the bride was on the warpath, crying on the phone to her bridesmaids and threatening to call the whole thing off. "Don't tempt me," said Sid through his hangover. By evening it was all back on schedule, of course, but now everyone in the gang is pulling wife or girl-friend duty for the next two weekends at least.

Everyone but me.

I'm single and free, and if tonight goes the way I want it to, I won't miss the guys at all. Beer, poker, camaraderie — I'll take them nine Fridays out of ten. Tonight, though, I've got a shot at the water of life.

All day at my desk it's been building in me. I could hardly keep my mind on the new account. It's a tough one, too. Art Jensen, a Queens beauty shop maven with a Mafia don's regard for our Tax Code. By rights he'll owe a couple of hundred grand, minimum, but if I can't figure a way to tell him "refund" come April 15, he'll be calling our senior partners at home. That's what I get for being the new guy.

I left the office at six, changed quickly at my place, then ran the sixty-hour work week right out of me. Started into the park in the last soft light of day, ran east to the water and then down along it, past the heliport, the ballfields, clear to the Brooklyn Bridge, touching the base of her and turning for home as the lights of the city came on and the cool spring night came down to meet me. After a long shower I poured a tall, bracing glass of Absolut and now I'm sipping it out here on the fire escape in shorts, looking down on the street below and thinking of the night ahead.

She'll be a tough one, all right. The toughest yet. But what a payoff. I change into a soft shirt and slacks, lock the door behind me, and step out of my walkup and into the Manhattan night.

Broadway is no misnomer. Thank you, Spring.

The women have put away their heavy coats and are out in blouses and shawls and hose. They are everywhere, stepping sensuously from cabs, gliding from the mouths of the subway. Alone, in pairs, on the arms of men. Even the billboards have caught the spirit. Angelina Jolie, wearing almost nothing, looks down from a movie marquee, and Drew Barrymore, in not much more, flashes by on the side of a bus. I turn onto Eighty-first Street, primed.

Her name is Melissa Clay.

Last Sunday I saw her for the first time in twelve years, the first time since I was a kid of fourteen and she, at eighteen, the hottest girl in our small American school in Tokyo. She was the eldest of three sisters, spaced two years apart, meaning that from the day I found out what my pecker was for until the day I left for college, there wasn't a two-hour stretch when one of them wasn't setting me off. Shana and Beth were star material, too, but Melissa was already a budding young woman, and to a kid of fourteen she was as magical — and as out of reach — as a princess.

The Clays were missionaries and summered, as we did, in a modest international resort community on a lake in the Japanese Alps. There were about a hundred of us families, most from the church but a few stray businessmen, too, like Dad, who rented the small log cabins from June through August each year for a couple of months of rustic living. There were no televisions, no telephones, even, and you hauled your drinking water from a well. They were simple summers, full of sun, exercise, and good country food. The missionaries came for the big church down by the lake, for their prayer groups and hymnals, and for the feeling of community they got from being with their own kind. The secular types, like my folks, came to beat the killer Tokyo heat, and when the religion in the air got too thick for them, they countered with the easy porch life of cards and afternoon drinks. As for us kids, we had the lake and, especially, the Boathouse.

The Boathouse was an old wooden wonder built onto the docks of the swimming area. It was open to the air, with low benches for lounging, a Ping-Pong table that worked on the challenge system, and a stereo in the corner, complete with a pile of last year's rock records from the States. I was a crack Ping-Pong player, true, and a music hound, but I wasn't thinking table tennis or the Clash when I grabbed my towel from the porch each morning, took lunch money from Mom, and promised her I wouldn't be late for dinner. No, I hurried to the Boathouse because from there you could see the whole swimming area, which meant that morning to sundown, every day but the Sabbath, you could see Melissa Clay.

Jesus, she was something. Close my eyes today and I can still see her in that black two-piece, sunning on her towel on the docks. Two, sometimes three times an hour I'd walk by her, feigning interest in a Jet Skier or parasailer out on the lake. She'd be on her back, her eyes closed against the sun, and

I'd get in a good two-second stare. Twenty minutes later, back in the Boathouse, I'd see her turn over, see Beth or Shana drip lotion onto her smooth back and rub it in, and I'd start down the dock again, gazing out at the mountains that rimmed the lake as if I'd just noticed they were there and needed to walk to the end of the dock for a closer look. The strings of her bikini top would be undone now, lying loose on the towel beside her, and if I timed it right, she would raise up on her elbows to read just as I passed and I'd get the barest hot glimpse at those magic breasts.

Once or twice a summer I'd hit the mother lode. I'd be horsing around with a buddy out on the raft and we'd look in and see her rise from her towel, walk to the diving board, dive gracefully into the cold lake, and start our way. As she moved smoothly through the water, her gorgeous face breaking the surface closer and closer with each breast stroke, even I — the smart-ass atheist — felt a bit of the divine spirit in the air. My buddy and I would lie down (on our stomachs, of course) and watch her through half-closed eyes, pretending to be jolted awake by the dip of the raft as she pulled herself up the short wooden ladder, dripping wet, her nipples hard as tacks through that black top. She'd smile beautifully at us and then, just as innocently as you like, tug casually at her suit bottom where it had bunched up under her sweet ass. Then she'd sit down, just inches away, squeeze the water from her blond hair, and ease onto her back, one golden leg straight out, the other knee pointed up at her grateful creator.

Gott in Himmel, as the German Lutherans used to say on bingo night, when Divine Providence delivered them the winning number. A half hour later she'd still be there, on her stomach now maybe, and we'd still be there, too, stealing looks up her legs, our hard-ons pressed into the raft, wondering idly what it's like to die of sunburn, because there sure wasn't a chance in hell that we could even turn over, let alone stand up, while Melissa Clay lay wet and perfect beside us.

One Saturday a month the teenagers were allowed a dance in the Boathouse. Man, the charge those nights used to give me. If the Mets go to the Series this year, and the Series goes seven games, and on the morning of the seventh game our firm's senior partner, Abe Stein, hands me two primo tickets and his granddaughter and warns me not to bring her home a virgin, then I might feel again the rush that would hit me as I walked down the quiet lake road, a kid of fourteen, to the Boathouse on the night of a dance. And not because I had any dance moves to try out or any real prospect at action, even. No, simply because I knew that Melissa Clay would be there and that she would come, as she always did, in a T-shirt and no bra.

I'm not saying she was a loose girl. Not at all. She was a sweet, healthy missionary kid who everybody loved — the pious adults, especially, because she never missed a Sunday service and always stopped to smile and talk when she passed them on the path. I'd bet all I have that she left for college in the States that fall with her cherry. She was a free spirit, that's all, and so innocent that if she didn't feel like putting on a bra under her tie-dyed T-shirt, well, she didn't and that was that. No one made anything of it.

Except us horny teens. We were a raw bunch. Across the pond, my American cousins were getting drunk at thirteen, high at fourteen, and into girls — literally — a year later. Over in Tokyo, meanwhile, we were still learning grammar and algebra, of all things, instead of backseat moves and self-defense, and making it through to graduation without ever catching a whiff of a joint. Sex? It was a rumor, and a distant one.

That last dance of the summer, in her last summer at the lake, Melissa Clay looked as good as a girl can look. Dancing barefoot on the wooden planks of the Boathouse, the strobe light freezing her in magic pose after magic pose, she had me at the breaking point even before Tim Crockett asked her for a dance — or rather, took her hand and coolly pulled her out onto the floor, because Tim didn't have to *ask* any girl. He was nineteen, in college, drank beer, smoked cigarettes, bought his clothes in the States, and, the word was, "knew what to do with it," whatever that meant.

In the corner, all of us kids started elbowing one another, and, sure enough, Tim wasted no time putting his hands right on her. Put them on her hips as they danced, and sweet Melissa smiled and moved in close, turning innocently in his hands even, let-

ting him drink in her taut ass, then moving away
just as his hands slipped down to it. Seconds later
he was in close again, and when this time he started
his hands up her belly, she let them climb up to
within a couple of inches of her carefree breasts and
then, still smiling, took his wrists in her hands and
moved them back down, then danced off a few
steps and came back to him, taking *his* surprised
hands in *hers* now and placing them on her belt,
smiling like an angel as he lifted them, lifted them,
lifted them to the very base of her perfect pair before she laughed, pulled them down, and danced
away again.

No matador ever worked a bull as well. Or left
one in worse shape. When the song set ended and
Tim, trying hard to keep his college cool, stood in
close and whispered a question to her, she laughed
and shook her head sweetly. Ten minutes later we
could see Tim sitting alone at the end of the dock,
slugging back a can of beer that he was using, I'm
sure, to ice himself down with between sips.

We kids were about at our limit, too, and when
ten o'clock came and the social chairman strolled
in, switched on the lights, locked the stereo cabinet,
and announced that the dance was over, we hud-
dled in a pack on the lake road, calling good-bye to
Melissa Clay as she disappeared around the bend
with Beth and Shana, her laughing "bye!" still in
our ears and the thought of those sweet breasts still
in our heads as we synchronized our watches, nodded that we'd all follow through on it, and then

raced home to our respective cabins to whack off, in
unison, at precisely 10:17.

Damn. It all comes back like a movie. And then
to see her again last week — unbelievable. I'd met
Pardo at the Howling Wolf for a quick Sunday
night drink and was walking home up Amsterdam,
passing one of the tiny, one-woman Benetton shops
that dot the avenues and stay open each night until
ten. I glanced in the window and stopped dead. I
walked to the glass. Twelve years, but I knew her
instantly. Knew those quick, blue eyes. That angel's
face, the long, blond hair swept back now with a
hairband. It was Melissa Clay.

I reached for the door but then checked myself. I
watched her as she talked to a customer, standing
as only a woman can, one small foot pointing in
front of her and the other off to the side. Her legs
were still thin and fine, but now they led up to a
woman's ass. I saw her customer laugh and turn
with her bags toward the door, and I ducked
quickly into a doorway before Melissa's eyes could
follow her and see me through the glass. I stayed in
the doorway as the customer walked to the curb,
waved down a taxi, climbed in, and sped away. I
stayed another thirty seconds and then, not risking
a last look in the window, started slowly up Amsterdam again, my mind already working a week
ahead.

I had another prospect, true. Debbie Collins, a
sassy dance major I'd known up at school and had
run in to again at an alumni mixer two weeks back.
She'd been a hot little number on the Hill and had

lost nothing in the four years since, and I'd lain awake just the night before working out a plan of attack. As I turned onto Eighty-second Street, though, and made for home, I knew that Debbie Collins would have to wait. She was a treat, yes, but this city was full of treats. It held only one Melissa Clay.

And now it's time. I turn onto Amsterdam at 9:55. She will be closing up in minutes. I stop in front of the bookstore next door, pretending to look at the same five fiction titles that have sat in the window all year. I take a breath.

She won't recognize me, probably, but when I say my name, it will land deep. Ours was a small community, and the ties strong and lasting. The Clays, I knew, had retired to a small Baptist town in the South years ago, so Melissa would have been cut off from the country where she was raised.

Through the glass I see her in the back, folding blouses at a small counter. She wears a sparse white dress, the impossibly thin straps just visible under her open red sweater. I walk inside and she looks up at the sound of the bell.

"Hi," she says.

"Hi. I need scarves," I say, walking to a rack of them, "and I've got no eye for them. Can you help?"

"Sure." She smiles and comes from behind the counter. Her dress comes just to her knees, and her legs are bare — *bare* — underneath. She wears a thin anklet and clogs. "You must have done a good deed today — we're having a sale."

She steps into the light, and I see her full for the first time. She's all I'd hoped. Beautiful, still, but working at it now. Aerobics, probably, and eye cream, and even so, just months, maybe weeks from the start of the long, gentle slide.

"Melissa? Melissa Clay?"

She looks into my face, startled. Smiling still, but caught between her store manner, her natural friendliness, and the reserve this city gives every woman.

"Yes. Do I? . . ."

"Japan. The American School. I'm Jake Teller."

"My God."

She puts her soft, white hand quickly on my shoulder. I see the ring.

"I was Shana's year," I say.

She steps back and laughs, quiet and friendly, the kind you don't hear often in this city.

"This is New York," she says. "It had to happen, right? I can't believe it. Teller . . . the lake, too, right?" I nod. "You weren't church?"

"IBM. They let a few of us heathens in, remember?"

She laughs. "I remember. We envied you — you could swim on Sundays. Jake Teller. You were . . ."

"Fourteen when you were eighteen."

She looks me over.

"Yes. You never left the Boathouse."

I laugh. "That was me."

"And you recognized me?"

"You stood out, Melissa. Still do."

She smiles easily and touches my shoulder again.

"Thanks. Jake Teller — all grown up, and a charmer. I'll tell Shana. She's in North Carolina now."

"Doing well?"

"Yes. Two kids."

"Wow." I shake my head. "Have you been back? To Japan?"

"Not once. You know us missionary kids: When we leave, it's for good. You?"

"I was back last summer. And I made it to the lake."

"Last summer! Jake, what is it like? The same families, still?"

"A lot of them. It's . . . hey, do you want to . . . how about a drink? I'll fill you in."

She pauses just a fraction of a second, looks down, then back up at me.

"I'd love to."

"When do you close?"

"Two minutes ago. Let me get my things."

She walks to the back counter and takes her purse and a light coat from a chair. I help her into a sleeve.

"Well, thank you, Jake. Across the street is P. J. Clarke's. Is that all right?"

"They'll let us in? You're wearing a ring and I'm not bald."

"Is it like that?" She laughs. "I've never been."

"We'll be fine."

She locks the door behind us, and we cross the

street and step into P. J. Clarke's, a dark, upscale singles bar, all mahogany and mood music. I've seen a few last calls here. I walk her to a seat in the corner, where the bar meets the window and you can see out into the street, see the shops and the walkers and, a block up, the green entrance to the park. A big ex-athlete in a pressed white shirt slides two coasters in front of us and smiles.

"Absolut, straight," I say.

"A sea breeze, please," says Melissa. She laughs at the look I give her and touches my shoulder again. "Since college," she says.

"I thought even caffeine was a no-no. Do the folks know?"

"I broke it to them at the reception. What could they say?" She offers her left hand and I take it, raise it, and give her ring a long look.

"Congratulations."

"Thank you. It's been a year."

Our drinks come, I clink mine against hers, and we take our sips. Her sweater is only pulled round her, and I can see the tops of her golden breasts.

"So, the lake," she says. "Tell me it's the same?"

"You didn't hear?"

"What?" Her blue eyes crinkle with worry.

"The Boathouse."

She puts her hand on my chest.

"No."

"It's coming down. This summer or next."

"It can't."

"The prefecture wants to build a boardwalk. With shops."

"How awful. They must be fighting it."

"Trying to, but it doesn't look good. It *is* their country."

"But the Boathouse . . ."

Her soft eyes look down at the bar for a moment, and she sips from her drink. I motion with my eyes at her ring.

"Is he one of us?"

She shakes her head.

"A New Yorker, believe it or not."

"Will you take . . ."

"Steve."

". . . Steve over? To see it?"

She pauses. "I don't know. Someday . . ." She looks for words and I wait. "It's . . . hard, you know?"

I nod.

"You belong, but you don't," I say. "Just like over here."

"Yes." She looks at me quickly, a little more in her eyes now. "It's hard to explain to people, isn't it? The community. The . . ."

"Innocence."

"Yes."

The bartender stands before us.

"One more?" I ask her. She pauses, then nods. "Should you call Steve?" I ask. She hesitates.

"It's okay. Some nights I do inventory."

Our drinks come; I raise mine, she raises hers and waits.

"To the Boathouse," I say.

"Amen." She looks at me and shakes her head.

"Jake, you've been a shock. I haven't thought of those days in . . ." She looks into her glass and, maybe, back through the years. "Do you remember the dances?"

"You used to dance with Tim Crockett."

She puts her drink on the bar and looks at me, amazed. Her hand goes to my shoulder again, this time with a little pressure.

"Tim Crockett . . . there was a randy one."

"He kept moving his hands up your shirt, and you kept moving them down."

"Yes, and I wasn't . . ." She looks over, sees me blush, and laughs. "It's true what they say about junior-high boys, isn't it?"

"All of it," I say.

I finish my drink and she does the same, struggling with the last long sip.

"Do you miss it?" I ask.

"When I think of it. They were special days."

I stand and reach for my wallet. I look at her.

"The crossover?" I say. "You made it okay?"

She looks at me, then down, pauses, and lifts her purse and jacket from the chair. The crossover is what we ex-pat kids call the move back to the States. Most aren't ready when it comes, and some — girls, especially — it marks for good.

"Pretty well, Jake," she says. She fingers her ring and smiles. "But this *is* my second."

I pay the bill, and we walk out and back across the street. A taxi corners too fast, before we quite make the curb, and I take her elbow until we reach the sidewalk.

"Which way are you?" I ask, and then, before she can answer: "The scarves."

"Jake. You never got them."

"My sister's birthday is tomorrow," I say. We're silent a second. "I can come back. What time do you open?"

"Come on." She smiles. "It'll take two minutes. I know just the ones."

"You sure?"

"Of course."

She unlocks the door and we walk in, the sound of the bell loud now in the quiet, dark store. She quickly turns on the light, and we walk to the rack of scarves. She flips through them, stops, unclips a silken yellow one, and holds it up with one hand while smoothing it out with the other.

"What's her complexion?" she asks.

"Like yours."

She slips it over her neck and the two sides fall evenly over her breasts. She tosses one around her neck again with a flourish, laughing at the gesture.

"It's perfect," I say. "I'll take two."

"Two of the same?" she asks.

I nod. She pauses. "Let me get the other one from the back."

The only sound in the place is the rattle of the hanging beads as she walks through them into the back room. I wait one minute. Two. I walk to the doorway and look in. The small back room is filled with clothes, dresses and blouses hanging along the wall and sweaters and leggings stacked neatly on the counter. Melissa stands at a small

folding table, looking down at the two scarves she
has folded and laid in a box lined with soft tissue.
She doesn't look up, though she knows I'm in the
doorway, and I see that her small hands are not in
the box but gripping the edge of the table. I walk to
her and stand behind her. She turns slowly, her
eyes rising to mine, and in one smooth motion I
pick her up by the waist and sit her on the edge of
the table. Her lips open in surprise and her palms
go to my chest, but her eyes give her away.

"You don't have a sister, do you, Jake?" she asks
quietly.

"No."

I turn and walk back into the front room and to
the door. I turn the lock. I switch off the lights. I
step back through the beads again. She hasn't
moved. I hit the switch in here, too, and she is a vision on the small table, lit only by what little light
from the street filters through the beads. I walk to
her and whisper into the back of her neck.

"You have five seconds to tell me to leave."

I can hear just her breathing and the last gentle
click of the beads. One. Two. Three. Four.

"Leave."

I lift her sweater off her trembling shoulders. She
closes her eyes and grips the edge of the table
tightly, at first resisting against my hands, then letting me pull her down onto her back. She closes her
legs and holds her dress to her knees. The narrow
table is just wide enough for her, and I lift her
hands off her dress and let her smooth, golden
arms fall over the sides. I take the yellow cloth from

the box and, kneeling, tie it in a tight knot around her slim wrist, then pass it under the table; she gasps as I tie it around her other one. I rise, take the second scarf from the soft tissue, and lay it across her eyes. She is shaking.

"Jake," she whispers, but she is with me now, and she knows I know it.

She lifts her head and lets me knot the scarf. I slide her hairband off and run my fingers hard through her long hair. She wants to come up off the table, but the strong silk holds and all she can do to slow the surge in her is bring one knee up to her body and then down again. I walk around the table and take a long look at her before touching her again. I take off her clogs and run my hands up her calves and back down. I can see under her dress now, all the way up her legs to the white mound of her silk panties. They are wet already.

I lift a pair of scissors from the counter, and she gasps again as I start the flat edge of the blade up her legs and over her dress. At her shoulders I cut first one thin strap and then the other, then pull the dress down and off her and let it drop to the floor.

It isn't pleasure but the promise of it that takes women to the edge. She is in just bra and panties now, and desperate to be touched, but I step away and slowly undo the buttons on my shirt, watching her as she strains to listen, her lips parting as I pull my leather belt through the loops.

I leave her dressed that way for ten minutes, tracing my fingers from her face all down the length of her and then back, and so lightly that when at last I put true pressure on her taut belly, I think she'll come apart. Her skin smells better than any I can remember, the faintest trace of light spring perfume on her neck and wrists.

Her strapless bra opens in the front, and the click of the clasp brings another gasp from her. I'm careful not to touch her hard, beautiful breasts as I gently lift the soft bra off her and pull it out from under her back. All those years ago, at the lake, I'd seen only the outline of her nipples through that wet top. Now they are just beneath me, soft and pink, and when I breathe gently on them, she turns her cheek hard into the table. Her eyes, I know, are shut tight under the silk.

"Please," she whispers.

Still I don't touch them. I look down at the small white triangle of cloth that covers her softest spot. It is all she wears now, and it is soaked through. I roll it slowly down her thighs, over her knees, past her calves, and off her ankles, then trail it back up her skin and swipe it back and forth across her breasts, watching the nipples harden into the silk.

"I can't take it," she says.

But she must. Because these are the minutes each week that I live for. The edge, I call it, and Melissa Clay is about to hit it. If she knew how long I will ride her along it, she would faint dead away.

I run my fingers between her breasts and just around them before finally taking both in my hands and pressing them hard together.

"God!" she gasps, her small hands fists now, jerking against the taut scarf.

She wants to grab her hair or beat the table with her hands. To release, somehow, some portion of the pressure I've built in her. She can't, and then I put my lips on her, her neck first and then hard on her breasts, and all she can do to hold herself off is lock her ankles and squeeze her thighs tight together. It is her last defense, I know, against the pleasure coursing through her, so I take even this away, lifting her left ankle off her right and holding them, a foot apart, to the table. "Damn you!" she gasps. She is helpless.

Women almost never lose themselves completely. Even in sex, they show you what they want you to see. Until you get them to the edge. At the edge they are past all that. Past any scheming. Past all reserve, even. Their social side vanquished. Melissa is reaching it now, a sheen of sweat on her cheeks, her breathing all soft cries. If Steve walked in now, she wouldn't recognize him.

And I've barely started on her.

Guys reach our mark and that's it, but women — handled just right — can crest and crest. Melissa has reached the edge, so I ride her along it, touching her, finally, where she needs it, but not with the pressure she requires. A little pressure, then none, then more pressure, then none, then still more, then none again. Thirty seconds of this, forty-five, a minute. She hangs in only because she can't believe what she feels. Still I keep on, watching her soft face slam from side to side, and only when I see that she is at her end, truly at her end, when I'm afraid I'll lose her or someone will hear her from the street, only then do I grab her thighs, pull her down to the edge of the table and lift her thin ankles up onto my shoulders.

"God, please, God, please, God, please," over and over from her now, and still I take my time. I'm past ready, too, but I lock her legs against me, holding her still, and as she cries out, arching her back in one last effort to stem the rush, to survive just one second more, I drink in the full measure of this night.

Melissa Clay lies beneath me. The first crush of my adolescence, my first true fantasy, and not just beneath me but at my mercy, helpless with pleasure and begging to be finished off.

I ease into her.

Her first cry is of relief. She can give in at last, surge and feel the hard answer she needs. Just a few seconds of this, yes, a few seconds and she can die in peace. She is in spasms now, but I keep a firm grip on her and build to a rhythm, and as I step into it, I hit something in her and she gasps. It can't be, she won't believe it can happen, not after all this, but yes, she starts to come back at me, then to arch again, and then she's got it, moving in time with me. It can't be, but it is — she's not finishing at all, not set to collapse but rising again, rising and turning back, back toward the edge for one final, crimson ride.

Her sounds are magic now, and her face, even with the silk over her eyes, so beautiful that it takes all my training to stay steady. And then I break one of my rules. I close my eyes. Always I watch a girl until the end — always. Watch her face, note every last detail of her finish so the memory of it can carry me through the week to come. Tonight, though, I close my eyes. Close them and go back in my head to the lake. I'm fourteen again, watching young Melissa dancing barefoot, watching her small feet and smooth arms and watching, too, Tim Crockett's hands as they rise up her belly. I can see her so clearly, see her *just as she was,* even smell the lake air, and feel in my spine the weight of all those nights, the nights in the cabin dreaming of her, the crushing innocence of us both, gone now but mine again — for an instant — when I close my eyes.

We live first in our heads and only then in the world around us. Well, I'm living in both, and right now I'm having them both, too. Both Melissas, the innocent princess of the lake and, opening my eyes again, the thirty-year-old beauty in the last golden hours of her looks. She's peaking now, outside herself with pleasure, and her cries and her sweet fucking take me to the turning point and past it, until finally I lean hard into her one last time, put my hands on her breasts, the same beautiful breasts denied Tim Crockett all those years ago, and join her, at last, on the edge, along the edge, and then over.

The bell rings softly behind me as I step out onto Amsterdam again. The cool night air greets me like a friend, and I start for home. A comedy is just letting out at the corner Loews, and I walk for a block through the happy throng, past young couples twined together as they wave for cabs and by college kids shouting the best lines at one another as they head in packs into bars or simply out into the New York night.

I turn onto Eighty-first Street, away from the din of the avenues, and walk the last quiet block to my building. I should be all done in, but I feel clean and electric, the spatial world around me trim and strong, the edges of buildings pressed close against the sky.

She was tremendous. The best I've had in the year I've been doing this. Her sounds alone — Jesus.

A suit walks by me, his cell phone pressed to his ear, querying some distant party about stock quotes. Stock quotes on a Saturday night.

I reach my building, climb the stairs, and let myself into my one-bedroom. I pour a half glass of Absolut, strip to my shorts, and step through the window out onto the fire escape again, to end the night as I began it. I sip my drink and lean my arms on the metal railing, letting the night air chill me.

Everything in our modern world is designed to protect us from true contact. The most we get of it is the jostling on the subway on the rush-hour ride to work. All day at our desks we speak to the business selves of others, saved from honest talk by our suits and our titles and our client relationships. And once home? We can order in our food, get our entertainment from a box, pay our bills by phone, and then, before bed, log on and reinvent ourselves on the Internet, sharing fantasies in chat rooms with people we'll never see and pretending that's intimacy, contact. It isn't.

True contact is the moment you drive inside her. You are face-to-face, with no escape for either of you. It is the one true moment of each week for me, the one I live for.

I look out at the lights in the quiet buildings across the street, and above them at the golden moon, which tonight seems to hang over New York alone. Next week's beauty is somewhere under that moon. Stepping lightly to a swing band maybe, or browsing in a late-night bookstore. She might even be asleep already, her slip riding up her pale leg as her soft lips part in dream. Who is she, I wonder, and how far along the edge will I take her?

CHAPTER TWO

The angels' share.

That's the term I was looking for. That precious day in wine country last summer, stepping with Mark out of the hot Napa sun and into the dark, musty champagnerie caves, drawing his arm around me and then stepping forward from under it when my eyes cleared and I saw, filling the room, those rows and rows of oak barrels. I've never seen anything so beautiful. There must have been hundreds of them, each working its magic on the juice of the first press, the finest juice from the best grapes in the vineyard. I looked at Mark, and even he, Mr. Beer Man, was struck by it. They were so simple, those barrels, but so solid and made with such care, and our guide explained that each one, while imparting its flavor, also lost some of its wine to evaporation. Yes. A portion of each barrel would pass right through the oak and disappear into the air. The American wineries, he said, simply write this off as "gross loss," but the French — champagne's creators — call it the "angels' share."

That's what I should have told Mrs. Brodeur. Sorry, *Madame* Brodeur. That you can't plan a wedding down to the last minute. That at every wedding, every one, there will be time that you can't account for, time that will . . . evaporate, I should have said. Like the angels' share. But I couldn't think of it, so I kept quiet.

Madame Brodeur is the wedding consultant — Mom's idea, of course — and if I let her, the woman will preside over our big day with a stopwatch. And to think she's from Paris. It hasn't taken her long to learn our American efficiency and lose all her home country's grace and sense of occasion.

She has allotted four minutes to get from the top of the church stairs to the limo. In my wedding dress. She has allotted five minutes for the best man's toast. Ten minutes, at the reception, from serving the first drinks until we gather at the edge of the lake for photos.

She's crazy. Our families, and all our friends, herded from place to place? And just the thought of following a script. We've been to three weddings this past year, Mark and I, and the best moments are always the ones you don't plan. They spring naturally from the magic of the day.

I might see Grandma in the church foyer after the recessional and stop for a minute to hold my new ring up to her failing eyes. Or maybe at the reception Uncle Ralph will get drunk and want to give a toast of his own. Or Sandy, who cried when

I named her a bridesmaid and cried when I showed her her reading and cries, her sister swears, at her neighbors' First Communions, will cry again when we gather for pictures, and we'll need to give her a few minutes to fix her makeup. Or something silly, even. The groomsmen will find a football and start choosing sides, and the bartenders will have to be sent out to coax them back. Or one of the UConn grads, probably Reece or Jason, will yell, "Huskie time!" like they do at any get-together, and all the young guys — and there will be twenty from school, at least — will charge onto the grass and build a human pyramid.

I want all those things to happen. Or others just like them. I want everyone to drink and dance and have more fun than they've ever had. I want it to be a day of joy.

For weeks I've been fine. Really. Because it's all been coming together so beautifully. We have the best band. Mark and I heard their tape and we went to see them, twice, in two different places, and they were wonderful both times. Any band that can get Staten Island boys away from the bar and out onto the dance floor can handle a wedding crowd. They can play anything, from ska to Sinatra. Mark rolls his eyes at Frank, but they *will* play "That's Life," even if I have to sneak it onto the song list in pencil. If Mark wants to hide when they start into it, I'll just dance with Dad.

The caterers, too, have been a dream. Judy, the woman in charge, was married herself just two months ago, so she can't do enough for us. Extras of everything. The flowers? Chosen, and beautiful. White roses for the altar and the steps of the church, pink ones to line the aisle. The brides-maids — all perfect. Calling or e-mailing every week now. Sandra has lost twelve pounds since November. "I'll be as thin as you, Mimi" was her e-mail today. She won't be, but she's fine — they're all fine, all six of them. I won't need slimming col-ors, or patterns, and I don't have to worry, as Mark puts it so delicately, about "stiffing one of the groomsmen." There are six of them, too, and in their tuxes they'll look sharp — even Lenny. The bridesmaids all want to see pictures and all look forward to flirting, though, okay, *flirting* wasn't the word Anne used.

So everything's been fine. Five weeks away still, but the day seems to be gathering a momentum all its own. And when I think of it, which is every fif-teen minutes or so, it isn't with panic at all. Until today.

I was at my desk, putting the last touches on the Cortez return in preparation for Mr. Stein's signa-ture. Stein is a senior partner, and he was trusting me, twenty-five years old and still a year from my M.S. in tax, to do solo work on a major client. The return had to be perfect, and it was nearly so. We'd taken an "aggressive approach," a favorite term among our Latin clients, and I had a spreadsheet and the return open, going back and forth, one good deduction away from bringing the total within our target. I'd zeroed in on overseas depre-ciation allowances. Yes, here was one that could work. It might just do it. . . . And then the phone rang.

"Honey, I saw Father Ryan yesterday."

"Mom . . ."

"I'll be quick. It's just this, dear. If you have a change of heart, he's offering his services. Full Mass and Communion. We would pay, of course, your father and me."

The Catholic thing again. As if I might change my mind at this point. Even if I believed, does she think I'd put everyone through a one-hour mass? The groomsmen would sneak beer into the church.

"Mom. We've been over this. Please."

"If you have a change of heart, dear, that's all. Sorry. I'll leave you. Bye."

I looked up to see Mr. Stein in the doorway, his hand raised to knock, his kind eyes, under the old-fashioned wire rims, trained graciously on a spot just past me. "Hi," I said, and the phone rang again. *Great. He thinks I'm a party girl.*

"Thirty minutes?" he asked quietly, ducking his head as if to be pardoned. "The Cortez return? In my office?"

"Of course," I said, then picked up the phone, hoping it was a client whose name I could repeat while Mr. Stein was still within earshot.

"Mimi Lessing?"

Madame Brodeur. And before I could remind her, delicately, that home is a better place to call me, she started in on the "schedule." Each precious element of my wedding day — the recessional, the tossing of the bouquet, the first dance — scripted with martial precision. And before I could tell her about the angels' share, explain to her that my wedding was not a military maneuver and wouldn't be planned like one, she was on to her "concerns." Had I asked the reception hall about a noise ordinance? What if the band is late? Or the caterers? Will there be vegetarians on the guest list? Who will tie the ring to the ring pillow, and with what kind of knot?

It was ten minutes before I was free of her and staring at the Cortez return again. Just minutes ago it had been as clear as dawn, the last figures set to fall into place, but now all I saw was a mess of numbers. I looked at the clock. I had twenty minutes. Where had I gotten these depreciation figures? They couldn't possibly be right. That last deduction — what was it again? Noise ordinance? I picked up the phone.

"Mark, what is a noise ordinance?"

"A law against making too much noise."

"Our wedding band — what if they violate one?"

"In the Boathouse in Central Park? Who's going to gripe — the ducks?"

"What if the caterers are late?"

"She called you, didn't she?"

"What if we have vegetarians, Mark? What will they eat?"

"Each other. Mimi, relax."

"The ring pillow. What if the knot is too tight?"

"Mimi."

"What?"

"What are the only two 'don'ts' at any wedding?"

"I know, but —"

"Say them."

I took a breath. "Don't run out of liquor, and don't run out of music."

"We've got liquor for an army and tunes for a dance marathon. Stop obsessing. It's sexy, but it's hell on your nerves. I'll see you tonight."

I put the phone down, walked to the window, and was all right again. I looked down at midtown Manhattan, at the row of trees that stretch in a pretty line up Park Avenue. Mark was right, of course. It is the day that matters, not the details. And the day will come. It will come and we will stand at the altar and he will ease the ring onto me, lift my veil, and give me my first married kiss. Then we'll turn and walk, to "Ode to Joy," through all the people we love, and step from the church doors out into the sunshine. (There's something Madame Brodeur can arrange, if she really wants to earn her pay.) And then to Central Park, all of us, to party on the grass by the lake, through the late afternoon and into the night, drinking and dancing under the trees and even, if luck is with us, under the stars.

I sat back over the return, and it was as simple again as a coloring book. Cows, yes, that was the key. On a cattle ranch you can capitalize cows. And they can depreciate. I put in the new numbers and printed it all out. Thirty-one pages in all. A marvel of compression, really, and it hit all our targets. Ten minutes later Mr. Stein smiled over the top of it from behind his large oak desk.

"A spirited return, Mimi."

I could have kissed him.

"Bold in places —"

He held up page 13. The cows.

"— but defensible. All of it. First-rate work."

Those are beautiful words from a senior partner. Anytime, but especially a month before your review. I glided through the rest of the afternoon, and then to the gym in the early evening, where I pushed myself through my best workout in weeks. Step aerobics, twenty laps in the pool, light weights, the StairMaster, aerobics again, ten minutes in the sauna for my pores, and then the brisk walk home. "Looking good," Manuel called out, from the lottery window of the little newsstand on Eighty-second Street. "Feeling good," I answered with a wave.

And I am, as I step out of my apartment and into the street again. I should really cab it, as it's almost eight o'clock, but it's too beautiful a night not to walk. I'll miss only the start of the game, and that's all right. The others went early and will save me a seat along the bar. I'm meeting Mark, his sister Sherry and her husband of three months, Alan, at a sports bar on Sixty-second. Sherry is a UConn grad, too, and Alan an honorary one, so tonight we'll root on the Huskies in the big annual college basketball tournament. March Madness, they call it. All the best teams from around the country keep playing one another until only the champion is left. It goes on for weeks every year and it's great fun, an excuse for us young grads to gather in bars and show our school spirit.

I need a night out. A night when I can forget, for a few hours, about all the wedding madness and about tax season, too. Maybe I can even forget about last Friday.

I cross the street at the corner of Eightieth and walk past the open kitchen door of Ernesto's, breathing in the smell of the bread they bake fresh each night. I continue down Second Avenue.

Last Friday. I can't believe it's still on my mind. It was nothing, really. Well, not nothing.

The firm sent me to an all-day tax conference at the midtown Hilton. At the reception afterward, a young associate from Peat Marwick, Robert — I don't remember his last name — turned from the bar, saw the face I was making at my red wine, and offered me his untouched glass of Italian white. "Never trust New York accountants to pick California wines," he said. I laughed and took the glass, and we started talking. The wine was refreshing, and he was, too. *Dry* is a kind word for most of these conferences, and for the presentations you hear at them, but he'd given a sharp talk on tax shelters. It wasn't your average accounting paper. He'd titled it "Gimme Shelters," and it was hip and funny, though dead on point, too.

He was psyched to hear that I was writing my master's thesis on offshore shelters, and over another glass of wine he asked some questions and suggested some approaches that I hadn't heard yet from my NYU adviser. True, he did recommend I title it "The Artful Dodger," but he was a real help and fun to talk to, even. It was a productive hour, and after he circled on my copy of his paper all the sources that might apply to my thesis, and after he wrote out the numbers of two senior partners I might call in Marwick's international division, Robert looked at my ring for a long second, then up at my eyes, and asked if I'd had enough tax talk for one day and wouldn't I like to, and here he leaned in close, "join him somewhere quiet" for a drink?

I flushed, I know — I could see it in his eyes. I took a sip of wine, smiled, and said that I was "joining" my fiancé but that I was sure we'd have the chance to talk again at the next conference. He was a good sport and very smooth, saying he looked forward to it, shaking my hand in that casually provocative way some men can pull off and drifting back to the bar to join the other young Marwick turks.

That was it. No big deal. Anne calls me VM, for the Virgin Mary, but I'm not naive. I field looks every day, like we all do, and turn down drinks in bars and deflect, gently if I can, the hard chargers. Robert had caught me off guard, that was all, coming on to me out of nowhere — and at a work function besides. That's why I flushed. I should have just taken it as a compliment, as I always try to, and forgotten about it. But even as I mingled, introducing myself to the other panelists, meeting senior partners from big firms, passing business cards along to potential clients, I found I always knew where in the room Robert was, and twice I caught myself watching him, first as he talked to a young woman from Grant Thornton and again, minutes later, as he joked with the bartender. Okay. He *had* come on to me, after all, and he was a standout in that crowd, young and the only one there with his suit jacket in his hand, his sleeves rolled up and, it seemed, some appetite for life. Naturally I'd keep an eye out for him.

Still. What shook me was the feeling I had inside. The . . . stirring.

It was the same stirring I had felt for the first time six years ago, when I stood with Mark at my dorm-room door after our second date. He kissed me once, then harder, then ran his fingers across my cheek, down my neck, and to the open top of my blouse. "Can I come inside?" he asked, and I felt the tightness in my belly and I felt my legs go light and I knew, all at once, that I would have him in and that we would make love and that Mark was the one for me.

I've felt it many times since. Always with Mark, of course, and always it leads to sex. We've been a couple for so long that I feel it less often now, but still it comes. Walking home from a movie on a warm night, say, when we've been a week without, and I picture, just minutes away, his strong arms holding me still. Or stepping from the shower on a Sunday afternoon, seeing his trail of clothes to the bed and tying my bathrobe tightly even as I follow it, for the pleasure the air will give me when he throws it wide. It is only now and then, but I do feel it still, this stirring. It is the stirring of sex, and it has only ever been a private stirring for Mark alone.

But there it was, at the reception. I felt it when Robert made his play and when he shook my hand so . . . carefully, and later, even after he'd walked off, when I'd spot him across the room. The tightness in my belly. My legs going light.

I tried to pass it off to the wine. I'd drunk two glasses very quickly, after all. But it wasn't the wine. And the thing is, it wasn't even Robert. Today I can barely remember what he looked like. It was simply . . . well . . . the possibility of sex with another.

There.

And that's why, when it didn't fade, I walked to a pay phone and called Mark and told him to be at my place in thirty minutes. He never stays over during the week, doesn't even keep clothes here, but he stayed that night, and we made love and I . . . reached that place and afterward, lying on his chest in the cool dark, I felt okay again. Pure and cleansed. When I woke up the next morning, to the fresh breeze from the open window, the reception and Robert and any worries about anything were a world away.

And that should have been the end of it. But it hasn't quite been. I keep thinking of that night. What would Robert have suggested, if I'd gone for that drink? How would he have suggested it?

I reach Sixty-second Street and see, just ahead of me, the garish awning of Champions. The windows of the bar are crowded with neon beer signs and pennants, and even from here I can see that half the city has hit on the same idea. Excited shouts pour out the open door, and as I search in my purse for my license, I shake my head at myself. Listen to me. If Anne could hear me now, she would laugh, and she'd be right to. A night of fun, and here I am worrying over nothing. Enough. I show my ID to the bouncer, he waves me inside, and I step into the joyous fray.

The place is a madhouse. Hundreds of people — a thousand, even — all in college wear, all drunk or getting there fast and all clutching tournament pools, those single betting sheets that get passed around every office before the games begin. Along the bar are four big-screen televisions, each showing a different game, and in the middle of the big open floor are bleachers, actual full-size bleachers like you'd find in a real stadium, and they're packed, too, jammed with fans and bettors, shouting or cursing as they watch the screens, stomping their feet when their teams go on a run. It's bedlam. I hold my purse tight to my chest and make it through the crowd to the bar.

"Hey, she made it!"

Mark waves me down to the far end, where Sherry and Alan give me hugs and Alan pulls his jacket from the barstool he's been guarding.

"My car's not worth what I got offered for this seat," he says, and I laugh.

The three of them are all decked out in Huskie caps and sweatshirts. They are drunk already and revved up for the game. "For you," Mark says, handing me a sweatshirt, which I pull on right over my blouse. Alan waves down a crazy UConn booster, a guy with his head painted blue and white, our school colors, who comes down the bar with a hand stamp and presses the school logo onto our cheeks. The bartender is another alum, and he puts Jell-o shots in front of us, blue and white again, of course, and we four hold them up and say, "To the Huskies!" Mark, Alan, and Sherry toss theirs back. I give mine to Mark, and he tosses it back.

We're playing UCLA, and down the bar is a good, rowdy crew of their fans, too, blond Californians all. They start chanting their school cheers at us, and we chant ours back at them, before the game and then during it, as first their boys go ahead and then ours come back to take the lead.

I sit on the outside, next to Sherry, and when she slips away to the bathroom, I move to her seat for a better view.

Alan is watching the screen, living and dying with every shot, and then suddenly, after we score a pretty basket, I feel his hand on my leg, squeezing the inside of my thigh so hard that I gasp. And as he does he turns, his eyes shining, his mouth a curl; when he sees I'm not Sherry, he jumps right up off his barstool.

"Jesus!" he says, and then laughs.

"She's in the bathroom, Alan," I say, and laugh, too.

Alan laughs again. "Hit me, Mark," he says. "I just put my hands on your girl."

"At halftime," says Mark, pumping his fist as the Huskies score, and then Alan is watching the game again and Sherry is back, too, and at the first commercial Alan turns to her and says, "I just strayed, baby," and tells Sherry what happened, and we all laugh again.

After a minute I walk to the bathroom and into the stall and sit down on the closed seat of the toilet. And I'm shaking. Shaking so hard, I drop my compact. And the spot where he touched me is . . . there's no other word for it, it is burning. I almost roll down my stockings to see if there is a mark. "Mimi, Mimi," I say, but minutes later I'm still shaking, and when I put my hand to my forehead, it is red-hot. What is going on? It was an accident, clearly, and there's been nothing, ever, between Alan and me, less than nothing, but . . . his touch was like an electric shock. Finally I gather myself, step from the stall, walk to the sink, and pat down my face with a cool towel, careful not to smudge the UConn logo. It is five minutes before I can join the others again.

After the game we all leave together. UConn lost in the last seconds, and there was some official's call that went against us, and Mark and Alan are lost in argument over it as we walk out to the street and up to the corner. Sherry asks me about the wedding, which I can discuss in my sleep now, but I'm only half there as I talk to her. I can still feel it, his tight grip on my thigh. More even than that, though, I can still see the look on his face. His mouth had been hard, his eyes . . . feral, and in that split second I saw how they do it. How they go into sex. Every couple goes into sex a different way, and I'd seen the look he gives her when they start. And his grip — it had been so rough. Sherry is no bigger than I am. She must like . . .

And then we are saying good-bye, and Mark and I are getting into a cab, Mark still shaking his head every few seconds over the game, muttering "damn" and "Christ" and then, looking at me, checking himself and pulling me to him. I smile and lean against him, but when he puts his hand softly on my knee, I almost jump. Outside the window the city flashes by, and I catch glimpses of faces, rough, then soft, and stabs of neon from the bars along the avenues. Mark would never grab the inside of my thigh in a public place. Never. He would never give me a look like that. Has never given me a look like that. Not that I'd want him to. No, not at all. It isn't that. It's just . . .

We reach Eighty-third Street and the cab pulls hard to the curb in front of my building.

"Wait till next year, right?" says Mark, smiling.

I put my hand on his shoulder. "Mark, come up."

"Now?"

I nod.

"I've got a production meeting at seven-thirty. And it's going to be a bear."

"Come up anyway."

He looks at me, then leans in and kisses my neck.

"Temptress. Tomorrow — and you'd better be ready."

I step from the taxi and watch as it pulls away up the empty street. The spring air, so refreshing just hours ago, makes me shiver now. I step into my building and walk the five flights up to my apartment.

There has been Mark and no one else for six years now, since sophomore year at UConn. No one else because I've wanted no one else, and in five weeks I'll pledge myself to him forever, and no moment in my life will be happier. I'm sure of that. As sure as I breathe. So what is going on?

In the kitchenette of my one-bedroom I pour out a glass of chardonnay. It is a weeknight, and tax season, and I've had a glass of beer already, but I'll have just the one. A glass of wine, a hot bath, and then to bed. I walk with my glass into the bathroom and start the water in the tub. I pour in bath salts, small blue crystals that scatter and dissolve under the force of the faucet's stream.

Robert at the reception was one thing. But tonight. The charge that went through me when Alan grabbed my thigh was stronger than any stirring. And there's more, too. I have started lately, on the subway or on the street, not to look — that's too strong a word — but to notice men around me. Attractive men. I know, I know. Like that's anything. What am I, a maid? I'm twenty-five. But I've never been this way.

I slip out of my sweats and panties and into the bath. The water is as hot as I can stand it, and I slide down into it until only my neck is above the bubbles. Maybe I can soak these thoughts out of me.

Nerves, Mimi. That's all it is. The wedding is so close now, and Madame Defarge — excuse me, Brodeur — has me obsessing over every detail, and Mom is on me about religion again, and all of it's . . . taking a toll. Not to mention that it's the height of tax season and I'm a month from my review.

And it's spring. Spring in Manhattan, which means that no one, it seems, can think of anything but sex. Take Anne.

Anne is my maid of honor and best friend. We grew up together. She has been single since she left Dan at Christmas, and when she has a "good night on the singles scene," as she calls it, she phones me up with the details. All the details. How many times. The different ways. I always have to stop her. My other friends, too. Five of us meet every other week for drinks, and though none are as . . . specific as Anne, sex is always topic A. Mark assures me that his buddies are the same. Worse. If it weren't for professional sports, he says, they'd talk about nothing else, and he promises that if I ever heard a tape of poker night, I wouldn't let any of them into the apartment again.

I don't understand it, this obsession with sex. Will she or won't she, on their end, and should I or shouldn't I, on ours. Isn't there more to life? It's in the air, I know — the whole culture is mad with it. The movies. The music. The scandals. The billboards. There is no escaping it, and I guess it seeps into everyone. Really, though, I don't ever think about it. Or didn't ever.

If there was a problem between Mark and me, any problem, I could understand it, but no, there is no problem.

Well.

It's not a problem, I would never call it that. It's not even a complaint, really. But since I'm trying to understand . . . there is one thing.

We . . . only ever go at it the one way. The usual way. It's wonderful. Safe and easy and natural, and he makes sure I'm . . . cared for . . . and three weeks ago I would have said I'm happy. I *am* happy. I'm a flower to Mark, and I love it. I can do everything with him that I dreamed I'd do with a partner. Suggest a museum on Saturday and he won't blanch. Talk to him about books and about ideas, even.

It's just . . . there is fire in me, I know it. And there are times I'd like to . . . give in to that side of me. And there are times I almost do. Mark and I have made love when I've gone after him and he's come back at me hard and it's been wonderful. But still safe. Always safe. And always, essentially, the same way. Even our way into sex is the same.

He'll touch me, then look into my eyes, and if I return his look, we'll walk to the bed, where I'll take off his clothes and he'll take off mine, and then either he will start down from my neck or reach down for me as we kiss. I swear it is this way almost every time. If I start it differently, he steers me back to this . . . routine. Gently, but he steers me back. If we are on the floor, reading the Sunday

paper, and I kiss him and smile back at his look and
try to pull him down to me, he will smile but he
will tense, and to save the moment I'll stand and
we'll go to the bed. Or, and this happened just once,
two weeks ago, we were in bed, and ready, and I
started to, to sit up, but I saw his eyes tense and I
stopped myself almost before I started, brought
him down to me, and we did it as always.

I should speak to him, maybe. We've never
talked about sex. Not once. There are couples, I
know, that discuss everything, that get videos and,
can I even say it, devices. We could never. Even asking him to take me . . . another way — impossible.
Imagine, the man I marry. But I couldn't. And I
wouldn't, either, because he'd think I've been un-
happy all this time, and I haven't been at all. There
has been, from the start, such comfort and safety in
our sex. And I've prized it. I grew up a good Greenwich girl, eighteen years in the same beautiful
stone house, loving parents, private school, and
happy, happy with all of it. And when as a girl I
thought of love, I thought first of a soul mate, and
yes, a protector, and I have that in Mark, absolutely,
beyond question.

So why do I see men now and . . . it's less than
imagining it, not quite imagining it, because I stop
myself, turn my thoughts away because . . . what
was it Daddy used to say . . . no good could ever
come of it.

But just once, to feel — what?

Dominated.

Mimi. See where the mind will go, when you let

it loose? When you start it down a way of thinking? It's not true. It is nerves, as I said before. Nerves and nothing else, and it will pass. Oh, I wish the wedding were tomorrow. I want to stand at that altar and hear the priest say his words. The traditional words. The magic ones. "Do you, Mimi . . ." and so forth, right through to the end. He will wait on my answer, the beautiful stone church dead quiet, and I will look at Mark and say *my* two words, the words that change everything, and as I do I won't remember any of this. What is it I'm obsessing about, anyway? Positions? The angle of our bodies? Stray half thoughts about strangers? What are they, next to love? They are nothing.

Tomorrow will be six months. Ten months since we lay in a rowboat on the pond in Central Park, Mark on his back in the cradle of the boat and me on my back in his arms. We bumped the shore, and Mark pushed us out again. We drifted through sun, into shade, into sun again, my eyes lazily closed as he stroked my arm, up and back down, up and back down, then opening to see, in his hand, the shining ring.

It still brings a surge to me. A true surge, one of love and happiness. I press my neck against the cool tile of the tub, finish the last of my wine, and rise from the water. I turn the shower on to its strongest setting and rinse off. The ring was so beautiful that day. Its diamond caught the rays of the sun, I remember, and sent them out again, up into Mark's eyes and off the leaves of the trees. I make the water hotter, then hotter still, and I can feel it pounding the last troubling thoughts right out of me. They disappear into the steam, and when at last I shut it off, step onto the bath mat and reach for my soft, white towel, I am clean and clear again. Minutes later, in my slip, I walk to the bedroom and climb in the bed. Just an hour ago I was tense and worried, and now I feel wonderful. One song before sleep.

The Pavarotti tape waits in the player by my bed. I switch off the light and hit the PLAY button, and in seconds his voice fills the dark room. "Nessun Dorma." The singer cannot sleep. Not while his love is away from him. Such beauty. Where does it come from, in a man? I'm a fool. I wish Mark were here. It is the worst of sins, to forget what you have and long for what you don't. And what I have is precious. The luckiest girl in New York, and I sit at home and worry. No more. Tomorrow morning I'll step out of the office and make it to the video store while there is still a selection. The Oscars are in ten days, and there are still two contenders we haven't seen. I'll get the one Mark wants, the crime one, and I'll have him over tomorrow. I'll put out candles and make popcorn, and even before the previews are over, I will come on to him. It will be perfect.

Pavarotti holds his last, soaring note, and then the room is quiet. My building is all the way east, on the water, and listening hard I can hear in the distance the horn of a boat. It is so peaceful. Plaintive. Sleep, Mimi. Tomorrow will be busy. Mr. Stein is assigning me a new account. Something special, he said. It's the last thing I need, this far into tax season, but he's giving me help. I'll work the returns with a new associate, a young guy who just joined the firm last month.

Jake Teller, I think his name is.

Please let him not be difficult. He won't be, I'm sure. Stop worrying, Mimi. Okay, I've stopped.

To sleep. Dream of veils.

CHAPTER THREE

Miss Lessing walks the same route home every day.
It is longer by nearly a block than if she kept to
First Avenue, but instead of squat bars and grim
scaffolding, she ends her commute with a vibrant
stretch of neighborhood shops. She passes first the
produce stand, with its bins of fresh fruit open to
the air; next the bustling deli, where they know her
by name; and then the newsstand, where she greets
the smiling Latino boy who, on her weaker days,
will sell her a lottery ticket and then lean out the
window to stare after her. At midblock her eyes
often drift up to the delicate stonework of the prewar walkup, then lower again as she passes the
tiny art gallery, with the watercolors she likes in the
window. Then a friendly wave to the Asian cleaners who press her suits and finally, just before the
corner, the smoked-glass window of Vine. Vine is
an elegant wine-tasting room, and Miss Lessing
rarely passes it without stopping to read the day's

selections. If one intrigues her, as it did today, she takes a pen from her purse and writes it down.

Each afternoon I see her first as she turns onto the block, see her from my window spot in La Boheme, the faux Parisian coffeehouse across the street. Today she wore a demure blue suit, offset by white stockings. I watched until she turned the far corner, and then I returned my cup to the counter and stepped out of aromatic La Boheme and into the teeming street. I walked east, then south, through what was once called Germantown. Forty years ago my father would bring me here on Sunday mornings, to browse in the sausage shops. They are bars now, or boutiques.

I walked down through the Seventies, and through the Sixties. At Fifty-seventh Street the clamor of York gave way to the quiet of Sutton Place, and from there it was but three blocks to the clearing, a small patch of grass and flowers between two gray buildings. The clearing commands an unobstructed view of the river and its walkway but is set back far enough that one can watch from the railing in peace.

As I do now.

Three nights a week Miss Lessing works out at her gym, but three others she runs along the river. Any minute now she will step into view. I hold to the railing and watch the river walkway. A young woman runs by in a garish sports bra, and now another in shorts cut to her hip.

There she is.

Dressed discreetly, as always, her long T-shirt

falling almost to her knees. Tonight her brown hair is pulled into a tight ponytail. Her chin is up, her runner's legs striding smoothly. Such carriage. And then she is gone. Seven seconds it takes her to pass from sight.

I watch the spring wind stir the dark surface of the river. When she appears again on her return pass, she will be beautiful in her exhaustion. Her head down, soft beads of perspiration rimming her smooth face. I look at my watch. 6:40. It will take her about twenty minutes.

I watch the waves and settle in to wait.

CHAPTER FOUR

The first rule of tax season is never to answer the phone. I do, though, certain that it's Pardo, calling to accept the offer of primo Knicks tickets I left with his assistant just minutes ago.

"Jake Teller," I say.

"Mr. Teller." I recognize the voice of senior partner Abe Stein. "What's the first rule of tax season?"

"Screen your calls."

"Good. Abe Stein here. Could I see you in my office, please?"

"Sure."

I look at the foot-high pile of tax returns in my in-box, then at the slew of pink message slips. Each will be a client wanting last-minute advice. Even the stodgy ones get pretty creative as tax day nears, and they call us for fresh explanations of the distinction between dodge and deductible. I walk down the long hall, through reception, then down the carpeted hall of the south wing, to Mr. Stein's corner office. A visit here can only mean more work, and as I knock on the heavy mahogany door, I already feel nostalgic for the fourteen-hour days of the past two weeks. Just let it be a straight return — nothing from out of left field.

"Come in."

Mr. Stein sits behind an impressive rosewood desk. He has the quiet air of a professor, but the word in the halls is that when the senior partners get together, he speaks last and loudest. In front of him, in one of the two leather client chairs that face his desk, sits a young woman.

"Hello, Jake," says Mr. Stein. "Do you know Mimi Lessing?"

"Just barely," I say.

We met for ten seconds on my first morning. In the crush of work ever since, I'd forgotten her, though I don't see how I could have. She is beautiful. Lithe, a runner maybe, with clear brown eyes and olive skin. Beneath her light suit she wears a camisole, which pulls away from the top of her smooth chest as she leans forward to shake my hand.

"Hi," she says, her hand small, warm.

"Hi."

"I'm putting you two on an account," says Mr. Stein.

I must be living right. Ten nice Jewish boys and her, and I draw her. I take a seat.

"Mimi," says Mr. Stein, "do you remember an Andrew Brice?" Mimi tries to place the name but can't quite, and Mr. Stein points with an open hand at the wall. "Go have a look at that frame, you two." We stand and walk to a gilt-edged frame that holds an ancient, dignified page of company letterhead. The page has yellowed and the corners have flaked away. The ink is faded but legible.

"It's a tax statement," I say.

"It is indeed. For one Theodore Brice, for the fiscal year 1924. Can you read the figures?"

I step closer to the glass. "One hundred ten thousand dollars?"

"That's right. More than Babe Ruth made. Theodore Brice served with our founding partner, Fred Hyson, in the Great War. Hyson came back and founded this firm. Brice came back and went to law school, and then to work for the Rockefellers. How is your American history?"

I look at Mimi.

"That was the time of Standard Oil," she says.

"Very good. Come, sit down." We do. "Brice was a shark lawyer back before these waters were infested with them. A pioneer of the big deal, and the practice of securing a hefty percentage for the lawyer who closed it."

"And we did his taxes?" she asks.

"Fred Hyson did them personally. And they developed a custom. Each year on April first, Brice took Hyson to lunch at the Algonquin. After their meal Brice would order a Rob Roy, spill a drop on his tax sheet for luck, and then sign his name."

Mimi leans forward, and the camisole parts from her skin again. She raises a hand and presses it to her. "Andrew Brice," she says. "I remember now. Last year at this time, at the elevators. You introduced us." Mr. Stein nods. "So he's a legacy." He nods again.

"And he carries on his father's custom?" I ask.

"After a fashion. The son didn't quite inherit the old man's spark or drive."

"In financial matters?"

"In all matters." Mr. Stein leans toward his desk, and I notice for the first time the two account folders on top of it. He picks up the heavier one. "Theodore Brice died in 1970 a rich man. A month later his only son — Andrew — liquidated all the assets, except for some property upstate. Preferred to take his inheritance in cash, apparently." He lays the folder back on the desk. "After estate taxes and what have you, that inheritance was ten million dollars. And as far as we can tell, he's lived off that and nothing else ever since."

"He doesn't work?" I ask.

"Not a W-two in thirty years." He picks up the second folder and opens it. "No record of any income, outside of interest."

"He made money in the markets, maybe?" says Mimi.

"I'm not sure Brice knows a stock from a bond. He's never bought either. His investment strategy was to split his ten million evenly between twenty accounts — five hundred thousand in each."

"He's afraid of bank failures?" I ask.

"Or war. Or famine. Or locusts. Brice is not your standard rational investor."

"But we must have advised him of other options," says Mimi.

"George Hyson, son of the founder, broached the topic in 1971, at their first lunch. Andrew Brice made it clear that it was not to be raised again. And it hasn't been." Mr. Stein takes off his glasses and wipes them with a soft cloth. "Every firm has its concessions to company lore. Brice is ours. You know the term for them?" He looks at me.

"Courtesy cases," I say.

He nods. "Brice's taxes take an hour a year. Which, by the way, he insists we bill him at staffers' rates. Thus, his annual worth to Hyson, Levay is eighty-five dollars." Mr. Stein replaces his glasses and looks at each of us again. "You're trying to think of a polite way to ask what all this has to do with you." He pauses.

"Something has gotten into our courtesy case. It's been five years since George Hyson retired and left to me the honor of accompanying Brice to lunch. In those five years Brice has never once called this office. Never had a tax question. Never solicited a shred of financial advice. He simply appears at noon on April first each year, takes me to lunch, signs his tax return and the bill. Until this morning."

"He called?" says Mimi.

"Yes. He's been doing some thinking, and he's concluded that an investment strategy would be prudent after all."

Mimi and I exchange a look. Her cheeks are high and fine, a hint of flush to them. "After thirty years?" she says.

Mr. Stein nods. "After thirty years." He's silent

again, his eyes leaving us for a French watercolor on the wall, resting on it a second, then coming back. "Mimi, you made a stronger impression on our legacy than he did on you."

"I did?"

"He's asked that you be assigned to his account."

"I only met him for a second."

"Yes. Well, he's requested you, and when we can, we try to keep our legacies happy."

He pauses again, and now leans forward. Here comes the hammer.

"Brice wants a crash course in modern money management," Mr. Stein says. He pulls a note card from the thin folder, then looks over it at us. "Money markets, Treasury bonds, mutual funds, commodities, derivatives — the history and prospects of each."

Christ. Why not physics and space travel, too? Mr. Stein looks at me. "Now you know why *you're* here, Mr. Teller."

The man read my résumé. Actually *read* it. Under "Specialties" I listed "financial instruments." A bit of a stretch, as my only exposure to them was a three-week winter-term course my senior year at Ham Tech. Jeremy was my roommate at the time, and my coursemate, too, and thanks to a torrid stretch at the dice cup, I spent my mornings sleeping off the winter-term parties while he trudged through the snow to class, notebook in hand. I don't think I made it to three of them. As for the notes, I have a clear image of standing in back of the frat house the night of finals, dropping them onto the bonfire.

"He wants five investment scenarios," says Mr. Stein, "with estimated exposure and rates of return on each — for both bull and bear markets. I'll need all of this on my desk the morning of the first— ten days from today." He looks at us. "You can manage this?"

Mimi nods. "I'm sure we can," she says. He looks at me, and I nod, too.

"At least you'll be spared lunch. Largesse is another quality Andrew failed to inherit from his father. Last year, if I recall, it was a sandwich and a tonic water at the Carnegie Deli." He leans forward with the two account folders. "I don't know what we can expect from Brice — nothing, maybe. But his account's been a nonperformer for thirty years. It's worth a shot."

We each take a folder.

"That's it, you two. Thank you."

We stand and walk together out of the office. Mimi closes the door behind us and looks at me, smiling.

"Are you as swamped as I am?" she asks as we walk down the hall toward Reception. Her perfume is light, alluring.

"Two weeks here and this is as far as I've made it from my desk."

She laughs. "I know the feeling. We'll have to do this at night, won't we?"

"Yes."

"Tonight's out — the send-off party for Diane Silio. Will you be there?"

"I will," I say.

"Shall we work out a schedule then?"

"Sure."

We're both quiet a second. "All right, then," she says, as we walk from Reception into the north wing. "Back to the salt mines. See you tonight, Jake."

She smiles and walks off toward her office. I watch her turn the corner. Ten seconds pass and still I'm standing in the hallway, staring at the far wall.

After my parents died, I was raised by my grandfather. "You won't see it coming, Jake," he told me once. "And you won't be able to explain it. But you'll know." I walk slowly back to my office and sit down at my desk. I reach for the phone. Jeremy answers on the second ring.

"Jeremy Nascent."

"Jeremy, it's Jake. How would you like to see the Knicks next week? With me and Pardo. Third row."

"Wow," he says, but I hear the note of nervousness that I'm always bringing out in him. "What do you need, Jake?"

"Two things. I need you to look over a client file for me. And I need a crash course in financial instruments."

"What for?"

"To impress a girl."

He laughs. "You'll be sure to credit me, right?"

"If it ever comes up."

"Okay, Jake. Come over tonight with the file."

"How about tomorrow at lunch?"

"Fine."

I hang up the phone and spin slowly in my chair to face the window. I look out at the bright Manhattan sky. Tomorrow I'll learn about financial instruments and the investment needs of Andrew Brice. Tonight is the farewell party for Diane Silio. Everyone in the firm will be there. Including Mimi Lessing.

See you tonight, Jake, she said. I close my eyes.

Yes, she will. And she'll see me in action.

Diane Silio gave her notice the day I joined the firm. This night has been coming ever since.

Diane is the first thing I see when I step off the elevator each morning, a coffee-eyed girl from the Brooklyn avenues, her snowy skin a cool come-on amidst the dark leathers of the reception area. She was hired out of high school seven years ago, back when our partners could still get away with choosing a receptionist for her ass. She's kept it, and a lot more, and yet is that rare Brooklyn looker who slips through the neighborhood gauntlet of cops and plumbers right out onto the open market. She's been an asset here, I'm sure, inspired to efficiency each day by the aura of money that soaks this place, but careful, too, to wear her slit skirts cut at the knee and her blouses open at the throat, letting her trim legs and creamy swell work on the guys here the way candy at the corner store tempts from beneath the glass.

There's been current between us from the first. We haven't said a hundred words in my two weeks here, but her calm eyes hold mine an extra quarter second each time I bring her a latte from downstairs, and her voice, crisp and distant when she puts through calls to the other accountants, is close, even warm when she puts them through to me. Part of it is pure good luck, catching her in the flush of her last days, her mind lulled already by the black sand of Maui, by the two weeks of tropical drinks and free license that she will escape to with a girlfriend tomorrow, before easing into her new and better life as a legal secretary uptown.

There's more to it than luck, though. The ten other guy associates here are steady, wire-rimmed plodders who read the Tax Code in their free time and might have three dates and one score between them in the past year. They may all make partner before I do, but none has what it takes to stir the blood of Miss Silio, and none would dare dream of cashing in on her giddy last day.

I was hired as much for being a regular guy as for any magic I'll ever work with a tax return. I earned a third-team all-NESCAC selection in hoops up at Ham Tech. As a basketball honor, all that means is that I could hold my own with any white kid under six-three between Albany and Buffalo, but in the interview room here at Hyson, Levay, that and my proud admission to being a TDXer put me over the top. Sol Levine, the hiring partner, knows the money business. He knows that the best accountants are grinders, and he's packed the firm with a dogged crew of them. But he knows the search for capital is still half the game, and he sensed that I might be able to go beer for beer with the goyim jocks and frat boys that this firm needs to bring aboard if its financial ship is to sail as tall in the new century as it did in the old.

Part of my job is to go after these guys, my classmates of five short years ago. Chi Psis and Psi Us who staggered across the stage at graduation, talking through their hangovers about Jamaica, Antigua, St. Martin, about the three months of sun and spleefs that would wipe out whatever scrap of their liberal education had managed to survive senior week and enable them to start fresh and ruthless at big Wall Street firms in the fall. Some of them are pulling down serious bucks now, and a few times a month I'll be expected to treat one to our floor seats at the Garden or to eighteen holes out on Amagansett or even, if he's that kind of guy, to a night at Scores, the thinking being that down the line, when they decide they need someone to count their money for them, they'll remember Sprewell dunking over Shaq or the three-wood they blasted to the green or the blond angel with the schoolgirl smile who rocked back on her golden ass, uncrossed her high-heeled ankles, and offered them a long, sweet look at heaven. They'll remember, and they'll reach for the phone and give us a call.

That's the theory, anyway. We'll see. And if it costs me? If I go so high and no higher, and watch as the grinders march past on their way to partner? So be it. Because right now all those grinders are staring into the dull green glow of the spreadsheets they took home with them for the weekend, and I'm watching from a limo as Diane Silio steps from a bar doorway into the soft light of a streetlamp, the wind tugging at the open collar of her blouse as she gives our secretaries a last hug good-bye and now walks, taut and lithe, away from her old life and toward a night she hasn't begun to imagine.

It is the custom of the firm, on the last day of one of its own, to fete them at the Porterfield, in the financial district, an immaculate homage to gentleman culture and a favorite of the partners. At five o'clock the secretaries and some of us junior associates took Diane over, and for two hours she sat in our center along the gleaming brass bar, sipping Kahlua and cream, her legs crossed demurely on the rung of a barstool. Her eyes found mine more than once, even after the partners started dropping in, each staying long enough for a martini or an old-fashioned and then each invoking clients or family, handing Diane a gold-edged parting envelope, accepting the hug they'd waited seven years for, and leaving for their garages and cars and Connecticut weekends.

As they took their turns with her, I looked toward the door and saw Mimi Lessing come through it. She shook her long hair once, softly, and walked toward the group. I ordered a glass of white wine from the bartender and held it out to her as she reached us.

"Jake Teller," she said, smiling. "Why, thank you."

"To life after tax season," I said, touching my glass to hers.

"Amen." In the soft light of the bar her dark hair shimmered, and again my eyes went to the smooth skin beneath her camisole. "My last glass till April first," she said. She took a sip. "So, you've been with us two weeks?"

"Yes."

"What brought you?"

"The odds. Two hundred associates at Grant Thornton and eight partners."

She laughed. "Here it's twelve and four. Well, you picked a fine time to start." Mimi's eyes looked past me a second. She lowered her voice. "You must know Diane well," she said.

"Why?"

"She's watching you."

She was. The last of the partners had gone by then, and everyone had relaxed. Diane, warmed by the two drinks, the attention, the dark outline of the crisp hundreds in the envelopes on her lap, had pulled the clip from her smooth hair and leaned into the last hour of her special night. "Who's been to Maui?" she asked, her eyes on mine, and when I said a buddy of mine had gone last year and come back certain that at twenty-six the two best weeks of his life were behind him, she moved aside so I could get next to her at the bar. "Excuse me," I said to Mimi, who tipped her wineglass to me. I caught the barest trace of rose in Diane's perfume as I slid next to her, counted six buttons on her cream blouse before it disappeared into her gray skirt.

"What did he like best?" she asked, and her brown eyes, soft as a teen queen's, filled with life as I told her of the warm ash she could wade in in the open mouths of the volcanoes and of the trained dolphins that would swim with the guests in the hotel coves. Her crossed legs started to bob gently. A minute later I looked at my watch.

"That's it for me," I said.

"Already?"

"I'm meeting friends uptown."

Her eyes stayed on mine, suggesting, as clearly as if she'd said it aloud, that the others would all have to leave soon and that if I could wait them out, this night might not have to end in a bar.

"You'll come by the firm when you get back?" I asked. Diane looked down, then back, the offer in her eyes dimming, then gone.

"With pictures," she said, holding out her slim white hand. I shook it and then said my good-byes to the others. On my way through the group I stopped at Mimi.

"Tomorrow night?" I said.

She nodded. "Eight o'clock in the conference room?"

"Okay."

"I'll bring the caffeine," she said. "Have fun with your friends, Jake."

"I will."

I walked out into the street. Through the Twin Towers I could just see the red sun dipping into the water. The night, with all its promise, would be here in minutes. I walked up the block to the black limo that waited at the corner, the familiar star insignia of Orion Car Service on its side. Thanks to the long hours of tax season, I knew all ten of their drivers. At the wheel tonight sat Rudy, his big arm on the open window, the *Post* spread out in his lap.

"Rudy."

"Jake."

"Diane Silio's car?"

He nodded. I opened the door, climbed in, and sat back in the leather seat. Through the open partition I met Rudy's eyes in the rearview mirror.

"You dog," he said.

"We'll see."

And here I am. Night is on us now, and the financial district is quiet. The skyscrapers have spit out the last of their moneymen and stand like sentries all down Wall Street. Through the floor of the limo I can feel the low rumble of the Broadway local. It rolls off, its fading clatter giving way to silence and now to the magic click, click, click of Diane Silio's heels. "Bye," she calls out behind her, and then the limo door opens and I see a gray skirt and, where it divides along its slit, a trim stockinged thigh, then a flash of blouse, and suddenly Diane's brown eyes, as shocked as a victim's but recovering in the same instant. She is half in the car, her wrist on the seat, her eyes on mine, on mine, on mine still.

She slides inside.

"Seven fifteen Clermont," she says, looking straight ahead as she pulls the door closed. "At De Kalb."

No man who makes do with a steady, or even pays for sex, will ever know the charge of this moment. The electricity. We pull away from the curb, accelerating smoothly through a yellow light, then up the curving bridge ramp, then easing into the streaming lights that flow together, away from the perfect skyline of Manhattan and toward the broken waterfront of Brooklyn. I lean forward and slide the partition closed; we are alone, three feet of smooth black leather between us in the cool dark.

"I live upstairs from my parents," she says. "It's private."

She looks out her window, at the dark, wide mouth of the bay and the emptiness beyond. Bridge light pours in, falling on her pure, unguarded neck, on the white of her stockinged knees, which are pressed tightly together. Pressed together to control the build that started in her two weeks ago, the build that rose to fever when she closed the door of the limo and that rises even now as we ride. She looks out her window, but I doubt it's the water she sees. It is the sweet, hard moment of release. How does she picture it? A rough first kiss, and then the slam along the walls?

If only she knew.

We glide off the Brooklyn Bridge and soon are onto Flatbush and into the guts of Brooklyn. We ride past the dark avenues, all concrete and shadow — another country. At a stoplight, over the hum of the motor, we can just hear the muted call of a siren, all its urgency dissolved by the distance.

"Give me your keys," I say.

She pauses, then takes them from her purse and gives them over. "Put your wrists together." She looks at me, her eyes wet with tension, and presses her small wrists together, watching as I loosen my tie and pull it through my collar. I wrap the tie around them twice, secure it with a tight square knot, then take a Swiss Army knife from my pocket and cut off the extra fabric. Our faces are close now, almost touching. I can smell the sweet Kahlua on her breath and the rose again of her neck, and it takes all I have not to start in on her, not to kiss the full lips that part, already, in excitement. I place her hands gently in her lap, lay her jacket on top of them, and turn to the window.

Minutes later we pull up to 715 Clermont.

Her place is a gated brownstone in a row of gated brownstones. I guide her up the walk, my hand on the small of her back. The crushed glass in the concrete sparkles like tinsel, and the night air smells of power. We take the steps quickly. On the landing, as I work the key in the lock, she looks back, at the block she grew up on, her eyes deepening, then catching fire as some tug of memory connects the girl who played on these very steps with the young woman who stands on them now, her hands bound, aching for the release that waits just on the other side of the trusted wooden door of her childhood.

We step into the hallway. In front of us are the stairs that lead up to her apartment. She is stepping onto the first one when I see it.

"Wait," I say, taking her elbow, my other hand still on her back. I guide her not up the stairs but to the right, down the narrow hallway that ends, twenty feet down, at a door with a centered nameplate reading SILIO.

"My parents," she whispers, trying to stop.

"It's okay."

Three feet from their door I stop and back her against the wall. She waits, trembling, for a hard kiss, but I take her bound hands, raise them above her, and press them to the cool plaster. Then I lift her by her small wrists, easing the tie that binds them over the curved edge of a stout brass plant hook, then letting it slide down to the lower base of the hook so that her feet just touch the floor again.

She is stretched taut, and she is ravishing.

Some women owe their looks to fashion or lighting, but hers are true, and each hot curve responds to the strict test of the binds. Her breasts, straining at her cotton blouse now, are so full and close that I look away to steady myself. I look back, at the pretty blue veins in her lean arms, at her knees tight together. Through her parents' door we can hear the low drone of the television. She wets her lips, desperate to believe I don't have this in me but burning at the thought that I might.

"We can't," she whispers.

But we can. I lift her chin and taste, finally, the soft neck that has killed me since her first day. She gasps. "Upstairs," she whispers. "We'll do anything."

Against the wall is a small folding chair her parents must use to put on the boots they store beneath it. I unfold it quietly, just in front of her, and sit down. "Please," she whispers, but I start in on her black pumps, each sensual *pop* of an ankle strap drawing a quick breath from her. I slip them off, and she is forced onto her toes, her tensed thighs in tight, perfect relief through her skirt. I run my hands up the back of her stockings, the cool silk warmed from beneath now, and stop just under her ass. I squeeze her trim thighs gently. Gently. And then hard.

Only her binds keep her standing. She pulls at them, shuts her eyes tight, and crosses her ankles against the current coursing through her. "No," she whispers, shaking her head, but as I make a second slow pass up her legs, her knees slip apart, an inch at first, then another, opening toward pleasure, toward the sweet torment she wants to give into, *is* giving into, until, through the door, the sudden spike of a laugh track brings her around again.

"Don't," she whispers. "Please."

I roll her stockings down and off her, careful to trail my fingers on the inside of her thighs. She squeezes them tightly together, gaining a moment's relief that melts away when I slide my knees between hers. "You can't," she gasps, fighting for her life now. I widen my knees, parting her legs a little more, and slide my hands up her thighs until I can just feel the moist cotton of her panties on the back of my fingers. Beads of sweat dot her forehead now.

At the first, tiny pressure on the private cotton, she turns her face into her shoulder. I press harder, and she bites the thin collar of her blouse to keep quiet; still harder, and she shakes her head violently, tearing off the top button and exposing, for the first time, her tight white bra and the gorgeous bounty it restrains.

"Stop," she manages to whisper. "They'll hear."

I part her knees another inch. She is swelling against my fingers now, and as I work them, she drops her head to her chest, then arches it back. I press harder, just where she needs it, hold it for a five count, and then release. Tears come to her eyes. If only she could close her legs, or cry out just once. She bites her lip against the next round of pressure and — when it doesn't come — bites harder against the lack of it. I make her wait fifteen seconds. Thirty. I press again.

It is their struggle that sends me. Always. Their sweet agony as I take them to — and then through — their sexual limits. Diane Silio is reaching hers now. Women manage their pleasure with their legs or release it with their cries, but my knees keep hers apart, and even a single cry now will betray her. Cool Diane, who has handled all comers. The smooth Manhattan suits, eager for a one-off with a Brooklyn beauty. The block toughs, all hands and persistence. Handled them at close quarters, on couches, in cars. Controlled them with her soft eyes, with the small permissions they could grant or take away. Tonight those permissions aren't hers to give. Tonight her battle is against her own body, and right now she is helpless to stem the pleasure rushing through it.

Diane Silio is reaching the edge, and as she reaches it, her soft face pressed to the wall, her breasts rising with each quick breath, I hit the stretch that I live for. The golden moments when the world falls away, when it is her and me and nothing else.

I find, through the wet cotton, the spot that will collapse her and I work the edges of it, giving and withholding, giving and withholding. A soft moan escapes her. Another. She is coming apart.

And through her parents' door comes a cough, and then the creaks and moans of an old easy chair surrendering its burden. Her eyes open and find mine, imploring, desperate. *You wouldn't do this*, they say. *You couldn't.* She tries again to close her thighs, and again I don't allow it. Footsteps now, coming down the long hallway. Close. Closer. Her old man, off to the fridge for a beer. Not ten feet from us now. If he looks through the peephole, he will see her. His jewel. Trussed. Trembling. Perfect.

I part her legs a final inch, her feet slipping off the floor, gaining it again, slipping off, her thighs tight against my knees, all her weight concentrated now on our one true point of contact — the shred of cotton that keeps my fingers from her softest spot. I find her eyes — pained, beautiful. Ten thousand times they must have melted her father's heart, and

never again if she can't keep quiet during the seconds to come.

I press, hard, on the very heart of her.

Her body spasms but somehow she keeps silent,
twisting what little she can away from the door,
her head sent back now, her white throat taut,
thrilling. I lean in. A tiny gasp escapes her but she
fights back, pulling with her wrists against the unrelenting hook, her fingers clasped as if in prayer.
Harder she pulls, still harder, desperate for any
sensation, even pain, that will slow the explosion
building in her. Her father's steps reach the door,
pass it, then continue down the hall, finally fading
just as Diane Silio lets out the soft moan she needs
to keep sane.

Her cheeks are deep red now, her shining bangs
damp on her forehead. One more hard touch and I
will lose her, so I ease off, my fingers calm against
the soaked cotton as I watch her tremble along the
brink, whispering to herself, searching inside for
strength, for some trick of breathing that will get
her through the next round, which will begin, she
knows, as soon as her father's steps start up again.

Through the door, faintly, comes the deep, metal-
lic thud of the refrigerator door. It must be a relic —
the one she knew as a child. She shuts her eyes tight
again. Escaping through the years, perhaps. Seeing
herself at five, her feet set, pulling hard on the big
handle with her tiny hands as she dreams of the
cold milk inside. I flick my fingers. A spasm rocks
her. "No," she whispers, opening her eyes, brought
back to the moment as if out of a dream. Back to the

binds, the pressure, the edge. "I won't," she whispers, shaking her head from side to side, but two more quick spasms rock her, then a third. My fingers are still now but her gasps come faster, louder, and her thighs go slack against my knees. I'm losing her. We hear the fridge close, the soft clink of a bottle on a countertop. Another spasm shakes her, another, and with the next one comes a moan, too loud, and then from the kitchen — silence.

I don't move. Two seconds pass, three, the only sound the sigh of the metal hook as Diane Silio strains with all she has against it, her head back like a saint. A single sound from her now and we're lost.

She bucks again.

I reach with one hand for her mouth, to quell the cry that will give us away, but just as I do I feel — first in her legs and then all through her — tension. She is rallying, struggling back from the edge, finding, at the last second, true will. And through the door now comes the gush of tap water. She's made it. A final spasm rocks her but she stills it, her breathing steadying, her thighs pressing hard against my knees again. And then her eyes open, open and find mine, and the look in them sends a charge clear through me.

Gone is any trace of fear, of panic. In their place, acceptance, and something more — fight. Diane Silio signed on when she offered her wrists in the limo, and now, at her breaking point, she wants not mercy but *more*. She is with me now, a full partner in this magic ride, and her beautiful eyes dare me to take her the rest of the way, even as we hear, through the door, her father's footsteps start up again.

I stand quickly and take my hand from between her legs. She closes them, at long last, buckling with relief even as my fingers find the clasp of her skirt, unhook it, and send it to the floor. She steps out of it, her eyes holding mine, daring me still. I take a side of blouse, from the bottom, in each hand and pull away.

Her smooth belly, taut from the gym, is so close it hurts, and her effort against the binds has lifted the top of her crimson nipples free of her tight bra, which opens in the front. I unhook it. Her full breasts are soft, her nipples hard, her father's steps just seconds from the door now. I reach in my pocket for the blade.

She shudders at the cold touch of the metal as I slip it between cloth and hip, flick once, then again, and send her final protection to the floor. Quickly I cut off her bra, too. She wears only her ruined blouse now, which hides nothing, and she's no longer alone on the edge. I loosen my belt, ready myself, and take the back of her glistening thighs in my hands, my grip slipping, then tightening, as I lift her free of the floor.

Everything in me wants inside her, but I hold her still a last second, taking her all in. The deep berry of her nails, pressing into the backs of her hands now, her sweet, exhausted muscles stretched taut. And her beautiful eyes, which hold mine as I lift her thighs higher, as I part them a final time, and close as she braces for the coming shock, gathering herself as a diver, glimpsing the pearl of a lifetime, gathers for the final plunge.

I let her father's footsteps pull even with the door, set myself hard, pull down on her thighs and drive up and into her.

Only my shoulder saves us. She bites hard into it, surviving, barely, the nova inside her as all her weight meets all my force at the one magic spot that now joins us. I pull her tight to me with my left arm and brace against the wall with my right. There's no question of movement, of rhythm or pace. I can only keep still and hold on as Diane Silio tears free of the pressure I've built in her since the limo. The first deep spasms come before she can even wrap her legs around me, rocking her as she bites into my shoulder; rocking her as her father's steps pass by the door, as they fade down the hall; rocking her still as the distant creak of his easy chair grants her, at last, freedom.

Freedom to breathe again, to release my aching shoulder and to release into it gasping whispers of "Yes!" and "There!" and "Yes!" again. Freedom to move, to arch against me, each tiny shift in position unleashing a fresh torrent of pleasure. Freedom, at last, to give in to that pleasure, abandon herself to it, surge hard against the source of it. And freedom to take me, quickly, to where she's been for too long. To the true edge. She takes me with her smell, sweet rose and Kahlua and sweat, a smell that becomes taste now as I bury my face in her neck and breasts. She takes me with her sounds, slipping now from words to soft, repeating cries. She takes

me, most of all, with those deep spasms, spasms
that will not end, that jolt her, a minute into the
fuck, as hard as at the start. Three seconds apart
they come, two, one, and then one long, cleansing
cascade.

All my training is no match for this. Without
ever moving, I'm to the breaking point, too, and
then past it, my resolve done in by the purity, the
fury of her surrender, by the sight, at the last, of
the tight red silk on her wrists. I'm just able to set
my feet and give a last, lifting thrust, her mouth
finding my shoulder again as I pin her to the wall,
letting the last shocks burst inside her, shake her,
then ripple away, and as they do, I accept her col-
lapsing body as it leans into mine and is finally,
beautifully still. I hold her until I can trust my
arms again and then raise her gently, letting her
lift her bound wrists clear of the hook, and then I
set her, more gently still, on the folding chair,
kneeling in front of her, kissing her closed eyes as
I brush the damp hair from her face, watching
those eyes as I reach behind me and free her ankles from my back, seeing them open, finally, as I
pull her ruined blouse close around her. Open to
my face, to the still hallway around us, and to the
realization, just breaking in them now, that the
fuck of her life is over.

I step through the gate out onto the quiet sidewalk,
the Brooklyn night tasting as clean and clear to me
now as mountain air. I can see, a block up, the neon
lights of a bodega and I head for it, feeling the way

I always do just after I leave them. Emptied out. At peace. I could walk for miles, but it would be three rough ones, at least, to the Brooklyn Bridge and another four from there, so I go to the old pay phone just outside the bodega and call the car service. Then I buy a tall, freezing can of beer from the man of the place, who drops it into a paper bag and hands it over, and I cross the street with it and sit down on the steps of a brownstone to wait for my ride.

The block is all brownstones, save one. Across the street from me sits a big yellow house straight out of a southern dream, with latticed windows and topped by a small tower served by a curving set of stairs. A widow's walk, I think they call it. It's easy to forget that this used to be a port town, that once Mrs. Captain could climb those stairs and look out over the sea. I take a long sip of beer, lean back, and look up at the dark sky.

I've got buddies out of law school now, bringing down one twenty-five per, pre-bonus. Putting in hours that would shame a farmer, true, lucky to stagger back to their posh pads by midnight or to make it twice a summer to the shares they rent in the Hamptons. Still. Playing the game and winning. Getting ahead.

I've got others going the romance route. Been with their girls two, three years now, and the spark's still there. Some of them under the same roof, even. Sure, they switch channels when the wedding ads come on, and grit their teeth come

Valentine's Day, but even so. Best friends and all the rest of it. Happy.

And if I had the chance to trade one of these nights for any part of their lives — forget it. Jesus, she was unbelievable. Clear outside herself. And her finish . . . I take another sip of cold beer. Down the line I may pay the piper for these nights, miss out on money, advancement — hell, on love — but at least I'll know what I paid him for. The chance to feel, for a few minutes, completely, electrically alive. To feel a rush that no amount of money, and no girlfriend, will ever give you.

The low lights of a limo turn the far corner and head up the block toward me. Diane Silio was incredible tonight. And two weeks ago Melissa Clay was just as good. But as I look up into the dark sky, the face that comes into my mind is a new one. The face of a girl I didn't know before this morning. A girl with soft hair, gorgeous skin, and a body as tempting in her work suit as any model in lingerie.

Mimi Lessing.

I know her type. I could never get near them up at school. She grew up in Larchmont, I'll bet, or New Canaan. Riding lessons, private school. Held herself apart from them, but even so, they shaped her. Thinks sex is a ballroom dance. Forget it, Jake. A coworker with a ring on her finger and the last girl on earth who would ever have that side to her. Still. I felt something this morning in the hall, and again tonight in the bar. And I saw something in her eyes when we talked, when she told me Diane Silio was watching me.

The limo pulls to the curb in front of me. Through its open window I see the big arm of Rudy and then his sardonic smile as he shakes his head and gestures with his thumb toward the back. I stand, finish off my beer, and walk down the steps, pausing at the limo door to take in a last breath of spring night air, then climb inside.

Yes, there was something in her eyes. A look I've learned to spot in women.

Temptation.

CHAPTER FIVE

I gained entry to Miss Lessing's private world on a workday morning a year ago.

At 8:30 I watched her descend into the subway at Eighty-sixth and Lexington. An hour later I caught the street door to her walkup on Eighty-third and York as another tenant was leaving. I checked the apartment directory, stepped inside, and climbed the stairs to the fourth floor. I stood for a few minutes in the deserted hallway, then walked to the door of apartment 4D. I knelt in front of it. From my coat pocket I took out the white cloth in which I'd wrapped the tools I would need. I laid the bundle on the hallway floor and spread it open.

Sunlight from the landing behind me streamed over my shoulder. I picked up the tension wrench and inserted it carefully into the keyhole. Holding the wrench steady and applying firm counterclockwise pressure, I took the lifter pick and guided it, too, into the hole. Then I lifted the pins of the lock one by one, until I'd brought them all to shear. After the last one clicked softly, I drew out the lifter pick, took a slow breath, and turned the tension wrench. The lock gave cleanly. I pushed on her apartment door, and it opened without a sound.

I stood up and stepped into her living room. It was not at all what I had expected from a woman of twenty-four. Surrounding me were two solid walls of bookshelves. On them I could see complete sets of gold-embossed Shakespeare, Dickens, and Twain. Above those shelves were framed pictures of family on one wall, and alone on the other a beautifully clean and elegant lithograph of a horse in snow country.

I stepped into her bedroom. It was immaculate, the bed made, the suits in her closet discreetly tailored and tasteful. Lying open on her nightstand was a hardcover book, open to page 247. *Van Gogh: His Life and His Art.*

I thought for a second that I might have entered the wrong apartment. But looking back at me from the bureau was Miss Lessing, her beauty undimmed by a graduation cap and gown, her diploma held to her breast as she smiled into the camera. I walked to the photo and ran my fingers along it, feeling an excitement rising in me as I had never known. I set about my delicate work.

The finest listening devices in the world were invented in Norway. Øres, they are called, after the Norwegian word for *ear,* and they can be purchased in either of two shops along Electric Row in Oslo. An Øre weighs five grams and is scarcely an inch in circumference. The device itself is encased in porous plastic, no part of its wiring visible to the naked eye, even on close inspection. If discovered, it looks like nothing; a piece of a curtain rod, maybe, or a part broken off a furniture joint. You would throw it away without a second thought. Yet with a speck of adhesive this tiny lump can be attached to almost anything; and once attached, it can pick up a sigh from ten feet away, a whisper from thirty. The Mossad have used them for years.

My work required just ten minutes. In the kitchenette I took advantage of the quarter-inch gap between the stove and the cabinet, securing one Øre, out of sight, to the side of the latter. A second I tucked into her telephone receiver. In the living room I attached one to the bottom of the couch. In the bathroom one lies hidden in the top corner of her medicine cabinet. And then I stepped again into her bedroom.

I walked to her bed and knelt beside it. I unscrewed the plastic plate of the electrical outlet, and with the aid of a hanger I ran an Øre up until it was level with her mattress. I pressed it firmly to the inside wall. A quarter inch of plaster would be no match for it, I knew. It would stay, silent and listening, not ten inches from her pillow.

The Øre transmits any sound it captures to its mother unit receiver, a black box the size of an electric shaver. This box I positioned beneath the sill outside her bedroom window. It is visible only from across the way, and across the way is the bare wall of another building. This mother unit, in turn, beams what it receives out into the air along a dedicated frequency: a radio transmission, essentially. Its range is limited, no more than two miles, but that made no difference. It is only a mile and a half from Miss Lessing's windowsill to my own.

And on my sill sits my own mother unit, collecting input from its twin on Eighty-third Street and feeding that input through cable wire into my stereo, where it is directed through my amplifier and so, magically, out my speakers.

Yes, I can sit in my living room at 1200 Sutton Place and listen to Miss Lessing. And listen efficiently, for each Øre in her apartment can be controlled from mine, activated or shut off by electrical impulses sent through the mother units. Thus I can follow her from room to room and not be held hostage to the sound of the dishwasher when in fact she has stepped into the bath.

The industrious Øres burn themselves out quickly. Every three months I must slip back inside to plant fresh ones. Five hundred dollars apiece, they are. Ten thousand dollars it has cost me to listen to Miss Lessing this past year. To hear her every spoken word, to drift off each night to the sound of her gentle breathing.

Ten thousand dollars to reclaim what I thought I had lost forever.

CHAPTER SIX

"We sin in the full knowledge that we are sinning."

Father Ryan used to say that in confession when I was a girl, anytime I pretended not to know if a lie or a mean comment counted as a sin.

It is nine o'clock Thursday night, and I sit with Jake Teller at the polished oak table in the conference room. Through the open window come soft sounds from the street far below. We are alone in the firm.

"The final piece," he says, handing me a page still warm from the printer. "Derivatives — a crib sheet."

"Thanks," I say. I three-hole-punch it and slide it into the presentation binder in front of me. I close the binder and look over at him. "We're done, aren't we?"

Jake nods. "I'll call for our rides."

I stare down at the binder and take a quiet breath. *Play it safe, Mimi.* All I have to do is let Jake

Teller call the car service, and our time together will be done. Six nights it's taken us, three of them late ones, but we've mastered the Brice account. Our report is ready for Mr. Stein, and because it's ready, my work with Jake Teller is finished. I'll see him only in the hallways. In the daytime.

"Jake?"

He looks up, phone in hand. I try to imagine what my fiancé is doing this very second. At his desk at the magazine, leaning over a sentence. Changing the passive voice to the active.

"You've been a huge help," I say. "Can I buy you a drink?"

The night is cool and the streets busy as we walk down Lexington Avenue. I'm a fast walker, but even so, Jake slows his pace for me. He is tall, an athlete, and I knew when he shook my hand in Mr. Stein's office that he wasn't like the other associates. I've never had to "handle" any of the men in the firm. The partners are my father's age, and they act it, and the other associates are . . . lost in their work. They come to my desk with account questions and with nothing, ever, in their tone or eyes. Jake is different. I shouldn't be doing this.

We turn onto Thirty-ninth Street and walk east, and two blocks later we reach the Gangway Pub. Music and light spill out the door as Jake holds it open for me. Earlier this evening Anne called me in the conference room, and I promised to meet her here at ten o'clock. Just forty minutes from now. My out, if I should need one.

We walk across a floor covered with sawdust

and peanut shells, past a long bar crowded with young grads. Guys with their ties pulled free of their collars buy drinks for girls who came for happy hour and haven't left. We find a small wooden booth near the back and slide in across from each other. The wall beside us is covered with college pennants, two hundred of them at least, in all colors, and in among them are plastic busts of old rock stars. Buddy Holly, Elvis, Janis Joplin. I can hear Alanis singing from the jukebox about broken trust as a waitress in a Duke sweatshirt smiles at us and takes a pen from her hair.

"I'll take a Bass," says Jake.

"A glass of chardonnay, please." She walks off to the bar.

"The friend you're meeting — she's in the wedding?" Jake asks.

"Anne's my maid of honor. She's in charge of the bridesmaids' dresses, and I've had to put her off all week. She said if I don't meet her tonight, they'll all wear jeans."

He laughs. "Can I see?" he asks, looking at my ring.

I lift my hand to show it to him. He takes it, his thumb resting on my pulse a second, then lets go as our waitress returns and places our drinks in front of us. Jake raises his pint and touches it gently to my thin-stemmed wineglass.

"The outside world," he says. "It's good to see it again."

"Thanks for all your help, Jake — it made the difference."

"Sure."

I take a sip of wine. I've been drinking a full glass before bed for a week now. Since the send-off party last Friday.

"This place reminds me of my frat house," he says, looking around. "Except for the girls. Is your school up there?"

I scan the colored pennants and find the familiar blue and white. "Between Duke and Syracuse."

He looks surprised. "You're a UConn girl?"

"Yes. Why?"

"It's a party school."

"That's an unfair rep."

"I meant it as a compliment."

"Where did you go?"

He motions with his eyes. "Up at the top, in the middle."

"Hamilton?"

He nods. "Thirty grand a year. Nonrefundable, it turns out."

I laugh. I can feel the wine starting to warm me. It's 9:40. If I'd put off Anne and gone home, I'd be in the bath now, soaking away my thoughts, the steam rising from the water as I slide down into it. *It's time, Mimi.*

"Can I ask you something, Jake?"

"Sure."

His green dress shirt sets off the blue of his eyes. There is something in them I can't place. Something buried.

"You got into Diane Silio's car last Friday," I say.

He takes the pint from his lips, surprised. Wary. He places it carefully on the table.

"She told you that?"

"No. I couldn't take the smoke in the bar. I went outside for air. You were speaking to the driver, and then you got inside."

Jake looks down at the table, then back at me. These past six nights, working side by side in the conference room, there's been something in the silence between us. Something rich. Narcotic. He understands it now.

"You watched her leave?" he says.

"Through the bar window. She opened the car door and hesitated."

"For just a second."

"Yes."

"Two more here?" asks the waitress, appearing again. My glass is empty, and I see that my fingers, gripping the stem, are white. I let go.

"Red this time, please," I say.

"The house cab?"

"Fine."

Jake nods yes to another pint, and the waitress walks off. I look down at the old wooden table. People have cut their initials into it. *LN. JB. TR loves BN.* We're quiet until she returns with our drinks, sets them down, and leaves. Under the table my free hand finds my stocking.

"What do you want to ask me, Mimi?"

I try to meet his eyes, but I can't. My legs feel light.

"Why were you in her car?"

"That's not what you want to know." His voice is different — harder. My face is crimson, and he sees it. "You want to know what we did."

The wine in my glass is so dark that it's black. I look up and see something new in his eyes — flint. "I'm going to tell you a story my grandfather told me," he says, his voice low but all I hear now. The clink of glasses, the music, the hum of the bar — all gone. "And then, if you still want to, you can ask your question."

I manage to nod.

"Grandpa married his wife at nineteen, and six months later he shipped out to Europe to fight in World War Two. She was pregnant when he left, and he was stone in love with her. She wrote him every day he was gone. And he wrote back. Even from the front, he wrote back. Wrote on anything he could find. Newspaper, and when that was gone, toilet paper. If the guys in the foxhole had found out, it wouldn't have been a German trying to shoot him."

Jake takes a sip of beer. His eyes stay on mine, measuring me.

"Her letters came in bunches, during breaks in the fighting. Two weeks would pass with no mail, and then ten would come in a day. He read them over and over. In trenches, by moonlight, by the light of artillery fire. Read about his new son. 'He's crawling now, he's standing up, he's got his first tooth.' Through all the fighting, he carried those letters pressed against his skin. Mud, blood, sweat, rain, everything got on them. Most dissolved away to nothing.

"One day he opened a letter to find a picture of her in a cotton dress, standing on the porch at sunset. I've seen the picture — she was beautiful."

Jake looks away a second.

"Grandpa used medical tape to tape that picture over his heart. Late in the war, his unit gets pinned down in a ditch at Saint-Mihiel, in France. Surrounded, nowhere to go. Getting it from all sides. They lose twenty-six of thirty men. Night comes, and they run out of ammo. Start throwing rocks. They run out of rocks. They lie still and wait for dawn, when the Germans will come to the mouth of the ditch and kill them. They draw their knives, hoping that between the four of them they might take one German with them. When the first rays of light come, Grandpa takes the picture from his chest and holds it to his face. He wants it to be the last thing he sees.

"Dawn breaks — no Germans. They wait — still no Germans. They crawl out of the ditch — no Germans. They left during the night.

"The war ended a month later. Grandpa spent his last night over there in Paris. Lying in a bunk, staring at the picture of the beautiful wife he's going home to in six hours. Rereading the few of her letters that had survived. At two A.M., he gives up on trying to sleep and goes for a walk through the streets. Paris is newly liberated — a carnival, right? He walks through the different quarters packed with revelers. Soldiers, British and Ameri-

can. Civilians. He keeps walking, and after a while
the streets thin out. They are cobblestone now.
Passing a small church, something in the doorway
catches his eye. It is a woman. A young Gypsy
beauty, standing alone, the light of a streetlamp
falling on her black hair, her flashing eyes.

"They stand looking at each other. And then she
beckons him, and he steps into the doorway. She's
eighteen, maybe, and smells as clean as the spring
rain. She speaks softly to him in French. He doesn't
understand, but her hands are on him now, touching his face, his chest. She feels the weight in his
shirt pocket and pulls out the picture. She holds it
to the light. 'Elle est très jolie,' she says. *She's very
pretty.* Then she takes his hand and puts it under
her dress, right on her thigh. He's never felt anything that smooth. That warm."

Jake looks away, then back at me.

"Then she says, in English: 'Ten francs.' "

Jake is quiet.

"She was a prostitute," I say.

"Yes. A whore."

"What did he do?"

"He walked away."

We are both quiet.

"He told me that story the day I left for college.
And he said this: 'God doesn't show you what
you're made of — that's the devil's job.' " Jake
leans forward, the sleeve of his shirt brushing my
bare arm.

"When is the wedding?"

"In a month."

"You met in college?"

"Yes."

He looks at the wall a second, his eyes on the pennants but not seeing them. He looks back at me.

"Ask me, Mimi."

My nails press through my stocking, into my knee. I can't say a word.

"A month ago I saw the first crush of my adolescence through a Benetton window. She was still a beauty. A week later I went back to her store at closing time. I took her for a drink, and then I took her back to her empty store." Jake holds my eyes until he sees I understand.

"Diane Silio was one of many, Mimi. Tomorrow it will be someone else."

"You have sex with them," I say finally, my voice far away.

"More than that."

I feel the blood in my head. I'm dizzy.

"You want in, Mimi — you have to ask in. Ask me."

My hand goes to the top of my blouse, and his eyes follow it. I look up at him.

"What do you do to them?"

Jake leans toward me, then puts down his pint. He looks at me, past me, then stands and smiles.

"You must be Anne," he says, and reaches like a gentleman for the hand of my maid of honor.

I'm all caught up, finally.

Seven o'clock Saturday evening and I sit in my office at the firm, grateful for the mountain of re-

turns and extension forms and client reports that
have kept me at my desk all day. Grateful because
they've kept my mind off of Thursday night and
Jake Teller and the question I can't quite believe I
asked him. Anne rescued me from an answer, but
two nights later, as I print out and now sign this last
tax return, I think again of the electric moment in
the small booth just before she walked up on us.
The heat in my face, the look in Jake's eyes. I think
of it and I look at the phone on my desk. His extension is seven two six. He must have accounts to
catch up on, too.

Enough. Back to work, Mimi. I pull out the Brice
account binder. One last pass through it, then I'll
stop for the night. I'll call Mark and ask him if he
knows anyone who can be at my place in an hour
with a bottle of wine and a Caribbean movie. Mark
booked our honeymoon today, and he called earlier
to say that the travel agency had given him a video
and that when I see it, I'll forget about the cere-
mony — and the reception, too — and beg him to
elope tonight. It'll be just the evening I need.
Maybe I can even forget Thursday night.

I open the binder and start in. Mr. Stein's lunch
with Andrew Brice will be delicate. "Dragging him
from the nineteenth century to the twenty-first," as
Jake said, "without pissing him off." I scan the
stock portfolio that Brice's father left him so long
ago. An investor's dream, really, filled with first-
tier stocks that would have risen like redwoods
these past three decades if Brice hadn't cashed

them in as soon as he got his hands on them. He'll have to start over now.

I turn to the investment scenarios we prepared. Clipped to the top of the first one is a handwritten note, and reading it, I feel the breath go out of me.

To answer your question, Mimi.
Tax Statutes: Volume 47, Section 38.1.
Jake

I look up suddenly, as if he might be in the doorway. It is empty. I sit still and listen to the soft sounds of the office — the hum of the air conditioner, the faint clicking of a keyboard down the hall. Another associate, logging weekend hours. I look down again at the note.

The firm keeps its tax statute books in the conference room. I take the Brice binder with me and walk down the hallway. I don't see anyone, and when I reach the conference room I find the light on but the room itself empty and quiet. It is my favorite room in the firm, smelling of wood and made cozy despite its size by the floor-to-ceiling bookshelves that line the walls, each filled with leather-bound volumes so beautiful that it's easy to forget they aren't classics but tax tomes. They always remind me of the gold-embossed hardcovers by my bed at home, my graduation gift from Grandma just weeks before she died.

I walk to the shelves and run my fingers along the black spines, down one row, up the next, until I reach volume 47. I pull it out and page through the statutes, the book heavy in my hands, its pages creamy and thin, like those in a Bible. Section 35, 36, 37. Here it is — 38.1. Tucked between the pages is a page torn from a magazine. It is folded in half, then in half again, so that all I can see is the back of it — a cigarette ad. I replace the book on the shelf and walk with the folded page to the window.

I could throw it out and let the wind take it God knows where. Not even look at it. Put an end, right here, to this . . . game I'm playing against myself. *You're a month from the altar, Mimi. A month.* I close my eyes. Mark wrote the check for the honeymoon today. Thirteen days and twelve nights in Jamaica. A stone hot tub on a balcony on the cliffs looking down on the sea. Long walks on the white-sand beach at sunset.

I step from the window to the conference table and sit down. I switch on a green banker's lamp and place the folded page in its light. I close my eyes, unfold it, and smooth it with trembling fingers against the hard oak table. I open my eyes.

A woman lies on a bed, wearing only bra and panties. A black blindfold covers her eyes, and her wrists and ankles are tied to the bedposts with white silk. In the bottom corner, handwritten in blue ink:

The bar at the Roosevelt Hotel — 10:00 Saturday night.

I fold the picture in half, put it in my lap, and open the Brice binder again. I turn to the investment scenarios. Three separate ones we designed, each a careful mix of blue-chippers and high-upside stocks. I try to focus on our "governing principles" — reward him in a runaway market, protect him in a slack one. A cautious approach, as Mr. Stein advised, but not a weak one. I close the binder and look at the picture again. Her lips are parted in a gasp, and each of the ties is stretched taut — she can't move.

I walk to the window, feeling dizzy. I look for the Chrysler Building, and there it is, to the west, its jagged metal spires sparkling in the night. I've always loved them. Tonight they look dangerous. I walk back through the quiet halls to my office, where I put away the binder, tuck the picture into my purse, and call Mark. I'll be later than I thought, I tell him. Tonight won't work. Can we have brunch tomorrow and watch the video then?

Yes, he says.

In the reception area, waiting for the elevator, I pull my sweater close around my shoulders. I watch the silent floor indicators light up one after another, and think of something my mother told me years ago. *Men see nice girls and want to ruin them. They can't help themselves.*

In the lobby my low heels sound loud on the marble floor. The night guard, smelling of Old Spice, opens the logbook for me and turns down the baseball game playing on his tattered transistor. I sign out and he nods kindly, then follows me with his eyes until I'm through the glass doors and into the street, the cool night air a tonic on my face. I raise my hand for a cab, and one cuts across traffic and glides to a stop in front of me. I slide inside.

"Where to, miss?"

Jake Teller must have been in the office this morning. He knew I'd come in and go over the presentation again.

"Miss?"

"I'm sorry. Eighty-third and York, please." I'll go home first. I'll change and run, and then we'll see.

The driver's ID tag reads NABOUSSEM. Akrika Naboussem. I watch his gloved hands on the wheel. They are leather and tight over his skin. Like Mark's golf gloves.

Last night I met Mark at Vine, the wine bar around the corner from my apartment. We drank a glass of wine and then cabbed to Anne's high-rise building at Fortieth along the water, where her Irish doorman, as Anne had arranged, led us without a word to the elevator, took us to the top floor, and then unlocked the fire door that opens out onto the roof. There, by the railing, in a chilled bucket, were two glasses and a bottle of Jordan champagne.

Mark was overwhelmed. Stunned at the champagne, at the city spread below and all around us. I hadn't counted on the quiet, so far up — we could hear just the wind and each other, and it was as if we had the island to ourselves. We stood close together against the wind and raised our glasses to the lights of the city and the dark, beautiful East River.

In the cab on the way home to my place, the driver's eyes went to the rearview mirror as Mark kissed my neck and slipped a hand between my knees. At my building Mark fumbled for the fare in his excitement. I tried to guide him to the couch, then to the floor, but he took me by the hand to the bed. He was fast with our clothes and strong inside me, and afterward, lying on his chest, I thought, *Yes, I can do this. Through the years.* I thought of the wedding, so soon now, of the processional, the sun filtering through the church glass, glinting off the ring resting on the soft pillow his nephew will carry down the aisle. I kissed Mark's chest, listened to his peaceful breathing, closed my eyes and saw, very clearly, the blue eyes of Jake Teller. And I realized what I'd seen in those blue eyes in the small booth in the bar Thursday night.

Cruelty.

"Which corner, miss?"

"The near corner."

In my apartment I change into my running clothes and then walk down the five flights and out onto the street again. It is my first run in a week and I go hard, over to the water and then down the lit river walkway. I run all the way to Twenty-third Street, touch the railing, then turn and really push myself on the return, *striding*, as I learned in track, leaning into the pain, letting it cleanse me. Six miles in all, and then I shower and dress in a blouse and stirrups, sweeping the hair from my forehead with a hairband, my hand on the Chanel bottle, the cap off, before I catch myself and put it back.

It is 9:30. I'll take the subway.

*   *   *

At Forty-second Street I rise from my seat into the
crowd of passengers and follow them out the subway doors. I move with them along the platform,
up the stairs, through the turnstiles, and up into the
swirl of Grand Central. I cross the main terminal,
with its ballroom ceiling, and walk out into the city
night. Food vendors are still working the sidewalk
from their wheeled carts, and the smell of
caramelized nuts scents the air as I walk past the
bootblacks, looking away from the last one, whose
eyes go to my blouse even as he keeps up his patter
and shines away. I turn north onto Madison, the
crowd thinning as I pass the scrubbed windows of
the delis, the well-dressed mannequins in the fine
boutiques.

Two hundred people in a church wedding. The
invitations already sent out. And I walk toward the
Roosevelt Hotel to meet Jake Teller. And if I close
my eyes and try to imagine my fiancé's face, I see
instead Diane Silio. I see her pausing at the door of
the limo and then getting inside.

*We will talk — nothing more. And then I'll be done
with him.*

In front of me now is the Roosevelt. I pass
through the revolving doors into its enormous
lobby. The ceiling is beautifully high, the decor that
of a 1950s gentleman's club: dark reds, velour. Gra-
cious porters weave their luggage racks among the
foreign businessmen who sit reading newspapers
in deep, well-spaced chairs, all under the sharp eye
of the graying concierge. On the far side, not set off
from the lobby at all but a part of it, is the elegant

hotel bar, intimate, the lights kept low, a handsome bartender in a chiffon shirt working the circular brass bar alone. I see couples and a few men, but no Jake Teller. I take a seat at the bar, and the bartender walks over.

"For the lady?" he says.

"A glass of cabernet, please."

In one smooth motion he plucks a glass from an overhead rack, flips it upright in front of me, comes up with a bottle of Sterling from under the counter and deftly pours out two-thirds of a glass. The wine smells of oak, of leather. The bartender takes my money to the register and returns with my change.

"Miss Lessing, yes?" he says.

I look at him in surprise. "Yes."

"For you."

He pulls a small envelope from his shirt pocket and lays it on the bar in front of me. He nods discreetly and walks down the bar to another customer. I look quickly around to see if anyone has noticed, feeling the deep red rising in my cheeks, then slip the envelope into my purse. I take a deep sip of wine.

It is five minutes before I open it, keeping it in my lap as I do. Inside is a hotel-room key, and wrapped around the key is another note. I look up to see the bartender glance over from down the bar. He looks down again at the snifter glass he is drying, and I read the note.

She will arrive in Room 740 at 10:30. The closet is less than ten feet from the bed. You will hear everything.

I put the note in my purse, and my hands on the bar. I'm surprised at how steady they are. My nails need a coat of polish. Did I bring any, I wonder? I take another sip of wine. It is 10:15.

I've always thought the soul was the seat of sex. How else could it be? You love and trust someone, and your desire springs from that. I make love to Mark because I love Mark. He's all I need. I look out across the busy lobby to the revolving doors. I'll walk out them and into a taxi and take it straight to Mark's apartment. I'll surprise him. I open my purse, take out ten dollars, and leave it for the bartender, as though to keep our secret. He nods from down the bar, then watches me stand and walk to the elevators.

I ride alone to the seventh floor and step out into the deserted hallway. My steps barely sound in the deep carpet. At room 740, I push the key into the lock and open the door a few inches. I listen, then open it the rest of the way and walk into the room. It is empty, the blinds drawn. I turn on the light. A modest hotel room like a thousand others. By the window is a desk without a chair. In front of the desk is a king-size bed. I close the door behind me and walk to it.

Tied to each of the four posts are strips of white silk. They lie on the bedspread, their free ends looped into loose knots. One for each wrist and ankle. I feel weak and sit down on the bed. I touch one of the ties, careful not to disturb the knot. I've never felt anything so soft. I try to imagine it against my wrist. Tight against it, restraining. On the pillow is a black sleeping blindfold, the kind they give you on airplanes, and next to it is a folded note.

This morning Mark and I argued about the wedding. He wants it on video, and I don't. He never once raised his voice, and I remember thinking that he'd never slap me, ever. Even if I deserved it.

The clock radio by the bed reads 10:25. I walk to the closet and open the slatted doors. Inside is the chair that belongs at the desk. I sit down on it and pull the doors closed. The slats are close on one another, heavy, and block out all light. I lay my coat and purse at my feet and run my fingers over the slats. I find a hook latch and secure it. There.

From the hallway I can hear voices. Male voices, nearing. A short laugh, the word *golf*, more laughter. I can picture them: stout, in heavy suits. Their voices fade, and it is quiet again. Maybe she won't come. Some of them must tell him no.

From far away I hear the soft *ting* of the elevator bell. Twenty seconds pass and now, yes, the click of the key in the lock, and the sigh of the door as it opens. Is it Jake or is it her? The door closes. Through the wooden slats of the closet comes the scent of perfume. She has come. The scent seems familiar, somehow, but I can't place it. Her steps take her to the bed, then stop. She is looking down at the ties. Seeing them for the first time — so pretty, so severe. Feeling the chill I felt, deep in the spine, but so much stronger. Looking down at her wrists, maybe, feeling the silk on them already. Wondering if she can tie them loosely or if he will notice and pull them tight. I hear the rustle of paper. The note.

I grew up in a house with rules, and I'm set to marry a man who won't set any. Is that it? I hear the voice of Father Ryan again *. . . in the full knowledge that we are sinning*. At the edge of my memory is something else he used to say. Something about *the path*.

I listen to the whisper of her clothing as she takes off her blouse, her skirt, her shoes. Yes, the note would tell her to strip to bra and panties. To slip her wrists and ankles through the knots. Like the girl in the picture. Jake Teller will have total control. She won't be able to move. I hear the give of the bed as she lies down. She is still for thirty seconds. A minute. I wish I could have a sip of water. The air in the closet is close and hot. In the room, too, I realize. He's turned on the heat. He wants her warm.

I hear the sound of the bedside phone lifted from the cradle. She is making a call? Who could she call? She's lost her nerve. She's calling to tell Jake Teller she can't go through with it. She will dress and leave, and I'll be alone. *Please don't*. I hear the sound of the buttons as she dials. Silence, and then a whispered voice. A voice I've known since I was six.

"Mimi, pick up. Mimi? Mimi, it's me, Anne." A pause. "A girl makes her own luck these days, right? I called him — Jake Teller. I'm at the Roosevelt Hotel. And you *will not believe* what I'm about to do. I'll call."

I sit stunned. *Breathe slowly, Mimi. Slowly, or she will hear.* I put my forehead to the wooden slats. Through them I hear her replace the phone in its cradle. Her breathing is quicker now. She tries to slow it, to calm herself. She whispers something I can't make out. And now I can hear, barely, the soft pull of silk. Father Ryan's words come back to me. *We can regain the path, but only if we keep it in sight.* And another sound now, from the hallway, faint but clear.

The elevator bell.

CHAPTER SEVEN

It is nearly 1:00 A.M., and neither one of us can sleep.

Miss Lessing returned home just after midnight. On her phone machine was a message from her friend Anne Keltner. Anne called from the Roosevelt Hotel, to brag in advance of a conquest. "You will not believe what I'm about to do," she said. Miss Lessing played her message three times, then began to pace.

For almost thirty minutes I listened to the soft sounds of her steps on the living-room floor. Then I heard the phone lifted from its cradle. She pressed four digits, then cut off the call. She pressed five digits and cut off the call again. And then she undressed. Not in her bedroom, as she usually does. Usually she hangs each article carefully in her closet. Tonight she shed her clothes in the living room — onto the floor, by the sound of it — and then stepped into a steaming shower. After fifteen minutes I heard the water shut off and the glass shower door slide open, and moments later Miss Lessing walked to the phone again. She pressed three digits and killed the call.

It was music that finally calmed her. *The Kreisler Album*, Joshua Bell on violin. It is an album that I sent her six months ago, in the guise of a radio station giveaway. The fourth track is her favorite. "Caprice Viennois." She plays it more than any other, and there is a moment, one minute and twelve seconds into it, that she loves especially. The aching violin refrain, which will find its mark in any heart receptive to beauty. She has learned precisely when it comes, and no matter what she is doing — dressing, bathing, preparing dinner — she stops and quiets. Tonight it worked again. Just before the refrain came, her slippers stopped sounding. And though I was twenty blocks away, I could picture her, standing quietly in her living room, her eyes closed. I stared into my black speakers, and together we listened to the pure violin notes.

And now minutes later, as the song ends, I listen to Miss Lessing cross to her stereo, take out the compact disc, and snap it into its case. I wait for her pacing to start again, but instead her steps fade away. I silence the living-room Øre and activate the one in her bedroom, in time to hear her footsteps and now the click of her bed lamp. And now the soft give of her bed as she climbs into it. Most nights she will read before sleep, but now I hear the bed lamp click off. Sometimes she will play a song on her cassette player. A minute passes, and now

two, and the only sound is her breathing, calm and
even.

It is late but I pour myself a small glass of wine
and walk to the chair by the window. I sit down
and look out, west into the dark night. Anne Keltner's phone message was not the only one this
evening. Miss Lessing's fiancé called as well. He
was sorry she would be stuck at the office all night,
he said. She should think of tomorrow, and of the
Caribbean, and be happy.

I take a sip of wine. Miss Lessing was home by
7:30. She went for a run, showered, dressed, and
went out again. Without ever calling her fiancé.

I look up suddenly into the speakers. Her breathing — it is different. Deeper. I hear other sounds.
The rustle of her comforter. I lean forward in my
chair. Her breathing, so smooth a moment ago, is
shortening now. Quickening. I set my wineglass on
the windowsill. Not once in a year have I heard
this. With her fiancé, yes. But not this.

Her breathing quickens further. And still further.
And now a soft gasp. A soft cry. And again. And
again. And again.

CHAPTER EIGHT

Nina Torring was a Delaware beauty with thin Scandinavian legs and hair like the noon sun. She was our dorm adviser freshman year, and she made you want to tank a midterm or get caught in the lounge with liquor — anything to be called to her room for a talk. She was the lone senior in the dorm, a woman among girls, but her delicate build fired all of us first-year men with aching notions of purity. Just maybe, we imagined, nothing had ever been done to her.

From my top bunk I could see out the big window to the clearing in front of the dorm. The library closed at eleven, and night after winter night I watched Nina come up the packed snow path at 11:15, hand in hand with Nick Simms. Nick was a senior, too, and a tough Jersey kid whose steady play at shooting guard was keeping me out of the starting five. I'd see their breath in the lamplight before they passed from sight, and then minutes later I'd see Nick start back down the path alone. If he didn't, I'd stare out at the falling snow, at the salt scattered along the empty walkway, and then up into the dark cement ceiling above me.

All season long I gained on Nick in practice. By March I was torching him daily, blowing past him when he crowded me and knocking down the jumper when he gave me room. Coach hated to trust freshmen, especially guards, but I knew that when the tournament came, and it was win or go home, he'd put his best five out there on the floor.

A week before the tourney, I was lying in bed with a beer when I heard low whispers in the hallway and the sharp click of a lighter. I dropped from the bunk, grabbed a towel, and stuffed it into the crack beneath the door. On the other side, I knew, were Pardo and Reeder, drunk on stolen fraternity beer and armed with the fireworks we'd bought in South Carolina over break. I heard the fizz of the fuses as I went for my own stash, and then one! two! three! sonic booms as the cherry bombs exploded in the narrow hallway. I lit the fuse on my bottle rocket, waited three seconds, and pulled open the door.

I could hardly see through the smoke bombs they'd laid down to cover their retreat, but I took aim and held the bottle steady, realizing a split second too late that the moving target at the end of the hall wasn't one of my pledge buddies but Suzie Carr, scared from her room by the blasts and racing for the safety of the lounge. My low tracer caught her right in the ass. She grabbed her singed pants with both hands and screamed and screamed, and

as her screams mixed with the din of the smoke
alarm and the shouts of angry students jarred
awake, I knew Pardo and Reeder were halfway
across the quad. Nina Torring stepped into the
hallway seconds later, catching me dead to rights, a
pile of spent fireworks at my feet and a smoking
beer bottle in my hands.

"Please clean all of this up," she said quietly, her
blond hair spilling down the long T-shirt she'd
been sleeping in. I nodded, and she turned and
walked away.

Three things could get a player suspended from
the team — bad grades, bad behavior, and alcohol.
The next day after classes I sat in my room, turning
a basketball in my hands and waiting for the call to
come. At five the phone rang, but it was Grandpa,
calling to tell me he'd be driving up for the tournament. I stared at the wall in front of me. He
wouldn't stay over, I knew, but would drive four
hours home after the game and, if we won, four
hours back for the next one. I was still staring at the
wall when Nina Torring called. Could I please
come to her room? I walked past the sulfur stains
I'd tried to scrub out of the rug, then through the
lounge, where Suzie Carr sat, pretending to study.

Nina closed the door behind me and turned a
wooden desk chair toward her bed. A blue sweatshirt hid her pliant body, but her gray tights ended
at her calves, and as she sat down cross-legged on
her covers, I could see her golden ankles, see the
small medallion scar on her left one. I sat down on
the chair just a few feet away from her.

"Somebody could have been badly hurt, Jake."

"I know."

"I have to turn you in."

I looked down at the floor. I thought of Grandpa, of the silence on the line when I'd tell him.

"Nick put in his two cents, I'll bet," I said.

Her blue eyes flashed. "Actions have consequences, Jake. I'm sorry you had to learn this way."

"Did Nick tell you Coach named me the starter in practice this morning?" I watched her eyes. "I didn't think so." I stood to go. "More power to him," I said quietly, walking to the door and from her room.

The next morning at 5:30 I crossed the silent white campus to the gym, my boots sinking deep into the crystalline snow. The janitor was just opening the door, and I dressed alone in the locker room in the cold quiet, breathing in the smell of rubber bath mats and tile. I laced up my sneakers and took to the court, rolling the ball racks into place and then moving hard from station to station, firing jumpers from the corner, the elbow, the top of the key, the elbow, the corner, and then back around the circle the other way. I shot for half an hour, finding my release point, repeating, repeating, moving and shooting even as I saw Coach in the doorway, even as he walked over to me, even as I waited for him to ask me into his office. "Hold your follow-through, Teller," he said. "One-thousand one, one-thousand two." A few minutes later, in practice, he put me with the first team, and all morning the offense seemed to run itself. Every time I came hard

off a screen, the ball was there, and if I wasn't rising over Nick Simms to knock down a jumper, I
was feeding one of the big men at the rim.

That night I sat in my room again, staring at the
phone. It never rang, and at 11:15 I watched Nina
Torring walk up the path. She walked alone, her
blond hair tucked inside a wool cap, her flushed
face framed for a second by the lamplight. I waited
twenty minutes and then went to her room and
knocked on the door. She opened it a little, saw me,
and opened it wide. The heat was up all the way,
and she wore shorts and a long pink T-shirt that she
pulled down over her knees when she sat down on
the edge of her bed. I turned the desk chair toward
her and sat down.

"Thank you," I said.

She smiled. "If there's a next time, I'll call the dean
at home."

"There won't be."

"Write Suzie a nice letter of apology."

"Sure. Nick was pissed, wasn't he?"

"I'll make it up to him."

We sat quietly for a few seconds. On the shelf
above her bed was a row of stuffed animals.

"He says you'll cost us in a close game," she said.

"He'll have a pretty good view of it."

She laughed. Her T-shirt slipped off her knee, and
she pulled it back down.

"You watch me come up the walk, don't you?"
she asked.

"Every night."

She drew a pillow from behind her and held it in her lap.

"Tell me, Jake Teller. When the boys talk — in the locker rooms, on the buses. What do they say?"

I looked at the flower bedspread, at the shape of her knees through her shirt.

"They brag about how much wood they're giving their girls. About how many days it takes them to walk right again."

"Nick doesn't say those things."

I paused. "No."

I reached out, slipped her T-shirt off her leg, and pressed my hand to her small knee. Her leg tensed, and she covered my hand with both of hers, but her eyes, on mine, were calm. I tried to slide my hand up her leg. "No, Jake," she said, and I stopped. She lifted her hands from mine, and I left it on her knee a few electric seconds, looking into her eyes, my heart racing, and then took it away and stood, trying not to shake as I walked to the door. "Jake," she said evenly. I turned around. "Shoot well — it's tournament time."

We swept through the field and took the trophy. I scored twenty-two in the final, and Nick, sent in to play the point when our starter fouled out, hit four big free throws down the stretch and found me in the corner for the long jumper that put them away. Grandpa took me to dinner after the game, then dropped me off behind the chapel, where Pardo and Reeder waited with sixteen-ounce Coors and a Psi U brother who, for five bucks a man, led us down an icy path to the back of the old fraternity house. He pointed to the window he'd jimmied open, and we climbed through, up a set of back stairs, and stood, magically, at the keg, dizzy at the thought of free beer and dazzled by the sight of the coeds dancing in the dark to "Rosalita." The old wooden floor shook as they answered the call to "jump a little higher," their arms above them, their jeweled wrists shimmering in the dark. We pounded down plastic cups of beer, then high-fived one another and headed into the swarm. I cut in on a girl in a black leather mini who didn't run when the music slowed but held my hand to her waist and pressed against me, her neck smelling of some forgotten spice, her fingers in my hair as I brushed at the glitter on her cheek. She was pulling me in for a kiss when the shrill burst of the sentry's whistle cut through the music.

I looked to the front door and, sure enough, there came the goon squad, the team of campus cops and turncoat students that raided frat parties to check IDs. I kissed the girl once, hard; said, "Sorry — freshman"; and then slipped down the stairs and out the same window I'd come in, pulling myself up into the snow in time to see two more cops slip-sliding toward me down the icy path. I escaped into the glen, starting the long way home across campus as, through the open windows of the frat house, the piano and harp intro started up and then, clear and strong, Bruce:

> *The screen door slams*
> *Mary's dress waves*

Like a vision she dances across the porch
As the radio plays
Roy Orbison singing for the lonely
Hey that's me and I want you only
Don't turn me home again . . .

The words faded as I walked deeper into the pristine glen, over the icy footbridge, the bark glittering on the white trees all around me. I felt vital, invincible, the cold air sharp in my lungs, the future stretching before me like a runway. I was still a month from my first fuck, but I could sense it now, had seen the possibility of it in the eyes of the girl on the dance floor. And tomorrow morning the school paper would lead with the story of the game. Twenty-two points. Ten of thirteen from the field. I closed my eyes and remembered the shots. The beauty of them, the purity. The way I'd known they were going in before they ever left my hand.

I came up out of the glen into the field behind the dorm. I could see into the windows of the dark rooms, the blinds left up because there was only the empty field and then miles and miles of farmland rolling away to the Adirondacks. In the corner room on the first floor I saw, in profile, a girl sitting up in her bed, looking down on someone I couldn't see, someone who lay beneath the window line but whose hands played with the buttons of the girl's shirt.

The corner room, I knew, was Nina Torring's, and the moon lit her like a soft candle as she pulled her shirt open and let it slip off her shoulders and down her arms. I walked closer to the window. The nipples were sharp and raised on her small breasts. I walked closer still. She took two of his fingers into her mouth and then put them on her breasts. I closed to within five feet of the window and dropped to a knee in the snow. She slid off the bed, sensually, stood beside it, pulled at the drawstring on her sweats, then looked out the window and into my eyes. For a full second we stared at each other. I waited for her to cry out, for Nick Simms's head to appear in the window, but she simply looked away from me and back down at him, then pulled the knot out of the drawstring and let her sweats fall to the floor. I saw the tight vee of her panties, and then, her eyes still on Nick, she rolled them down her legs and stepped out of them.

She would reach for the blinds now. No. She climbed back into bed and lowered herself onto him. And then, as I watched through my breath in the cold, Nina Torring began to move. Not up and down, as I'd always imagined, but back and forth, as if on a rocker. Slowly, at first, her hands on his chest for leverage, then, as she found her rhythm, moving those hands up her belly, to her breasts, squeezing them together.

I remember the taste of metal in my mouth as I watched. One minute, two. She rocked faster, then faster still, closing her eyes, grabbing her golden hair and shaking her head violently from side to side. Faster and faster she rocked, so fast that I wondered how he took it, and then she finished, not in one short collapse but easing to a stop, her spasms shortening, softening, her shoulders clenching and relaxing, clenching and relaxing, and relaxing, and relaxing, and then still, her eyes opening slowly as if from a dream, her hands settling onto her breasts and then finding, beneath them, her heart.

Without looking at me again, she vanished beneath the sill of the window, leaving me to stare at her empty desk, at the blue school flag that hung in the entrance to her closet. I rose from the snow, my soaked knee burning from the cold, and walked around to the front of the dorm, the taste of metal still in my mouth as I walked inside and down the hall to my room. I stripped to my shorts, climbed up into my top bunk, and lay on my side in the dark, looking out the window at the clearing, where the snow had started to fall again. Pure and white and endless it fell, covering up the footprints along the path.

A year later I opened my box at the campus mail center to find a plain white envelope with no return address. Inside was a photograph of Nina Torring, in her wedding dress, smiling into the eyes of Nick Simms. Written on the back, in a feminine hand:

To Jake Teller — may you find happiness.

Last Sunday, the day after the Roosevelt Hotel, I drank too many vodkas at an alumni mixer and let a classmate rope me into a night of calls for a fund drive. Two nights ago I received my list. The first name on it was Nina Torring.

On the phone, when I told her my name, she was warm and personal. She runs an art gallery now on West Fourth Street. Yes, it is going well. In boom times, people can't pay enough for beauty. She asked me sharp questions about accounting and the corporate climb.

"School seems like a long time ago, doesn't it, Jake?" she said.

"It does. There are a few questions here they want me to ask, Nina. For the database."

"Of course."

"Married how many years?"

She paused. "Married four years," she said. I sensed something in her voice, so I waited. "Divorced for two."

Neither of us said anything for several seconds.

"Can I buy you a drink?" I asked. "Friday night?" I looked down at the bare kitchen table and listened to the soft buzz of the line.

"Yes, Jake," she said finally. "You can."

"Somebody owes forty cents at the library."

Mark said those words when I walked in the door last night, and when he did I felt something inside me give way. All week long I'd grown stronger and stronger. At work Mr. Stein assigned me to what the partners call "midnight duty," putting me on call to three of our firm's biggest clients. I spent the days buried in the Tax Code, researching their last-minute ploys. Calling them personally, the heads of companies, to advise them or reassure them or gently dissuade them. An exciting relief from the drudgery of returns, but high-pressure work. Twelve, thirteen hours of concentration a day. All-consuming. And at lunch, at my desk, I took on Madame Brodeur. She wanted to know if the readings could be done in five minutes instead of ten. No. The roses would cost more than we thought — did we still want them lining the aisle? Yes. The check for the caterer was due in three days. Okay.

Work and wedding and work and wedding and little else. And it restored me. Centered me. For long stretches I shut last weekend out of my mind. Shut out the hour in the closet at the Roosevelt. One weak, mistaken hour of my life, behind me now. I'd get home at eleven, or even midnight, too late for my run — or for anything, really, except a warm bath and a little soft music and bed. And then up early and back into the office and into the tax books again. A hard pace, but just what I needed. I felt my life returning to me.

Yesterday, Thursday, I told Mark to come over after he put the magazine to bed. Come and stay the night, I told him. I wanted to touch him, to feel him next to me, to lie together in bed and talk. And when I walked in at eleven, he was already there. Sitting on the couch, holding up a book I'd borrowed from the library weeks before, his finger pressed to the time stamp.

"Somebody owes forty cents at the library."

I must have just stared at him because he said, "Mimi, what is it? Mimi?"

I broke out of it, shook my head, and smiled.

"Nothing," I said, going to him and touching my hand to his face. "You're marrying a space cadet, that's all." But inside, I felt all of my resolve slip away. The resolve I'd built hour by hour through the week. And later, as I lay in the dark, his sleeping arm over me, his breath on my neck, I started to tremble. I tried to think wedding thoughts, to picture the church at sunset, only three weeks away now. Instead, I saw the dark closet at the Roosevelt, and the white silk ties lying still on the covers. I tried to remember our recessional song, "Greensleeves." The first notes would come, so haunting, so beautiful, and then I'd lose them. Lose them and hear Anne's breathing. Her rising, desperate breathing as Jake Teller worked her, so very slowly, on the bed at the Roosevelt. Her breathing and then her cries, and then her hushed voice on the phone the next night.

"Mimi, there aren't words . . .

"Mimi, I didn't know who I was. I *could not* have said my name."

This morning I dressed so quietly that Mark asked if I was okay. "Tell you what," he said as I walked him to the door. "The company gets you until eight tonight — then you're mine. I promise wine, candles, and exercise." I kissed him. "Hold that thought," he said, and then he walked out and I closed the door behind him.

At the firm, Mr. Stein called me into his office to tell me that my work, all week long, had been first-rate. Our star clients were happy. I had a way with them, it seemed. "If I told Herb Sloan he was trying to run a tax dodge, Mimi, he'd see to it I was barred from the Harvard Club. You told him and he took it with a smile. Keep up the fine work." I walked back to my office, sat down at my desk, and saw the pink message slip tucked under my lamp. I pulled it out and unfolded it.

Tonight, you can watch.

I stared at the note until it blurred.

Tonight, you can watch.

I stood, walked to the window, put my hands on the sill, and closed my eyes. I'd known this moment would come. All week I'd steeled myself against it, and until last night I'd known just what I would say.

"No, Jake. Don't ask me again."

I took a calming breath and walked slowly back to my desk. I picked up the note again. Four simple words on a piece of paper. I stood over the phone, my hand on the receiver, and then picked it up and dialed Jake's extension.

"Jake Teller."

"It's Mimi. I can't."

The line was quiet. I took the receiver from my ear and held it over the cradle. And then I heard Mark's voice again, as clearly as if he were in the room. "Somebody owes forty cents at the library." And I lifted the receiver to my ear.

"Do you have a cell phone, Mimi?"

"No." I shut my eyes.

"Buy one after work today. Write down this number — six four six, seven one one eight." I opened my eyes again and wrote the number beneath his words on the pink message slip. "Call it and leave your cell phone number on the machine."

I did as he asked me. I walked to an electronics shop on Lexington and bought a small black cell phone. Two hours later, in my apartment, I dialed the number he gave me. "Seven one eight, eight one eight three," I said into the machine, my voice sounding strange, distant. I put the cell phone down on the couch beside me and sat in the silent apartment, waiting. I sat very still, my back straight, as I'd learned in ballet as a girl. I stared into the painting on the far wall, the one Dad gave me for Christmas two years ago. An etching, actually, of a horse standing in deep snow. I concentrated on the details — the muscled flanks, the wet mane, the eyes that seemed, somehow, to look back at you, no matter which angle you viewed them from. So very beautiful, those eyes. Wild. Knowing. When the sleek ring of the cell phone broke the air, I jumped, answering it quickly, as though someone might hear.

"Mimi Lessing." The way I answer my line at work.

"Mimi, it's Jake."

"Hi."

"She keeps an apartment on Sullivan Street. I don't know the address. Be in the Village from eight o'clock. When I'm prepared, I'll call."

I stared straight ahead at the painting.

"Mimi?"

"Yes?"

"No heels. And no perfume."

And now I sit at a table at an outdoor café on Bleecker Street, wearing a cobalt cardigan, three-quarter sleeve, with a deep V neck, over a pink dress. *When I'm prepared.* A spring chill is in the air, but I'm warmed by the electric heaters tucked into the awning above me. Moroccan music is playing somewhere. Faint, sensual. At the next table a young couple hold hands on top of the red tablecloth, while underneath it their legs touch shyly. A tall waiter serves them white wine, then pivots and sets a glass of red in front of me.

"Arrowood cabernet," he says.

"Thank you."

I take a long sip. On our trip last summer, Arrowood was our favorite winery. I can picture the tasting room, its veranda cut into the steep, dusty hillside, looking out over a sea of vines. I remember Mark touching his cool glass to my sunburned shoulder, warning me what would happen if I got drunk and dropped my guard. "The inn is five minutes away," he'd said. We were three weeks into our engagement then. We're three weeks from our wedding now, and just an hour ago I called him from my apartment and told him that I was still at the office. I would be stuck there until midnight, at least, I said. Our date would have to wait until tomorrow.

I take another sip. At the next table the girl is

tracing her finger along her sweating chardonnay
glass as the young man leans in closer and says
something in her ear. She ducks her head and
smiles. Beneath the table their ankles are twined
now. He glances toward me, and I quickly look
away.

Mark's love is unconditional. It is precious, and
all I've ever asked for, but who will test me? I've always turned away from desire. I see that now. I've
picked safe boys because I could have them without ever letting go. I can tell what Mark is thinking,
can almost finish his sentences. A month ago that
gave me such comfort. A month ago, when I
thought of the two of us at the altar, true partners, I
would fill up inside. Now I sit in a café and think of
Jake Teller. Of what he does to women. Did to
Anne, as I listened just ten feet away. A part of me
cannot imagine it. Bound. Helpless. And a part of
me can think of nothing else.

The lie to Mark was thrilling. It's terrible, but it
was thrilling, and ever since I've felt an . . . excitement, an urgency I've never known. As if, at last,
I'm truly living. Living in the moment, the colors
around me — the blue of the awning, the black of
the maître d's suit — close and vivid, and the
sounds — the snap of a purse — sharp, alluring.

The young man's hand is on her thigh now. He
whispers something, and she blushes, looks down
at the table, then back at him, and nods. He signals
the waiter, hands back the menus, and asks for their
bill.

I drink the last of my wine and look down at my

hands against the red tablecloth. At the sparkling engagement ring I picked out almost a year ago. "Clarity," the jeweler had said. "People obsess over carats and wind up with a muddy diamond. See how this takes in light?"

It does. Takes it in and sends it back out.

"Another glass?"

The waiter stands above me, looking down. I press the top of my dress to my chest.

"Yes, please."

I stare again into the sparkling ring and remember something Anne told me a year ago, when she broke up with her boyfriend of two years. I asked her why she'd done it, and she said for his birthday she had told him that for one night he could do anything he wanted to her. Anything at all. No limits, she'd said. He'd taken her to Le Cirque, and then to bed at the Waldorf, between satin sheets. "I don't understand," I'd said. Anne had just looked away.

She called me this morning. "He's a bastard, Mimi," she said. "Jake Teller. Six days, and he hasn't called. Have you seen him?" I told her I hadn't. Anne leaves for Spain on Sunday. Two weeks in Barcelona, Madrid, and Valencia. "I'll have the only tan in the wedding party," she said, promising she would be back in time to keep the bridesmaids in line.

The table beside me is empty now. The couple is gone. A twenty lies in the bill tray, weighted down by a half-filled wineglass, its edges lifting in the breeze. The waiter returns with my Arrowood and places it before me. I reach for it but then I freeze.

From inside the purse at my feet comes the muffled ring of the cell phone. I look up at the waiter, as if he might answer it. "The bill please," I manage to say, and he pulls it from his pocket, lays it on the table, and turns away. The ringing is steady, insistent. I pull the small black cell phone from my purse, close my eyes, and press the pulsing button.

"Three sixty-four Sullivan," Jake Teller says, his voice a whisper. "Apartment two. We're ready."

Miss Lessing is not herself.

All her delicate routines have fallen to the havoc of the season, and with them mine as well. No longer do I wait in the window at La Boheme and watch her step onto her block in early evening. Or stand at the clearing by the river for my cherished moments along the rail. A company car returns her home late each night now, and an hour later I lose her to sleep. This separation is cruel, but it will pass with the season. More troubling is her behavior tonight.

I sit on a plastic folding chair at a bus stop in the Village, letting the buses go by, one after the next. Across the street Miss Lessing sits alone at a café table. She is just now ordering a second glass of wine, pressing the top of her dress demurely to her neck as the waiter looms over her.

An hour ago she lied again to her fiancé, calling him from her apartment and telling him that she was at work. And that she would be there until midnight. Minutes later I heard the sound of the shower, and then of her hair dryer. Then the rustle of her jewelry box, and the soft swish of a dress lifted off a clicking hanger.

Another bus pulls into the stop and blocks my view. It discharges its riders and then rumbles away, and I turn my head into my collar to escape the exhaust. I look up again to see Miss Lessing reaching down for her purse, then into it. She brings out a black cell phone, listens for only a few seconds, and replaces it in her purse. She pulls her sweater, a royal blue cashmere, tight to her neck, and places money in the bill tray. And now she stands. She is leaving. Abandoning a full glass of wine. The waiter looks after her as she steps through the small iron gate that sets off the café from the street.

She looks around, as though to orient herself, and then starts east along Bleecker. I rise and follow her.

CHAPTER NINE

I turn the corner onto Sullivan, and the nighttime noises of Bleecker give way to the quiet of a residential block. In place of bars and street musicians are small trees and wide, empty sidewalks. The wind is stronger here, and I pull my sweater closer around me. The buildings are not like city apartment buildings at all. They are low and pretty, only two or three apartments to a building, and the street doors are wooden, carved, with ornate knockers of silver or brass. The numbers go down as I walk. 382 . . . 380 . . . 378 . . . I touch my hand to the black wrought-iron railing that separates the properties from the street. 376 . . . 374 . . . Flowers grow along the window grates. I can hear my steps on the sidewalk, and I try to walk more quietly. 372 . . . 370 . . . Across the street is the lone shop on the block, the Caffe Lune. A man sits by himself at an outdoor table, stirring a drink. 368 . . . 366 . . . Bleecker seems a long way behind me now.

Three sixty-four Sullivan Street.

I stop. Two large flowerpots, low to the ground and filled with rich earth and roses, stand on either side of a beautiful mahogany door. The door is closed, but something has been folded and slipped between the lock and the frame. I turn the knob and the door opens in, and a handbill falls to the ground at my feet. I pick it up.

WHITE SWAN GALLERIES. A brochure for an art gallery. At the top is the crest, a sleeping, long-necked swan, its bill tucked into its breast. And below: NINA TORRING, DIRECTOR. I look from the brochure to the nameplate beneath the buzzer for apartment two. TORRING, N. The name is written in a woman's hand, in fresh ink, as if she might have just moved in. I lay the brochure on the flowerpot, step inside, and close the street door behind me.

I stand in a carpeted foyer that smells faintly of forest. Of pine. Someone has put potpourri on the marble credenza outside of apartment one. Straight ahead is the door to apartment two, and even from here I can see a sliver of light between it and the jamb. I walk to it. I push it softly, and it opens without a sound. I step inside, into a small kitchenette, and close the door quietly behind me.

The living room in front of me is beautifully spare. Two silver Kaese folding chairs by the window, a glass coffee table with a vase of flowers on it, and a couch of black leather. On the far wall hangs a single painting, lit from below, the way you would see it in a gallery. This is the only light in the room, and it draws the eye to the painting, a stunning Parisian streetscape. Beyond the painting is a short hallway that leads from the living room to the rest of the apartment. And from down that hallway comes music.

Violin music, playing very softly.

I look down at the hardwood floor. I slip off my shoes and place them together by the door, then take a quiet step, and another, until I've crossed the living room and stand at the mouth of the hallway. It is six feet long, no more, ending straight ahead at the bathroom and, to the right, at the open door to the bedroom. I can't see into the bedroom, but I can see the strange, muted light that comes from it. And I can hear the soft music. I press my damp palms to my dress. It is just a few steps to the bedroom door, but I can't take them. My heart is moving too fast and my breathing . . . she would hear me. I step back into the living room. I need just a minute. I go to the painting.

Breathe, Mimi. Slowly. The painting is of one block in Paris, and the artist has captured everything. The crumbling print of a tattered flyer on a bus-stop pole. The reflection of a leaf in the top corner of a café window. *In truth lies beauty.* My art history teacher would say that, whenever an artist stunned the class with detail. I concentrate on my breathing and begin to steady. The colors in the painting are beautiful. The rusted blue of a roof shingle, the red of a child's dress. And the light. This must be what they mean when they talk about Parisian light. It seems to pour from the painting, bathing the shops at one end of the street and then giving way, store by store, to shadow. I look again down the hallway, at the light from the bedroom door. And back at the painting. I listen to the violin, each soft note achingly clear in the quiet apartment. It is as if the music were written for this painting. I can imagine standing on the street itself, a busker playing this very piece just a few feet away from me. "We'll live in Paris someday," Mark said once.

A sharp gasp cuts through the music. My legs go weak as I look down the hallway. It was a woman's gasp. Of pain, it sounded like. Or of fear. Or . . . something else. I look across the room at my shoes, paired neatly by the door. A part of me wants to run to them. But I look again at the light from the bedroom, and after closing my eyes for a second, I hold my sweater to my neck and walk toward the door. I stop just before it, listening for another sound. From her, or from him. I hear just the violin. I put my hand on the cool wall and step into the bedroom doorway.

The room is lit only by the light of three lamps. All three are trained on a four-poster bed. And on that bed is Nina Torring. Her eyes are covered by a black blindfold, and each of her wrists is bound tightly to a bedpost with a tie of white silk. Her legs are free. She wears a thin silver camisole with drawstring pants, and I see now what made her gasp. Jake Teller sits at her side, in corduroys and a shirt of rugged blue. He holds a pair of scissors in his hand, and he is touching the flat metal edge of them to her bare belly. His eyes look straight into mine.

I clutch the doorsill to keep from falling. Nothing — no picture in a magazine, nothing I imagined — has prepared me to be here. To see this. Her. Real, in front of me. I feel the blood rushing to my head. I force myself to breathe. Jake's eyes on me are steady and appraising. He waits a second, then looks from me to a hard-backed chair he's placed three feet from the bed. He nods toward it. I look down at the floor. Carpet. The soft violin concerto is coming from a tape player on a dresser just above the head of the bed. She won't hear me. I walk to the chair and sit down. I don't know where to put my hands, so I clasp them together in my lap. And I look again at Nina Torring.

She is beautiful. Her short blond hair is the gold of Ohio corn, uncorrupted by a single dark root. Her features are delicate, precise . . . Nordic. Her eyes, beneath the blindfold, must be ice blue. She is almost exactly my size.

Two of the lamps are standing lamps, one on each side of the bed. The third is a snaking desk lamp that Jake has clipped to the headboard and brought so low that she must feel the heat of the bulb on her skin. He's angled it forward, creating a line of light from her face down the center of her, leaving all beyond it in shadow.

Jake lifts the metal blades to the camisole and begins to cut. He cuts straight up the middle, leaning forward as he does, lifting the collar away from her soft neck for the last, careful clip. Then he cuts each strap and pulls the ruined fabric out from under her. Her bra is white lace and opens in the front. Victoria's Secret. Jake lays the scissors on the nightstand. He leans down and pulls the knot from her drawstring pants. Her ribs lift and settle as she breathes. Jake lifts the pants over her hips, then pulls them down her legs and off her, dropping them to the floor beside the bed. Her panties are white and spare. Not thong, but almost. They cover so little. She brings her legs together, bending them at the knees, angling them into the covers, away from him. She has the skin of a swimming queen, lineless, the same color beneath her hips as above them. Her legs are athletic and smooth, and on one small ankle is a raised scar, in the shape of a coin.

Jake traces the backs of his fingers from her hip down one thigh to her knee, and then in a curving path down her calf. She lifts her chin, and her lips part.

Jake reaches down beside the bed and comes up with a bottle. It is body oil, and he turns the top and pours some into his hands. It smells of vanilla. He lifts her right ankle, so small in his hands, and rubs the oil into her foot, then pours another dose into his hands and works it into her calf. She gives a deep sigh as he glides up her leg to the top of her thigh, stopping just where the lace of her panties begins, then pouring out more and starting down her other leg, working it into her thigh, her knee, into her ankle, pressing the tiny white scar with his thumb.

He finishes and places her foot back on the covers. Again she closes her legs tight together. Jake slides up the bed, to the middle of her. He shakes drops of lotion onto her belly, then presses it in with his hands, rubbing in small, tight circles, stop-ping just beneath her bra, his thumbs grazing the bottom of the thin cotton. She bites her bottom lip. He pours more lotion into one hand and works above her bra, rubbing it into her sternum, into her neck, the rich vanilla scent pervasive now, tantaliz-ing. She needs him to touch her breasts, but he won't, though each of her breaths lifts them toward his hands. He slips the straps of her bra off each shoulder and works his hand across from one to the other, pressing hard, his fingers lingering on her throat, dipping to the top of her cleavage, but never straying to the swell just beneath. She moans softly, bringing her legs up toward her, then back down.

I press mine tight together.

Jake stands, crosses to the other side of the bed, and sits down at the head. He pours lotion into both hands and starts on her right arm, moving up from the shoulder, slowly, working the soft knot of her biceps, her thin forearm, and up toward her bound wrist. Her fingers close into her palms, open, close again, her beaded matte nail polish glit-tering like sequins in the lamplight.

Jake crosses back to the far side of the bed and oils her left arm, climbing just as slowly as he did with her right, finally reaching her pulse point, her wrist, pressing the oil into her palm with his thumb. She swallows hard and rolls her wrists against the ties.

The final notes of the concerto hang in the air, then fade away. The room is quiet except for the soft rustling of the covers under her legs. And her quickening breaths. Jake lets go of her left hand, then takes hold of it again. And leans toward it. And bends her wrist toward the light. She resists, trying to curl her fingers, but he straightens them and holds them still. What is it he sees? I lean forward. And now I see it, too. A break in her perfect color. A small white circle on her ring finger.

Jake lets go of her hand. She closes it into a fist, then opens it again, nervously. He is looking into her face, as if he might see through the blindfold into her eyes. He reaches for the nightstand and, still watching her, slowly pulls open the drawer. She wets her lips at the sound, bites her bottom one. I can't see the drawer from where I sit, but I see Jake reach into it, and he comes out with something. He holds it to the light. A gold wedding ring. He turns it quietly.

She is married. He didn't know.

Jake slips the ring over the tip of his index finger and presses it into Nina's cheek. She gasps, her whole body tensing. She turns her cheek into the bed, then turns it toward him again.

"Please," she whispers. "I —"

Jake presses a finger to her lips. He lifts her chin. "It's still Nick, isn't it?" he says.

"Yes. Jake —"

He tightens his hold on her chin and lifts it another inch, straining her now. His thumb presses gently on her throat.

"No more words. If you speak again, I'll leave. Nick will find you like this."

He lets go of her chin. She swallows, breathes deeply, and nods.

Jake places the ring on the nightstand and picks up the scissors. He slips them between her breasts and closes them around the clasp of her bra, one cool metal blade resting on her skin. The bra springs open, the fabric falling away on either side. He cuts through each half again, pulls them off her, and drops them to the floor. Her breasts are small, but her nipples are hard and . . . swollen. I stare at them. She wets her lips again and gathers herself, bracing for the touch she knows is coming at last.

Jake leans down close and breathes, hard, on one swollen, ruby nipple. She gasps and rocks against the ties. He breathes hard on the other.

"Pl —"

She stops herself. He does it again, first one, then the other. She shakes her head, grabs at the few inches of silk between her wrists and the posts and twists them in her fingers. He breathes on her nipples again. I look away, down at the floor. My chest is aching. Not my chest. Above it. I hold my arm tight against my sweater, against my breast, leaning forward so that Jake won't see.

He puts his left hand on her hip, gently, and holds his right hand above her breast, lowering it until his palm makes the barest contact with her nipple. The touch is so soft that she thinks it is breath again, but he keeps it there, until she knows, and then he starts to move it back and forth. Slowly, an inch either way, touching just the tip of the nipple, nothing else. Back and forth, back and forth, then over to her other breast, and now back and forth between them. A little faster, but still just grazing the very tips of her nipples. She lifts her chest toward him, to force more contact, but he raises his palm the same distance. I press my arm harder against me. I try to look away but can't take my eyes off his hand. He moves it a little faster. He is giving her a fraction of the pressure she needs, a whisper of it. Faster, he moves, and now he lowers his palm the slightest bit. A gasp escapes her, a short gasp of gratitude. She bites her lip and lifts her chin. It is so little, what he gives her, but it is something, at last. Friction. Pressure. She accepts it, accepts it and begins to rock, lifting and dropping her crossed ankles, opening and closing her fists. If he'd give her just a little more. The smallest bit more. Jake lowers his hand a fraction of an inch and moves it faster. Yes. It is almost enough. Almost just barely enough. She lifts her chin higher. Faster, he moves his hand, and faster, and still faster, and she is climbing now, climbing toward release, trusting him. She clenches her fists tighter, jerks faster against the ties. She is almost in rhythm with his passes now, her mouth open, the cords of her throat tight, pulsing. Faster, he goes. Faster. His hand is a blur now, drops of oil coming off it. I lock my own ankles. She is almost there. Faster. A few more seconds. A few more. One more —

Jake takes his hand away.

She doesn't cry out or stop rocking but lifts herself toward where his hand was, where it must still be, straining against the ties to rise another inch, half an inch, to stay in contact. She feels nothing but air. Higher, she lifts herself, to the limit the ties allow — nothing. His hand is gone, finished with her, and now she cries out, one sharp cry, as if an iron had been pressed to her skin, and with it she collapses back into the bed. Jake stands and walks quietly from the room.

I put my hand to my mouth, to my forehead. My fingers are clenched, white. I look to the empty doorway, then back at Nina.

She is shaking all over. She tries to turn onto one side, to press one of her nipples into the covers, into anything, but the ties won't let her. Her ribs heave and small spasms rock her. She moves her legs, still pressed together, from side to side, then brings them up to her waist and back down. I try to look away, but my eyes are drawn back to her, to her delicate face, pained now, to her swollen nipples, each one slick with oil.

A sound comes from beyond the doorway. Nina hears it, too, and turns her head, realizing for the first time that Jake has left the room. It takes me a second to make out the sound, to understand that it was the soft *pop* of the refrigerator door. I hear it close again. Nina's breaths are short and desperate, almost sobs, but as it sinks in that she is alone, she begins to calm, and I see a new resolve come into her face. A strength. For a few moments, at least, she is safe.

She lets her wrists go limp in the ties. She takes one ankle off the other, then quickly crosses them again, moaning softly. She brings her legs up

toward her belly, but more slowly than before. And
now back down. She takes control of her breathing,
the way they teach in yoga, slowing it, slowing it,
finding her center. She uncrosses her ankles again,
gently, and this time she is able to leave them uncrossed, though still tight together. Her body still
trembles, but less now. She tightens her calf muscles, then relaxes them. Tightens her quad muscles,
relaxes them. Her thighs. Her stomach. Breathing
in as she tightens, exhaling as she relaxes. Her
shoulders. Her wrists. She is gaining control, muscle by muscle.

"Soon," she whispers. "Soon, soon."

I watch her, mesmerized. Her breathing slows
until it is almost natural, just a little quicker than
my own. Quietly, I take a deep breath, too, and take
my arm from my side. It still aches, so I look back
at the empty doorway and then slip my hand under
my sweater and press on my breast, careful to keep
silent. I can feel the heat in my face, the flush that I
know he will see. I pull my hand from my sweater
and sit up straight. I try to relax my legs, but they
tremble, and I feel my control start to leave me, so I
keep them tight. I smooth my dress quietly with my
hands. I'm preparing for his return, I realize, just as
she is.

Jake walks into the room again. Nina senses him
as much as hears him, breathes once more, deeply,
and then lets it out. She rolls her wrists once against
the ties, and then cups her fingers into a loose fist.
A runner's fist. I remember it from track. Pretend
you're holding a bird in your hands. Tight enough

to keep it from flying away, but gentle enough not
to hurt it. She is a runner, too. It will help her. Jake
walks past the bed and to the dresser, holding in his
right hand something that the angle of his body
keeps me from seeing. He presses the fast-forward
button on the cassette player, and when it clicks he
takes the tape out, turns it over, puts it back in, and
hits PLAY. He turns; I see what's in his hand and feel
my legs start to go again. He sits down on the bed.
Nina waits beneath him, calm now, feeling the bed
give under him, knowing that any second he will
start in on her again but thinking that she has prepared herself, that she is ready. She can't see the
rocks glass in his hand.

Filled to the top with ice.

Jake places it on the nightstand, silently. He
looks down at her, down the shining length of her,
from her bound wrists, relaxed now, to her small
ankles, pressed together but not crossed. The scent
of vanilla fills the room. And now, from the tape
player, comes music. Piano. Slow, meandering
piano. I've heard it somewhere. I don't remember
where, but I've heard it. It is haunting, beautiful.
Nina listens, too, seems to strain toward it, as if it
will save her, delay what is to come or help her
through it. Allow her to think of something other
than where he will touch her next.

Jake reaches into the glass, into the rough pyramid of cubes, and takes out the top one. He leans
toward her face, toward the beads of sweat that
have broken on her forehead, on her cheeks. Sweat
from the heat of the lamp, from the heat inside her,

the denial. Jake presses the frosted cube to her fore-head.

She gasps in shock, her mouth opening. She tries to turn her cheek into the bed, but he holds it still, her face tiny in his hand. He moves the ice across her forehead. She gasps again but calms, almost sighs. She needs this. She is burning up, and it cools her. She licks her lips, suddenly aware of her thirst. He touches the cube to them and takes it away. She waits for him to return it, but instead Jake looks down her body again, and as he does, I start to dis-solve.

He places his left hand on her hip, steadying her, and then presses the cube to her throat. She surges in shock. Her hands are fists again, true fists, jerk-ing against the ties. She brings her legs up sharply. Jake puts his left arm across them and, still holding the ice to her throat, forces her legs down to the covers and pins them there. He starts to move the ice again, down her neck, lifting his arm off her legs as he does. She bends her knees and brings them up again. Jake stops the ice. Again he presses it into her, just under her neck, bringing a gasp of pain. He pushes her legs to the covers again, and only when they are still does he start to move the ice, up onto one shoulder, then back down it and across to the other. He frees her legs, and again she instinctively starts them up. Jake stops the ice, pressing it into the small hollow beneath her collarbone. She gasps, but not just from pain now. She gasps because she understands. Moaning softly, she lowers her legs to the covers. When they are still, Jake starts the ice in motion again.

It is torture. She can't take the ice without moving her legs, but if she moves them he stops it, and that is worse. And so she lies still, gasping, her ankles crossed tightly again as Jake slides the ice between her breasts, up on its edge so as not to touch them, and now down her belly, the cube melting quickly in the heat of the lamp, leaving a thin trail of water on her skin. Her fists pull so hard against the ties that I can hear the creak of the posts.

The ice is down to a sliver now, and she gasps in relief as Jake lifts it from her and presses it to his forehead until it disappears. The piano continues its soft wandering. I can see that Nina is trying to concentrate on it, to give herself to it. To focus her mind on something, anything else. And now I remember. Convento . . . Convento . . . "Convento Di Sant'Anna." From the soundtrack of *The English Patient*. Mark bought me the CD for Christmas. I'd hardly noticed this song at first, but it is beautiful. Soft variations off a pure, simple, entrancing theme.

Jake takes a new cube from the glass. He holds it to the lamp, lets the burning bulb melt drops onto Nina's forehead. Then he slides down the bed and presses the cube to the raised white circular scar on her ankle.

Nina spasms and jerks up her legs again, but Jake keeps the cube pressed to her until she lowers them with a soft cry and is still. Then he starts it up her leg, in small circles, up to her knee and past it, up to her thigh. He lifts it off her skin, grants her twenty seconds of relief, then presses it to her belly, waiting out her spasms, her reflexive kicks, keeping it pressed to her until, with a cry of frustration, she stills her legs yet again. Now he starts the ice down, in the same small, agonizing circles. Her breathing is quick and desperate, her cheek turned into the covers, but somehow she is able to keep her legs still. At her belly button he lifts the ice off her again and holds it away from her, out over the carpet, watching her closely, her trembling body, her parted lips.

I look away. I am burning up now, the heat not just in my face but all through me. She can't take this much longer. Through a crack in her closet I catch sight of her suits — designer, expensive. I close my eyes. I can see her in her gallery, among her paintings. Graceful with clients, assured, in control. A professional woman. Married. I open my eyes, jarred, riven by the sight of her, the actual sight, the beautiful, helpless arms stretched above her, the strict white ties, stained now with oil and sweat.

Jake is working her again. Sometimes he starts the ice above her waist, sometimes below, but always he works it toward the center of her, toward the scant cotton that is her last protection. And as the music grows more insistent, so, too, do his forays. He moves the ice cube in ever smaller, ever tighter circles, and each pass ends closer to her panties. Before, he stopped at her belly button or, if he was coming up from below, at her thigh, but now, from either direction, he comes to within an inch of the cotton. The closer he gets, the harder it is for her to keep still, and twice she gives in, moving her legs, enduring his punishment, the pain of the pressed ice worth the chance to move but quickly so unbearable that she lowers her legs again and is still, crying softly, her nails digging into her palms, the ice leaving a mark like a red brand on her golden skin as it moves away.

Only the reprieves keep her fighting. The twenty-second, thirty-second breaks when he lifts the ice from her skin, when she can gather herself, twist the silk ties slowly in her fists, try to focus again on the soft, saving piano that is her only distraction. He gives her another break now, holding the ice out over the carpet. She turns her head, almost imperceptibly, toward the music. The beautiful piano music that is forever wandering off its theme and then returning to it. I try to concentrate on it now, too, to slow the feeling that is starting beneath my dress. Jake takes a fresh cube from the glass. *The music*, Mimi. *Focus*. Wandering and then returning. The eternal theme — the journey and then the trip home. Jake holds the ice but waits to press it to her. I lean forward. *Wandering, then returning*. Could it be? I watch Jake. Still he waits, holding the ice just above her. And still the music is digressing, digressing, digressing, and now, as it finds its way back to its theme, I see Nina brace, and as the piano settles into the theme again, Jake Teller touches the fresh cube, hard, to the inside of her thigh.

He is timing the ice to the music.

Her breaks, her saving breaks, come only in the digressions. As soon as the piece returns to its theme, in whatever subtle variation, Jake starts in on her again. I put my hands to my knees, to keep them from shaking and to keep them pressed together. He is taking everything from her. Every defense. The music is her only distraction, but by concentrating on it, she is driven back, always, to her torment, even the breaks unbearable now because she knows the piano will find its theme again, and she knows that when it does, the ice will resume its slow journey along her skin. And the deeper the piece progresses, the closer the ice will come to its final target, to where Nina knows it must go, *needs* it to go, and cannot imagine it.

The piano holds to its theme longer than ever now. A minute, a minute thirty, the ice winding up her still thigh, finding a vein, tracing it, bringing out its blue. Drawing soft, stuttering cries from her parted lips. It climbs higher than ever, almost to the cotton, reaching it now as finally, mercifully, the piano trickles away into a digression and Jake lifts the cube from her skin.

I feel it now. Beneath my dress.

Spasms are starting to jolt her as Jake drops the sliver of ice into the glass, moves quickly to the head of the bed and takes her bound wrist in his hand. He presses his thumb to her pulse point, hard, harder, and Nina, with a gasp of pain, opens her fist and lets the silk she's been clutching fall from her fingers. Jake presses her open hand to the covers as the piano hints at its theme, starts back

toward it, then wanders off again. He moves
quickly around the bed and presses on the pulse
point of her right hand until Nina opens it, too.
"N —" she cries, stopping herself, barely, and turning her cheek into the bed, toward me, her mouth
open in shock as she realizes what is happening, realizes that Jake isn't close to finished, that he is
merely making the rules more severe. Her legs
won't be enough anymore, he is telling her. He
wants her wrists still, too.

I've never felt what I feel now. Not without being
touched.

Jake takes her chin in his hand. He isn't, he can't.
Her last defense. She tries to press it into the covers,
but he turns it up, toward him, holding it firmly a
few seconds and then letting go. She doesn't try to
move it. The piano is circling now, finding its way
back to the theme, on the verge of it. Jake takes another cube from the glass. Nina starts to brace, to
close her fists, but she stops herself, opening them
again just as the piano locks onto its theme.

Jake leans over her and presses the cube, for the
first time, to her breast.

She cannot stay still, but she does. Absolutely
still, in every muscle, her head up, her legs together
like a diver, her wrists flat on the covers, fingers
spread, the white silk ties lying slack beside them.
Jake moves the ice up to her nipple, tracing it
around the soft aureole, to the tip, and down again.
Her lips whisper soundlessly, pleading, but she
doesn't move. He takes the ice, slowly, across to her
other breast.

I slide my hands down my dress, pushing it deeper between my legs.

She is a vision. Completely, completely still. I watch her face, her delicate face, the sweat coming down it in rivulets now, soaking the black blindfold, rolling in drops down her flushed cheeks, shining on the tight, pulsing cords of her neck. Somehow I'm sure her eyes are open. They are open beneath the blindfold, and in them, and in the arch of her still body, and all through her is a look of   pure . . . effort — no . . . pain — no . . . something past pain, even. That moment in a terrible run, after miles and miles, when you cannot go on but do and burst, suddenly, through pain into total clarity. Into transcendence.

She is with him now.

Nina is about to break, cannot bear the ice another second, but she is with him. And Jake sees this. His eyes are shining. He takes his left hand from her hip, lifts it to her face, and touches it to her cheek.

Still the music holds to its theme. The soft piano holds to its simple theme, repeating it, repeating it, ruthlessly repeating it even as Jake moves the ice off her breast and down, to the only place left to go, down past her belly button to the cotton of her panties, and along the edge of them, tracing them as carefully as a master tailor marking a suit for a cut. Still she doesn't move. Up to her hip he goes, down into her vee, up to her other hip, across, and, finally, onto the cotton itself. Nina gasps, from the very heart of her, gasps but stays motionless, stays beautifully, perfectly still as the ice reaches the center of her panties, where he stops it, a moan escaping her as he presses it hard to the cotton, holding it there while the piano, still playing, holds to the outer edge of its theme; holds, holds, holds, and now wanders off it, and she is saved.

Jake lifts the ice off her, leans forward, and kisses her gently on the forehead.

She drops her cheek to the covers again, her breathing coming in explosive bursts. She is afraid to move but she must, a little at least, and so she takes the silk up in her fingers again and makes quick, quiet fists. And then relaxes them, straining for any sound from him, any clue. Could he be finished? Could he possibly? She's done all he asked. From the first she wanted only to surrender, but when he didn't let her, she hadn't broken. He put the ice to her breasts, to her panties, put it *right there*, and she hadn't broken. And then he'd kissed her. Could that mean she'd made it? That he was through? She waits, pleading with every muscle as the piano, still in digression, starts to work back to the theme. Please. No more. She's gone to her limit. Past it. The piano turns onto its theme again and settles along it. And Jake makes no move to reach for the glass. He looks down at her, watching as she strains to hear, as she dares to believe. And then he moves to the head of the bed and unties the silk tie from the post.

Nina feels the slack in her wrist and collapses into herself, breathing silent prayers of thanks. Jake lets her bend her arm at last, lets her bring her wrist in toward her body, and then pulls it, hard, back to the post. She cries out, startled. Jake doubles the tie around the post, triples it, taking up all the slack, every inch, and now reties her wrist, reties it so tight that it is immobile, the back of it pressed hard against the bare wood, the tie itself almost cutting into her. She cries out again, turns her face to him, as if to ask why, but Jake moves quickly to the other side of the bed and ties her right wrist the same way, Nina crying out again as he pulls it to the post, spreading her arms out wider than before, so wide now that the muscles along each of them stand taut and glistening in the light.

I want to tell him to stop, to reach out and take his arm and tell him he has to stop, but I let him walk right past me and cross back to the other side of the bed and sit down again. And I know that if he were to ask me, that if we had some silent code and he were to ask me, right now, I wouldn't tell him to stop. Just as I can't make myself look away from her, even though I'm rocking now, rocking slowly with my hands clasped between my thighs, my ankles tightly crossed. He sees me, but I can't help it. It isn't just heat beneath my dress now. It's dampness. And so I rock slowly, and breathe quietly, and watch Jake Teller reach down beside the bed and come up with two more ties.

They are white silk, like the others, and he ties each one in a strong double knot low on the remaining bedposts. Nina can't hear him over the piano, the beautiful piano that I will never listen to again and that stays, faithfully now, on its theme as it begins its rise toward the finish.

She is moaning now, softly, over and over, turning her face from side to side, pressing first one cheek into the covers, then the other, moving her legs from side to side, too, her ankles crossed so tightly that each has raised a mark on the other. Jake moves to the foot of the bed and takes them in his hands. She cries out and fights to keep them together. He has to press down on her right ankle and pull up on her left, and even then it takes him seconds. When they come apart she drops her head back into the covers, and as he starts to pull her left one toward the post, she moves her other leg with it, breathing in frantic, negotiating sighs. If he will just let her keep them together. Nothing else but that, at least. But her right leg can go only so far, and when Jake takes her left ankle the rest of the way, to the post, it parts her knees for the first time, and then her thighs. She gasps as if bitten, and when she feels the silk close around her ankle and understands all that is in store, she comes apart.

"No!" she cries. "No, n —"

"I'll leave," Jake says sharply, closing his fist on her ankle and squeezing once, hard. Her head falls to the covers, rises, falls again. Jake takes her right ankle in his hands. She is trying to hold it close to her left, to keep her legs at least partway together, but Jake pulls it slowly the other way, parting her legs truly now, parting them farther, parting them so far that I want to cry out, parting them almost into a split, and then looping the loose end of the final tie around her ankle and tying it tight.

She is too small for either ankle to quite reach to the post. The taut silk ties hold them dead still, six inches away. And I see for the first time, in the center of her, the soaked cotton. When her legs were together it was hidden, but now I can see the dark stain on her panties, and I see that it is spreading. It can only spread, because there is no give anywhere now, no way for her to stop, or even slow, the torrent he's built up inside her. Nina Torring is spread-eagled, and she is helpless.

Jake sits down on the bed again and reaches into the rocks glass for the final cube. She hears it clink against the glass and cries out. She tries to pull her wrists straight out from the posts but gasps from the pain. The ties are too tight, and if she pulls again they will mark her wrists deeply. She would have to explain. She cries out again, but softly now, futilely, her face no longer turning sharply into the covers but drifting from side to side, as if in a trance.

He presses the ice to her forehead and starts it down.

He knows he has to work quickly now. Down her flushed cheek he takes it, down her neck, between her breasts. She can't escape from it in any way, can't move, can't resist, can only cry out, and so she does, short, sharp cries as he takes the ice down her belly. He can feel her giving way beneath it, can feel the last of her control leaving her muscles, feel her trembling giving way to spasms and her spasms coming quicker and quicker. He moves the ice down to her panties and along the thin edge of them one last time. And then he gathers himself. He braces himself against the bed with his left hand and slips his right, the hand with the ice, underneath the soaked white cotton of her panties.

She cries out as if he's shocked her with current.

I stare at the cotton. I can see the shape of his hand beneath it, and I see that he is not just inside her panties but inside her, too, inside her and moving. He is rubbing the ice against her, searching hard with it. "Ah . . . Ah . . ." in broken cries now as she pounds her head into the covers. He rubs rhythmically, still searching, and now locking in, working one spot, up and down, up and down. Nina is gone, her cries trailing away into gasps and coming back louder, cries of agony and of much more. Of deliverance. He is giving her, at last, release. Punishing release, yes, punishing and cruel, but release, touching her where she must be touched, answering, finally, the need he built in her so slowly. Up and down, up and down he moves it, so hard that I can see his tensed knuckles through the cotton. And then he takes his hand from her panties. His *empty* hand. But still the spasms jolt her, harder than ever, and still she cries out, just as if he were —

He left the ice inside her. And it is setting off charge after charge.

Jake takes the scissors from the nightstand, slips them beneath the thin line of cotton on her hip, cuts once, again on the other side, and pulls her panties off her. I feel light-headed. She is trimmed very close, the way you read about in magazines. Cropped. A thin blond line, nothing else, and because it's so thin, and she is . . . spread, and has been through everything, it is . . . she is . . . I look away.

To be seen like that. Against your will. No one should ever. I'm dizzy now. Rocking, still, but with my head down. I look up just once more, not to where I've been looking, I can't, but to her hands. Her small, delicate, bound hands. Her nails are so deep into her palms that one has drawn blood. I look down at the floor again, telling myself to rock, to rock slowly, rocking and listening to her cries and to the music, which is just ending, following its torturous theme one last time, holding its final note and then dying away, leaving the room to her cries.

I feel a hand on my shoulder and almost jump from my chair. I look up to see Jake Teller kneeling in front of me. He lifts my chin and looks into my face, his eyes blue, so very blue, the deepest blue I've ever seen. He is mouthing something. The word *Go*.

I stare at him. Again he mouths it: *Go*. And I stand, somehow I stand and back quietly to the door, my hands over my dress, afraid that he will see, afraid that I've stained myself, just as she did. I back out into the hallway and start down it, then lean against the wall. I feel my legs going, so I sit down on the hardwood floor, my back against the wall, my arms clasped over my knees.

I hear the whoosh of his belt through the loops,

and then the clink of the buckle, loud in the quiet apartment, and I realize why he sent me away. I hear the sound of the bed giving beneath his weight, and then a catch to her cries, a final, desperate catch as she summons the last of her will. He is touching her now, lining her up. I hear a single sound from him, a single, hard sound from Jake Teller and then, from Nina, everything.

Words at last: "God" and "God" and "God," rising and rising. "Oh God, Oh God, Oh God" now, and beyond her words another sound, a steady, fast clicking, over and over. The sound of the headboard, of the posts, as they strike the wall. Again and again they strike it, and then her words dissolve into cries, drawn-out cries, louder and louder. I hug my knees tighter to me, bury my face in them. If I could just hear Jake Teller, hear anything from him. But no. He is silent. I hear only her cries, filling the apartment, and the clicking of the posts against the wall, so fast, so impossibly fast. And then, slowing. Slowing and deepening. I can't take it. They are slowing because Jake Teller is slowing, slowing himself so that he can drive into her harder, deeper. She is so small, so very small. I struggle to my feet, the sound of the posts growing louder. Deep thuds now, and further apart. Three, four seconds apart, and with each thud, sharp cries from Nina Torring, piercing cries, wordless, soaring, as if something has torn loose inside her.

I rush into the living room and to the door. I slip into my shoes. Still her cries come, and then she is . . . there is no other word for it, she is screaming.

I leave the apartment and close the door behind me. And still I hear her. I hear her through the door, hear her even as I cross the foyer, hear her until I step out into the night and close the big mahogany street door behind me. I rush to the black gate, fumble with the catch, step onto the sidewalk, and hurry away, almost running and now, yes, running in my dress to the corner of Houston, where I stop, breathing hard, and lean against a newspaper machine. I need to touch something solid, to feel the cold metal of this machine with my hands. A drop of water falls onto my wrist, and I realize it is mine, that I am crying. I wipe at the tears with my sweater and I stand, holding on to the machine, until my breathing slows and I start to come back again, back from the apartment into the night around me, from the cries of Nina Torring to the rustle of the trees on Sullivan Street and the noise of the traffic on Houston.

A full minute it takes me, and then I look around. Behind me is a corner store. I walk slowly into it, startled by the bell over the door. Even the ordinary store sounds inside — the *ching* of the register, the voices from the television — sound strange, alien. I walk to the back, slide open the door to the standing refrigerator, take a cold plastic bottle of water from the shelf and press it to my forehead. I see my reflection in the glass, see that my hair is damp on my face, see the burning red of my cheeks. As red as hers. I put the bottle to them, then to the back of my neck. I open it and drink two, three long sips, almost half the bottle, and then I walk with it to the counter. I can't look into the face of the man behind it. It is as if he might see, in my eyes, where I've been, what I've done.

"Are you okay?" he asks. The white of his shirt is dazzling against his dark skin.

"Yes," I say, paying him and walking out the door into the street. I look up at the sky, the New York City sky with its strange light, the glow we have instead of stars. I wish I could see just one right now. In the yard in Greenwich I could always see stars. As a girl, when I couldn't sleep, Dad would take me out there, hold my hand, point up into the sky, and tell me which constellation would be guarding me that night. One of the Dippers. Orion's Belt.

I look up Houston Street and see a taxi a block away, coming fast, its bright indicator light dipping and swerving. I lift my hand; it rattles to a stop, and I climb inside.

"Where to, miss?"

"Take me home, please. Eighty-third and York."

I sit back against the leather. I put the bottle on the seat beside me and sit with my hands in my dress. When I get home, I'll wash it in the sink. I look out the window, at the city streaming by. In the bathroom sink, in warm water with a little soap. It will dry by morning. I roll down the window and move closer to it. The air is cold, biting, more winter than spring, but I close my eyes and turn my face full into it, into the pure, cleansing wind.

CHAPTER TEN

"Watch this," Pardo says, standing and cupping his hands to his mouth as the players come off the floor for a timeout. "Hey! Hey you, Coach! Hey you, you bastard! Room three thirteen, right?"

Even in the raucous crowd here at the Garden, Pardo's voice stands out, and the Minnesota coach shoots a look toward its source before squatting in the middle of his sweating players and pulling out his clipboard to diagram a play.

"That's right, you bastard. The Penta Hotel — room three thirteen. Lock your door, champ!"

Coach Saunders turns again and looks hard into the crowd. We aren't more than twenty feet away, thanks to the firm, but Pardo is back in his seat now and just one in a sea of hostile faces, all of whom saw, in today's *Post*, Saunders's quote that he'd never cared for New York, and many of whom came early to let him know the feeling was mutual. "What are you looking at, prick?" yells a guy just behind us. "Don't you got a game to lose, asshole?"

comes from our left. Saunders turns back to his team, and Pardo drinks his beer, smiling. Thirty seconds later, when the scorekeeper's horn sends the players back onto the court, he puts his hands to his mouth again.

"Room three thirteen, you bastard! Wait'll you see what room service has for you!"

Saunders looks back again, and then he motions an assistant off the bench and whispers to him, and the assistant walks to the end of the bench and calls over a plainclothes security guard from the first row. Pardo looks triumphantly at Jeremy and me.

"That's really his room," he says.

I look at him.

"No bull, Jake. I'm banging the desk clerk at the Penta."

"Jesus," says Jeremy.

"Am I in this guy's head, or what?" says Pardo.

The security guy wades into our section, a wire running from his ear down into his dark blue suit. His eyes are on the three of us. "Who's yelling out room numbers?" he asks. Pardo looks at him defiantly and taps his chest with his beer cup. The guard looks him over. "Good for you," he says. "The prick's too good for New York, let him take care of himself."

We watch the guard walk back to the bench and shrug at the nonplussed assistant coach.

"Jesus," says Jeremy again, his eyes widening in the look of wonder that Pardo is forever bringing to them.

"Go, Spree!" says Pardo, as Sprewell knocks the

ball away off the coach's ill-designed in-bounds play and streaks the other way for a dunk, bringing us and the sellout crowd to our feet. "Nice play call, asshole!" Pardo calls out.

Pardo and Jeremy are an unlikely pair. Pardo was a classmate and fellow pledge up at Ham Tech. An athlete, like me, admitted into the '93 freshman class because our football team had managed a school-record five wins the year before and our trustees, harboring visions of a winning season and grateful alumni, decided the heavens would hold if we relaxed our standards enough to let in a few guys who scored a lot better in the weight room than they did on their SATs. Or in Pardo's case, a guy who proudly claimed "a year abroad" on his college application without mentioning that it would have been four years, courtesy of the U.S. Navy, had his stint not ended suddenly and dishonorably when Pardo invented a new salute for the MPs who tracked him down in the back of a bar after a three-day Bangkok bender.

Still, he was all Ham Tech could have asked for and then some, a bruising six-foot-two, 230-pound fullback who could run a 4.7 forty and would've rewritten our meager record book if he hadn't blown out his knee on the first play from scrimmage. Blew it out all the way — anterior, posterior, and medial collateral ligaments — and thus there he was, two weeks into another four-year hitch, marooned in a full-leg cast at a rainy liberal-arts school in upstate New York, a hundred miles from a good time in every direction.

Pardo grabbed at the only lifeline he could see —
the fraternity system. He fell in with the good-na-
tured guys of Theta Delta Xi and gained sixty-five
pounds his freshman year, earning a spot on the
Wall of Fame at the local brewery. The next fall, on
the strength of his party credentials, he ran unop-
posed for social chairman, vowing to make TDX
"the beer and trim center of Ham Tech."

Jeremy is Pardo's polar opposite. He first came
to the Hill in December of '94, a seventeen-year-old
high-school senior and 125-pound bag of nerves up
for one night — his first ever away from home — to
see the school he'd set his mind on applying to
early-decision. Awed by the library tour, blown
away by the math center, he emerged into the main
quad at 9:00, fingering the packets of Ovaltine in
his coat pocket and wondering if it could really be
true that the reading room stayed open all night.
He would've headed straight across campus to the
room of the nerd who was hosting him if he hadn't
promised his father, a TDX from the class of 1970,
that he'd stop in on the fraternity and bring back a
picture of Dad's old room.

Pardo's current one, as it turned out.

Figuring Jeremy was a "prospective," as we
called potential brothers, Pardo told him he could
have his photo, but not until he'd had a "sip of the
duck." And then he led an uneasy Jeremy down
into the basement.

The "duck" was the beer bong that about twenty
of us were passing around as we plotted our strategy for House Party Weekend. Jeremy had never

seen one before, and it must have looked harmless
enough. At one end, a plastic funnel with Donald
Duck's head painted on it, and running from that
a couple feet of rubber tubing. Pardo pitched it as a
lesson in physics and told him it would only take a
few seconds, then handed him the rubber tubing
and told him to put his thumb over the opening
and have a seat. Jeremy did so, and someone
promptly handed him a *Playboy*. Apparently he'd
never seen one of those before, either, and while he
paged slowly through the twelve-page spread of
Miss December, his eyes widening under his
glasses, Pardo poured two and a half beers into the
funnel I was holding up in the air.

"Okay," Pardo said, "put the tube in your
mouth, and when I say, 'Go,' take your thumb off
the tube and open your throat. It's that simple.
Ready?"

Jeremy nodded.

"Go!"

Turns out the kid could open his throat. Gravity
did the rest, and ten seconds later Jeremy had thirty
ounces of beer in him. He leaped from the chair,
staggered in circles for a few seconds, then started
to hiccup, then giggle, then got control of himself
and decided, as the head rush of all head rushes hit
him, that he was in no hurry to head back across
campus and hit the hay, but rather he'd just hang
with his new brothers for a while, if that was all
right with us. It was, and when someone suggested
he try a beer the regular way, in a can, Jeremy giggled and took it, and when someone else gave him

back his *Playboy* and asked him what he thought of Miss December, he giggled again, turned to the centerfold, and, at our prodding, read to us her turn-ons and turnoffs. Just like that, he was one of the guys, and he was still with us an hour later, when Pardo pointed out that it was the ten-year anniversary of the change in the drinking law, the rise of the legal age from eighteen to twenty-one. This realization, mixed with the beer, aroused the latent political consciousness in all of us, and soon we'd decided there was nothing for it but to round up some freshmen girls and road-trip to Albany, an hour away, where we'd drink with them on the steps of the state capitol in protest of the heartless law that had doomed so many of our brothers to celibacy.

We couldn't come up with the girls, but Pardo pulled his 1985 Ford Granada (TDX spelled out along the doors in black electrical tape) around to the front of the frat, and seven of us piled in, including little Jeremy, who sat in the middle, clutching a beer ball between his legs and singing, in full voice, the rugby song we taught him as we headed for the highway.

> *God made pretty white ankles*
> *And God made big golden beers*
> *God made pretty white ankles*
> *To hoist up over pretty white ears*

We handed Jeremy a penknife and told him to carve his initials into the ceiling, an honor usually reserved for the brothers, and he was doing just that when Pardo hit a patch of Thruway ice and the car started to fishtail. We clipped a pickup coming the other way, and the jolt brought the penknife, clutched in both of Jeremy's hands, down hard into the beer ball, which exploded like a balloon. Jeremy pissed himself as we spun out of control across the median, and he shat himself when we broke through the guardrail and rocketed down the steep embankment.

In most other cars we would have been finished, but the Granada was a boat, built for balance, and she kept her feet even as we plunged two hundred feet down the hill, narrowly missing three different trees, any one of which would have killed us. We slowed, finally, as the hill leveled off, and then slammed to a stop, fender first, against a tree stump, the four doors crushed shut, the grille of the Ford into the ground at a thirty-degree angle.

Our stuck horn led the state troopers right to us. From inside the car, bruised, shaken, but essentially okay, we saw their bright lights bobbing down the long hill, then saw them brighten as they reached the bottom and started toward us. Four state troopers stopped in a semicircle around our wrecked cruiser, their lights illuminating its cargo — six of TDX's finest and one seventeen-year-old high-school senior, all soaked to the skin in Matt's beer and reeking of human shit.

We spent the night in a Utica jail cell, six of us at one end and Jeremy at the other. After soiling himself both ways in the car, he completed the trifecta in the cell, when his maiden hangover kicked in, and though he was a sorry sight and we were responsible, not one of us was man enough to brave the mess and lend him a hand. He lay sprawled there through the night, clutching the toilet with both arms, apologizing between sobbing dry heaves to God and to his parents and to his high-school math teacher, promising all of them that if he could just survive this night, he would go to a state school, any state school, if there was still one left that would have him.

Jeremy started out at Ham Tech the next fall. It seems his old man had given enough money over the years that it would take more than one night of legal trouble to keep his son out of the freshman class. We rushed him, of course. He was already a legend in our halls, and we needed every curve-killer we could get our hands on to keep the administration off our backs. Pardo became his big brother, and soon they were inseparable. Jeremy, who would pass the CPA exam as a sophomore, saw to it that Pardo kept up the C– average he needed to get his diploma, and in return Pardo showed Jeremy that life on the Hill was more than math and econ.

Both wound up in the city after graduation. Jeremy put in two years at Coopers & Lybrand and then was snapped up by the venture capital firm he works for now, where he hauls in big bucks telling his bosses which greasy startups might grow into the next Microsoft. And Pardo? He works for the governor. Splits his time between Albany and the city. A "roving political aide" he calls himself, which seems to mean part bodyguard and part hatchet man, standing to the left of the podium at the old man's speeches and working "in the field" the rest of the time, digging up dirt on anyone who might make noises about mounting a campaign.

As often as I can get away with, I treat Pardo, a true Knicks fan, to our client seats here at the Garden, and tonight I comped Jeremy, too, as thanks for his help on the Brice account.

As the fourth quarter starts, the game is tight and the crowd into it, chanting, "Deee-fense!" when the 'Wolves have the ball and rising as one every time the Knicks score. Tonight has been a Sprewell special, Latrell alternately shooting the Knicks out of the game and then running them back into it, all the while giving Coach Van Gundy the look that only Spree can give him; a pinched, tortured expression as if Coach were just then, at that moment, passing a stone the size of an apple but knew it was a baby next to the one behind it. Now Spree takes a pass, darts into the lane, draws three defenders, ignores a wide-open Houston in the corner, and hits an impossible, twisting runner to give the Knicks the lead back. The crowd goes nuts, and the Minny coach raises his hands in exasperation and signals for a timeout.

"It's a different game from down here, isn't it?" I say to Jeremy as the players leave the floor.

"I'll say. Thanks for the ticket, Jake."

"Sure."

"How did I do in prepping you? Did you get your girl?"

I take a sip of beer. "I don't know yet."

Pardo looks over. "Good luck getting trim details out of Jake," he says. "He treats them like state secrets."

Jeremy takes a sip of his beer. "You know, I've been thinking about that account, Jake."

"And?"

"Well, there were some funny things in that file."

I hold up a hand. "I don't want to know, Jeremy. We gave the partner our report already. If Brice is a tax cheat, I'm on his side now."

Jeremy smiles. "Okay," he says.

"Would you look at that," says Pardo, as the Knick City Dancers bounce onto the court, fan out into formation, and sit down on the wooden floor, facing us. They cross their legs in perfect unison, open them, and cross them again.

"How's the desk clerk?" I ask him.

He shakes his head dismissively.

"New York women — forget 'em. L.A., Jake. I was out there last week. Goddamn."

"What do you mean?" asks Jeremy.

"They get their tits done in high school," he says. Jeremy's eyes widen. "I mean it. If you aren't a C cup by senior year, they boo you out of homeroom." Pardo shakes his head wistfully.

A cell phone goes off in the middle of us, and we all look down.

"Not me," says Pardo.

"Not me," says Jeremy.

"Not —," I say, but it is, and I look in surprise at my jacket pocket.

"Since when do you have a cell phone?" asks Pardo.

"Last week," I say, rising. "Work. I better take this out in the hall."

They stand to let me by, and I walk through the crowd, then down the aisle and up the ramp into the quiet back halls of the Garden. I walk to a pillar, my back to the ramp and the crowd beyond it. Only one person has my cell phone number. I take the phone from my pocket.

"Hello?"

"Jake?"

"Yes."

"It's Mimi."

"Hi."

"Hi."

She doesn't speak for a few seconds. I touch my hand to the cool gray pillar. We've passed twice in the firm's hallways since last Friday night. Since Nina Torring. Neither of us said a word.

"Can I see you, Jake?"

"When?"

"Now."

"Yes."

"I don't have much time," she says.

"You're a runner, aren't you?" I ask.

"Yes."

"Do you know where the river walkway starts?"

"On Sixty-fourth Street."

"Meet me there, along the railing. In twenty minutes."

I put the phone back into my jacket and walk back down the ramp and into the Garden crowd again. Into the high-priced seats, through perfume and cologne, pretty people in designer clothes. I reach our section and shake my head at Pardo and Jeremy. "Tax emergency, guys. I gotta go."

"Heartless," says Pardo. "Only ten minutes left. McSorley's at midnight?"

I look at him. "Maybe."

He looks hard at me. "You sly bastard," he says.

Jeremy salutes me. "Thanks for the seats, Jake."

I make my way through the crowd again, up the ramp and into the Garden lobby, gauging the game by the sounds behind me, groans and staccato shouts when the T-Wolves score, mass roars when the Knicks pour it on. I walk through the big doors and out onto Seventh Avenue, the night clear and cool as I cross the street, wave down a cab, and slide inside. "Sixty-fourth Street, on the East Side," I tell him. "By the river." He swings onto Thirty-fourth Street and heads east.

Not a word between Mimi Lessing and me since I crouched beside her Friday night and mouthed, "Go." Since I cut the panties off Nina Torring and Mimi couldn't watch any longer. The driver turns north on First Avenue and heads up the quiet streets, past the dark and silent UN, the river just a hundred yards east of us now, a breeze coming through the open cab window. Friday night was all I could have asked for. More. A seduction like none

other, ever. A seduction charged by the history between us, by the gold ring gleaming in the nightstand drawer. But charged most of all by Mimi
Lessing, not just listening this time but sitting close
enough to touch her and seeing everything. Seeing
Nina stripped and oiled and spread. Seeing her
helpless. Seeing it and knowing, as only a woman
could, what it was doing to her; what the ties, the
music, the ice, the cruel denial were doing deep inside Nina Torring.

By the end Mimi couldn't watch. She could only
rock slowly, her hands in her dress. I lifted her chin,
touching her for the first time, and she was beautiful, her cheeks on fire, her eyes . . . there's no de-
scribing them. I sent her away and finished off
Nina Torring, and it was the fuck of my life. But
when it was over, when I'd cut her wrists loose and
watched from the doorway as she covered her
breasts and turned her face into the bed, too weak
even to free her ankles, I stepped from her apartment and closed the door behind me, and I wasn't
thinking of the delicate, untouchable adviser I'd
just broken so slowly, so beautifully, so completely,
but of the girl who'd watched me break her. I was
seeing again the shock in Mimi's eyes when I told
her to go, her halting steps as she backed out of the
room. And as I stepped out onto Sullivan Street and
felt the air on my face, I knew that I'd either drawn
Mimi in for good or lost her forever.

The cab turns east again, onto Sutton Place, and
we glide past wide, clean sidewalks, past posh
buildings with gilt awnings. A four-block enclave

that gives way to York as we speed out of the Fifties
and then up into the Sixties and, suddenly, we're
here. "Right here," I tell the driver, and he pulls
over to the corner. I pay him, step from the cab,
walk up the steps of the overpass and then along
the concrete bridge that leads over the street and
toward the water. And I see her. Alone, tiny, standing at the railing fifty yards away, wearing a white
sweater and a blue dress that the wind, stronger
now, lifts away from her bare calves. I walk to the
end of the overpass and then down the curving
ramp and onto the river walkway. She turns and
sees me, watches me walk toward her, and then
turns and looks out again over the water. I step to
the railing, a few feet away from her, and we look
out together at the black waves.

The artist's name is Iliati.

He paints village scenes in dazzling color. The
town plaza on market day; an olive field at dusk; a
stone church, with the faithful converging. Somewhere in each painting is the brilliant Tuscan sun.

I step back and look across the room. In the
muted light I can see her, moving gracefully among
the other enthusiasts. She looks over. I walk to the
next painting. A water tower in silhouette, set
against the flaming hills. She breaks from the others
and starts across the room, and I remind myself
again of the painter's career details. His appren-
ticeship in Arles. His love of cinema.

"Hi," she says. "May I help you?"

"Yes. I'm here to buy."

She laughs. "So much for small talk," she says, extending a delicate hand. "Welcome. I'm Nina Torring."

"Tell me about your first one, Jake."

Jake Teller looks at me, then down at the black railing, and out at the lights of Roosevelt Island. He doesn't say anything for so long that I think he's not going to answer.

"It was a year ago," he says quietly. "She worked in the building across from mine." Jake looks at me, then out at the lights again. "My office was on the fourth floor, and hers was on the second. The street was narrow, maybe fifty feet across. I could see right in."

The wind is cool on my face and neck. On my bare calves. Mark expects me at his apartment in twenty minutes. We'll rent a movie, he said.

"I couldn't see her features, but I knew she was a beauty. I could tell from her posture, from the way the guys in her office lingered in her doorway. And there was something else about her, something . . . lonely, restrained. She wore her hair up every day. Sometimes if she worked late and everyone was gone, she would take it down. Take the pins from it and shake it loose."

"How did you meet her?"

"I didn't. I just watched her."

Jake looks at me again, then down into the dark water.

"For a month, at least. Then one night I was finishing up my work, and I looked across and saw her lock her desk and take her coat from her chair. I went downstairs to the street and there she was, just coming out of her building. I followed her to Grand Central. Down the stairs, through the turnstile, down to the platform for the uptown trains. An express came, the one I always took home, but she didn't get on it, so I stayed on the platform. A local came next, and I watched her step into it. I stood there, staring at the open doors, and just as they closed, I jumped in. I took a seat down and across from her, and I saw her face close-up for the first time. She was beautiful. Delicate eyes, very little makeup. She sat with her knees close together, a book in her lap. At Sixty-eighth Street she got off, and I followed her all the way to her apartment building. I watched her go inside."

I look at Jake, and he meets my gaze.

"For twenty minutes I just stood there. Then I walked home. The next morning, at work, I pulled the blinds down in my window. I never watched her again."

Jake steps away from the railing and looks down the walkway at the distant lights of the Manhattan Bridge. He puts his hands on the railing again, looks at me for a second, then back down into the dark water.

"Three weeks later, I worked late on a Friday night. When I finished, I walked to Grand Central. I waited on the platform; when the express came, I let it go by. I took the local to Sixty-eighth Street and walked to her apartment building. I was still in my work suit. I sat down on the steps of a building across the street. At eight-thirty, she walked out the door. I stood up and followed her. Onto the subway, down to West Fourth Street. To the Waverly Theater. She went to the window and bought a ticket. An erotic movie was showing. A Japanese erotic movie. It wasn't porn — there were write-ups from the big papers outside the theater. It was an art-house movie. I bought a ticket and went inside, and I took a seat right behind her."

I try to picture it. The dark theater. Jake in his suit, sitting just behind her. Bodies on the screen. I feel the weakness in my legs, the color rising in my face.

"I couldn't take my eyes off her hair. When I leaned forward I could smell it, rich and dreamy. It was held up by a single long pin, passed through a wooden hairband. Deep into the movie, I reached forward and pulled the pin out of her hair. Her whole body convulsed, but she didn't make a sound or turn around. I watched her hair come down, and then I reached forward and touched it. Still she didn't move. And then I got out of my seat, crouched in the aisle beside her, and held out the pin and band in my open palm. She looked at me, and I saw in her eyes that she was terrified. She took the pin and the band, and then she stood and walked past me and up the aisle and out of the theater.

"I took my seat again, and I was shaking. I stayed in it through the end of the movie. Through all the credits, stayed in it even after the lights came up. I was the last one to leave. And when I walked outside, there she was. Standing in front of the theater, waiting."

Jake is quiet again. And still quiet. And now I realize he is through. I want to hear more, to hear everything. To know where it comes from, his cruelty. But he is through. Past him, I can see almost half a mile up the river walkway, see the light from the well-spaced lampposts, light that catches the bright clothing of two runners who come toward us at a steady pace.

"Mark wanted to videotape the wedding," I say. "I couldn't imagine it. The first dance ruined while we watch out for wires and mikes and lighting. We fought about it. He was adamant. 'Think of twenty years from now,' he said. 'We'll have all the magic of it preserved.' "

Jake's eyes are on me again. Bottomless blue.

"Last night he covered my eyes and steered me to the dining-room table. He took his hands away. Spread out on the table were photographs. Black-and-white photographs. He had fired the video-man and found a photographer in Brooklyn who does weddings in black and white. The pictures were so beautiful. The bride and groom. The priest in his collar. Panoramic shots — the wedding party with the whole of the reception hall behind them. Everything looked timeless, permanent. I saw them and I knew."

The runners reach us now, the sound of their breathing loud as they pass, then softening and disappearing as they start up the winding overpass, leaving us again to the sound of the waves against the concrete wall, the distant hum of traffic from the streets.

"I'm going to marry him, Jake."

Jake looks out over the water again. He is quiet for almost thirty seconds.

"Friday night, when I kept her still, you almost couldn't take it."

I close my eyes.

"And when I told you to go, you didn't leave the apartment."

I hold tight to the black railing. I can see her again. Her tiny hands, lying open on the covers, desperate to clutch the silk but not permitted to.

"What do you want from me, Jake?"

He is quiet again. I look into his eyes, and there it is. Steel.

"Do you have your cell phone?" he asks.

"Yes."

I reach down into my purse and take out the small black phone. Jake motions with his hand at the water.

"Drop it in. You'll be free."

I hold the phone against the railing and look down into the river. The wind has stirred the waves into small whitecaps.

"The girl in the theater, Mimi. She went into the lobby and asked for the manager. She was going to tell him to call the police. It took them a few minutes to find him. When they did, and he asked her what was wrong, she couldn't answer him."

I stare hard at the ring on my finger.

"I'm going to take the next one further, Mimi."

My sweater is tight around me, but even so, I feel it. The thrilling flush that starts on the back of my neck, as if I've just been touched there, and now spreads all through me.

"You've dreamed of it, Mimi, without ever admitting it."

I can't look at him.

"Pain," he says.

I close my eyes again. When I open them, Jake is gone. I turn to see him on the overpass, crossing the bridge back toward the city streets. I turn back to the water and look out over it, holding the black cell phone in my shaking hands.

"Powerful work."

"Isn't it?" she says. "We're lucky to represent him. Was there one in particular you were interested in?"

"I buy collections, Ms. Torring, not paintings."

"I see." Two new customers enter the gallery and shed their coats. They look our way. "All told, we represent more than forty of his works."

"Then my investment would be serious." The newcomers stand expectantly back at the gallery door. I nod at them. "I wonder if I might return when I could have your full attention."

"Of course. We offer after-hours appointments for collectors at your level. You could come back any night this week, and we'd have the gallery to ourselves."

"Very well. How is tomorrow?"

She nods. "Fine."

"Eight o'clock?"

"Fine again." She takes my hand in both of hers and smiles. "Tomorrow it is, then. I look forward to it."

I walk to the gallery door and step out into the evening air. I walk to the corner of West Fourth Street. From my coat I take the crumpled handbill that I rescued Friday night from the flowerpot outside Nina Torring's apartment building. Rescued just moments after Miss Lessing emerged, shaken and crying.

I tear the handbill in two.

CHAPTER ELEVEN

I had my first drink the night the Berlin Wall came down.

I was sixteen and living with Grandpa on Long Island, a year after my parents were killed in a car crash in Japan. I was asleep on the cot in my room when he woke me with a rough shake. "Let's go, boy," he said. "We've got business." On the way out, Grandpa stopped at the rolltop desk in the corner of the living room. I'd never seen him open it, but he slid a key into the ridged top, pushed it up, and pulled out a small green pouch.

It was almost midnight, the streets quiet, and he didn't say a word until he pulled his '77 Chevy into the driveway of Artie Moore's house. He was about to hit the horn, but we could see Artie through his living-room window, and he could see us. He stood on a small stepladder, hanging two stars high up in the window.

"Know what those are for?" Grandpa asked.

"No."

"Families used to put 'em in the window when a son went to war. In 'forty-three, 'forty-four, you walked around these streets, every other window had one."

"One of them is gold."

"Gold means they didn't come back. Artie's brother, Donald. We all called him Dooley — I can't remember why." We saw Artie step down and pull the curtains closed. "Go give him a hand."

I walked up the driveway and reached his front door as he opened it.

"Hi, Mr. Moore."

"Jake," he said, nodding and taking my arm, his grip strong. He leaned heavily on me, and we walked carefully through the wet leaves to the car.

We drove a mile through empty streets to the Veterans Club, a squat building of chipped paint tucked away at the quiet end of Main Street. Other cars were parked or pulling up, and men were walking over the short grass to the open door of the club. Men in their sixties and seventies. Grandpa's war friends, the ones who, like him, came back from World War II to their hometown and stuck around. Plumbers, dentists, admen. Most of them retired, all of them woken up just a while earlier by Grandpa's call.

Inside the one-room club, they took the stools down off the worn wooden bar. Smitty found some glasses and opened the taps and then pointed at me. "You're tending bar tonight, Jake," he said, and then started a fire in the small fireplace and joined the ten others around the television at the far end of the bar. Grandpa took the green pouch from his jacket and shook out his dog tags. All the men had brought theirs. Some laid them on the bar, and some held them in their rough, spotted hands or worked them between thumb and fingers as they drank their beers. And together they watched the Wall come down.

They watched kids stand on top of it, their arms locked, swaying and singing. Watched two women at a crossing point dance over the line and then back, over again and back. Watched men bury their faces in the shoulders of other men. All along the Wall, people with chisels and hammers chipped away at it. Chipped away and then moved off a few feet to stare, stunned, at the bits of wall in their open hands. One man kissed the pieces; another dropped them on the ground and crushed them beneath his feet.

They watched in silence, looking from the television to the floor, or out the window at the quiet streets. After a while the beer got into them. "Patton," said Artie, lifting his glass high, and everyone raised theirs in answer. "Elsenborn," said another, and they raised them again. "C rations." They raised them. "Fuckin' pillboxes." They raised them. "Carole Lombard," said Grandpa, to a round of "hear, hear"s. And then Charlie Bell, the oldest among them, raised a hand for silence, rose slowly to his feet, paused for effect, and said, "To Monty!" and they all roared with laughter.

Smitty tossed me the keys to the storeroom. "Jake, find some whiskey, will you," he said, and when I came back with Jack Daniel's and shot glasses and started to pour, Grandpa pulled over another stool. "Make room, men," he said. "This might as well be the night."

Artie poured a shot for me, right to the top of the glass. "Whoa," said Grandpa as I picked it up. All the men lifted theirs. "Anyone ever asks you what I did, boy," said Grandpa, and then pointed at the television, where a young man sat straddling the Wall, his arms in the air, his head back in triumph. "There it is." They all touched their glasses to mine, and in their company I had my first taste of whiskey.

I come up from the subway into the cloudy late-afternoon sky. I walk east to Third Avenue and up to Twentieth Street. Just past the house where Teddy Roosevelt was born is a green common set back from the street, and just behind the common is the Columbarium. It is an old marble building with the look of a church, but instead of spires it is topped by a dome. The path to it winds through a garden. I walk to the arched doorway and through it into the quiet lobby. High above me, in the open center of the building, are windows of stained glass. All three floors are designed as circular walkways, and built into the walls of those walkways are small niches. Seven thousand of them, each holding cremated ashes.

Classical music plays softly from hidden speakers as I start up the winding staircase. Even the stairwell landings are filled with niches. Most are glass, allowing you to see into them, to see the urn, or urns, inside and the keepsakes the families have placed beside them. Photographs. A square of lace. A baseball card.

On the broad third-floor landing I pass a family: a mother, father, and daughter gathered around an empty niche. The mother holds a small ceramic urn in her hands, and a director in a dark suit stands to the side. I step past them and start around the walkway, the air scented by the flowers in the hanging vases spaced along the wall. I pass hundreds of niches until, a third of the way around, I reach Grandpa's.

He died a year ago today. It was Artie Moore who called me. "Chopping wood, Jake," he said. "Couldn't ask for much better." I look through the clear glass at the two silver urns inside. Grandpa hadn't wanted any keepsakes put in. And nothing inscribed on the urns but names and dates. I can hear his voice: "What good will words do me, boy? I'll be dead." I take a cloth from my shirt and clean the glass. The first time he brought me to see Grandma's urn, he said, "Make sure mine is just like it." Then he shook his head. "Fifty years, Jake," he said. "The war. Three kids. Six grandkids. At the last, she didn't know me. Patted my hand and asked if I would send in her husband. You leave this world alone."

I squat down and press my fingers to the floor. The music stops, and for a moment the place is quiet. From another floor I can hear, faintly, a woman's heels on the marble. And now, from be-

hind me on the landing, where the family is gathered, the grinding sound of the heavy key the director uses to open a new niche.

In my summers home from college, Grandpa got
me a job at the Veterans Club, tending bar, even
though I was years too young. Saturday night was
poker night, and all his war buddies would come.
After the game broke up, they would sit and drink
and talk. If they had enough in them, they'd talk
about the war. Never the heavy stuff — wounds,
friends lost — not when I could hear. If they talked
about battles, it was quietly, in a kind of code.
"Hürtgen," someone might say, and those who
fought there would grunt or nod their heads. They
talked freely about machines and about the brass,
how the generals kept bragging about the Sherman
tank when any GI knew it took five of them to
knock out a Panzer. But mostly, if they could see I
was listening, they talked about the carousing,
about the nights they'd managed in spite of it all.
French girls. Belgian beer. Shots for the clap.

After the rest of them went home, Grandpa
would sit at the bar and drink a last beer while I
cleaned up. One night I was drying glasses and
thinking of the story Smitty had just told, of how
his unit got separated from their regiment, then got
so lost that they crossed from Germany back into
France, and instead of reaching the munitions plant
they were supposed to attack, the one surrounded
by dug-in Germans, they wound up on the steps of
a whorehouse, and after the savvy radioman called
in their position, mentioning only the coordinates,

they were ordered to hole up there until nightfall. Grandpa was sitting quietly, as he always did just after they'd gone, his mind still back in that time. "Sounds like you guys miss those days," I said to him. He looked up quickly, his eyes flashing, but he didn't say anything. He stayed quiet while I put the good liquor away in the cabinets, quiet while I counted out the register, quiet still while I turned the barstools upside down and lifted them onto the bar. I knew I'd said something stupid, so I took my time cleaning up, sweeping the floor twice, even dusting the liquor bottles on the back shelves. Finally there was nothing left for me to do, so I locked up and we walked to the Chevy in silence. He crossed to the driver's side, then looked at me over the roof of the car.

"Nobody misses the war, boy," he said. "You understand?" I nodded. We got in, but Grandpa sat there, the keys in his hand, staring into the wheel. "Every glass of beer was your last. Every letter home. So you got drunk any chance you could. And when you wrote, you made your words count." He looked out the window, across the lawn to the quiet town streets. "It isn't the war you miss. It's the spirit of those days. Some of us, who got lucky and lived through it, learned how to live. Like we'd be gone tomorrow. Because a lot of us were." He looked at me. "You got me, boy?" I nodded. "Okay, then," he said gently. He slid the key into the ignition, then looked at me again. "Find something that gives you that charge, Jake. That fires your blood."

I stand and look into the niche. *Harold Teller,
1922–1999. Charisse Teller, 1919–1992.* The first time
he brought me here, I asked him why he wanted to
be cremated. He said he'd seen what time does to a
corpse.

There was never any b.s. to Grandpa, or to any of
his war friends. They were the best men I've
known. Men in their sixties and seventies, and in
my summers tending bar, I never heard any of
them bitch about their aches or their ages. Three
more of them are gone now. Smitty — cancer. Charlie Bell — cancer. Roger Tamper — stroke. But I can
close my eyes and see them all again, see them as I
saw them that first night in the Veterans Club as
they watched the Berlin Wall come down. There
was a light in the eyes of those men that I've never
seen again in anyone.

From the stairwell landing, the words of the
mother drift out to me. "Brought more light in sixteen years . . . Remains in our hearts . . . Would
have wanted this beside him . . ."

Watching that Wall come down, those men must
have felt their lives come full circle. They'd been a
part of something vital. They'd meant something. I
think of my friends, try to imagine where we might
meet in thirty, forty years. What will we toast — the
Dow?

I breathe onto the glass, wipe it a last time with
the cloth, and walk away. I reach the landing,
where the family stands now with bowed heads,
then walk down the winding stairwell, through the
lobby, out the doorway, and into the late afternoon.

I hurry up the path, across the green common, to Twentieth Street, and back to the subway, stopping on the stairs to let the strong tunnel wind blow over me.

It was a week after Grandpa died that I followed the woman to the theater and then took her home. She walked ahead of me into her bedroom. On the door handle hung the silk belt to her bathrobe, and when she turned to me, I held it in my hands. "Give me your wrists," I told her. She started to lift them toward me but then backed away, her eyes on me, and sat down on her bed, running her hands over her stockinged thighs. I nodded and walked out and down the hall to the front door. I was unlocking the deadbolt when she touched my shoulder. I turned around.

"Please," she said.

"If I stay, I stay," I said. She leaned back against the wall, hugging her arms to her, rubbing them.

"Please," she said again, but I shook my head. She closed her eyes, but when she heard me turn the lock she opened them. "Stay," she said.

I ride the 6 train to Forty-second Street and then, instead of catching the express for home, walk to the shuttle and take it across to Times Square. I take the express to Seventy-second Street and then catch the No. 1 local to 116th. I walk through the turnstile and up the stairs, out into the last fading light of afternoon.

Just ahead of me stand the black iron gates of Columbia University. I don't know what made me come here, but I step through them, joining the flow of students, guys with dangling backpacks and coeds in sweatshirts and tattered jeans, books pressed to their chests. I haven't walked these red bricks since I was ten, since before IBM lured my father from the business school and sent us to Japan. I climb the stairs onto Low Plaza and stand for a minute in the fading light. Above me is the familiar black statue; a woman in robes, holding a staff in one hand, a book open in her lap. Above the statue rise the majestic white stairs of Low Library. And beside me, just as I remember them, are the fountains. I walk to one and sit down on its wide rim. The last of the sun glints off the rippling water. I look out over the campus, feeling the gentle spray on my neck as I spot the field where we played baseball in the summer. It looks impossibly small. I dip my hand in the cold water. I used to wade in these fountains, once cut my toe badly on a piece of jagged metal. I remember the shock, staring at the blood spilling back into the water, then being lifted up into Dad's arms, the world over his shoulder, close and jarring, as he carried me, running, to the hospital.

I rise and walk back down the stairs to the brick path. I remember these red bricks as endless, as stretching as far as I could see, but really it is just a few minutes' walk from end to end. I look back at the Broadway gate. I should go through it and home to my apartment, but instead I turn and follow the bricks the other way, to the far gate, and walk out onto Amsterdam Avenue. I turn left and walk the old familiar four blocks, uptown but downhill, the buildings of the campus to my left. I stop at the corner of 120th Street. The light is green, but I don't cross.

The A&P is a Red Apple now. There is still a cleaners on one corner, a drugstore on another. The same ones? I can't remember. And there, on the far corner, is the towering, gray prewar. U-shaped around a walkway that leads from the street to the front door. Eight twenty-three West 120th Street. I cross to it. The mailbox is still here, the solid green mailbox that marked one end zone in sidewalk football. I glance at the walkway, but just for a second, then walk past the building and up the block, across the narrow street to the raised clearing above the entrance to Morningside Park.

As a kid, this was the boundary of my world. I was never allowed down into the park, so the wide staircase and the path through the trees below held magic for me, terror. Even today they look mystical, cinematic, the thick stone walls along the edge of the park looming like the walls of a castle. The trees planted on the hillside below rise to the clearing, their branches dipping over the metal spikes of the railing. I pull off a leaf and rub it between my fingers.

Mimi Lessing. Grace, beauty, purity. I want to take her hand, to stand with her, to wake to those eyes. And I want to take her apart, button by button. So much inside her, to be taken away. More than she even imagines. A gust of wind finds the skin under my collar. The sun is gone now, gone behind the trees of the park. I want them both so strongly — to protect Mimi and to break her. Equally, I want them. I turn from the park entrance and cross the street again.

Not quite equally.

I walk back down to the mailbox in front of my old building. I run my hand along it, thinking of the day three black kids came down from Harlem and challenged us to a game. I led Tony Collins a step too far, and though he hauled in my pass, he hit the mailbox at full speed and broke his wrist. I turn and look up to the fifth floor, to the corner window. My old room. Mom would sit on the radiator and watch out the window as we played. When I scored I would hold the football up to her, and she would wave.

For the first time, I take a good look at the walkway that leads to the front door. It, too, had seemed so long, but it isn't even twenty yards. I can see the doorman in the foyer, looking out. It could be Clete, if he stood a little straighter. Clete, who always stood like a yardstick, his hands behind his back. I'd stand next to him, as straight as I could, my hands behind my back, too, and when one of the older tenants turned into the walk with her groceries, I'd say, "Can I get the door, Clete?" and if it was one who never tipped, Clete would say, "She's all yours, Jake." I walk up the path to the stairs. It could still be Clete, and now I see that it is. Bowed, but the same hard nose, the same mole just under the eye.

"Evening, sir," he says.

"Hi. Clete?"

"That's me." He looks closely at me.

"I used to live here a long time ago."

"You did? What's the last name?"

"Teller."

"Teller . . . Teller. Apartment fifty-three."

"That's right."

"Mr. Edward and Mrs. Gail. And the boy, Jake. Well, I'll be." He offers his hand, and I shake it. "Teller. Left in . . . 'eighty-three?"

" 'Eighty-four."

" 'Eighty-four. Went off to Asia, or some such."

"Japan."

"Japan. And here you've come back. How are your parents?"

I pause.

"They're . . . they're fine," I say.

"You tell them Clete says hello."

"I will."

He turns with me into the lobby and sits down at the small front desk. In front of him is a big leather book that I recognize from years ago. The tenant book.

"That's not the same one," I say.

"The same one." He runs his hand over the creased cover. "Columbia housing, so we don't get computers."

I look around the small lobby. A sofa and chairs. The fireplace. The mailroom just off the elevator.

"You been okay, Clete?"

"Oh, I been good, I guess. Still livin' on the wrong side of town. Few more years, though, it just might turn around." His hands, clasped together on top of the tenant book, tremble slightly. "Jake, you the boy used to stand with me in the window?"

"That was me."

He laughs. "Damn, you got big. And here I'm getting smaller. Well, it's good to see you again. We don't get many, come back after all that time."

"I'm going to go walk around, Clete, if that's okay."

"You go ahead."

I walk past the elevator to the stairs. I turn around.

"Who's in fifty-three now?"

"Three girls, Jake. Stewardesses, I think. Gone a lot."

I climb the stairs, my hand along the wide stone handrail. I was always running down these stairs. Racing against the elevator, against the envelopes I'd drop down the stone mail chute on the fifth floor. I walk quietly now, as if I might give myself away. I reach the fifth floor, turn right, walk to the end of the hallway, and turn left. There it is, down at the far end. The same small lettering in the middle of the door. 53. I walk to it. The buzzer is where it's always been, just below the eyehole. From inside I can hear music and laughter.

I press the button.

Ten seconds later the door opens to a young woman in a white belly T and gold drawstring pants. She is beautiful, her shining black hair falling almost to her waist. One tan arm is braceleted to the elbow, and she has four small silver earrings clipped to the top of one ear.

"Hi," she says. "Who are you?"

"I'm Jake Teller," I say.

"Sasha's friend?"

"No. I wasn't invited. I used to live here a long time ago. I just wanted to see the apartment again."

She considers this. "Prove it," she says playfully.

I smile. "Behind you, to the right, is the main hallway. Straight ahead is the living room. Off that, the dining room. To the right, the kitchen. The bedrooms are to the left."

"Wild," she says, smiling. "Come on in. Look around."

She turns and walks down the hallway. In the small of her back, in the tanned skin below her T-shirt, is a tiny tattoo. A sideways figure eight. I look up from it to see the old living room, the far windows where they should be, looking out onto Amsterdam Avenue. Mom hung the *Casablanca* poster in one of them, so that I could pick out our window on the walk home from school. Nothing else in the apartment looks the same. It is clearly a woman's place now — soft furniture, soft colors. And on the couch, another soft young woman, maybe twenty-five, a guy next to her. On the love seat beside them is another young couple. A third guy stands alone by the stereo. The guys wear Dockers, khakis, confidence. Everyone holds a drink. A couples night in.

"Hey," says my guide, "this is Jake. Believe it or not, he lived here." She turns to me. "When, Jake?"

"As a kid."

"And he picked tonight to come back," she says.

"I'm Tracy," says Tracy, from the couch, with a wave.

"Pierce," says the guy next to her.

"Sasha," says the woman in the love seat.

"Kevin," says her guy.

"Scott," says the guy by the stereo.

There's a second of silence. "Would you like a drink, Jake?" says my guide. "I'm Elise, by the way."

"Our reservation's at seven," says Scott, looking at Elise, then down at the CD case in his hands.

"And the restaurant's ten blocks away," says Elise. "Jake?"

"Sure."

Elise steps into the kitchen. The rest of us are quiet as I take in the living room, the dining room, the tiny room off the kitchen that Mom used for her paintings.

"Does it look familiar?" asks Pierce.

"Barely," I say.

Elise comes back with a bottle of beer.

"Thanks," I say, and after another second of silence I gesture down the far hallway. "Do you guys mind? I'll be two minutes."

"Go for it," says Elise. Scott shoots her a look.

I walk the few steps down the hall and stand in the doorway of my old room. The closet is the same, that's all. It smells of petals now, of oils, of a hundred soft scents. I see bracelets on the dresser. From the living room I hear Scott's voice, not quite a whisper. "I just think it's weird, that's all."

Her bed is where mine was, against the far wall.

I had a bunk bed, for some reason. It must have come with the apartment. I slept on the bottom, always, defeating my eight o'clock bedtime with the tiny transistor radio I kept pressed between pillow and ear. I remember its tinny smell, the voice of Marv Albert calling the Knicks. "Yes! And it counts!" he would say. "A gorgeous move."

Beneath the window is the radiator. I walk to it and sit down. I can see the mailbox on the street below, see the whole wide block. A streetlight flickers on across the way.

"Your old room."

I look up to see Elise in the doorway.

"Yes."

"You like what I've done with it?"

I laugh. When she moves, she dips her head to keep her long hair behind her. Her dark eyes are direct.

"I'm all done," I say, rising.

"It's okay."

"I'm interrupting."

"Third and final date," she says softly, just before Scott appears in the doorway behind her. He pulls her into him. She allows it but doesn't relax against him, and her eyes, on mine, explain everything.

"How's that beer coming, guy?" Scott asks. "Jack, is it?"

"Jake. It's finished," I say, tilting it back.

"It's just that we've got dinner plans," he says.

"Me, too." I walk toward the door.

"Scott," says Elise. "I'm going to need one more. Will you?" She holds her empty glass to him. Scott glances at me and then takes it. "Thanks. I'll show Jake out."

Scott walks out of the room. Elise and I stand in silence for a few seconds.

"Did it hurt?" I ask her. Her dark eyes hold mine. "The tattoo."

"Yes," she says.

"He's leaving," I hear Scott say from the living room.

"Sasha said he was my type," says Elise. She touches my arm lightly. "Go say your good-byes, Jake." I pause, but she motions with her head, so I walk out to the living room and lift a hand at the four of them.

"Thanks," I say.

"Sure, Jake."

"See ya."

"Bye."

"Bye."

Elise joins us again from the hall as Scott comes out from the kitchen. She takes the glass from his hand and walks with me down the hall toward the front door. We turn the corner into the foyer.

"What made you come back tonight?" she asks.

"It's a long story."

Before she can answer, Scott appears behind her. "Later," he says to me, reaching past her to open the front door.

"Thanks," I say to Elise.

"It was nice to meet you, Jake." She holds out her hand, and as I shake it, I feel the slip of paper. I palm it and walk out, and the door closes behind

me. I walk down the hall, turn the corner, walk to
the elevator, and push the button. Beside me is the
old stone mail chute. I run my fingers along it. Only
when I'm inside the elevator and the door closes do
I open my hand and unfold the piece of paper.

    212-6128.

CHAPTER TWELVE

It's been years since I thought of Eileen Post.

Of the day in seventh grade at All Grace girls' school in Greenwich when Eileen walked into homeroom five minutes late, her French braid ruined, her headband in her hands, her blouse pulled out of her uniform skirt. One white sock was at her ankle, the other was smudged with dirt.

"Eileen Post, what in the world —," said our teacher.

"It's nothing, Miss Anders," said Eileen. "I tripped on the bike rack." But as she slid into her seat near the back of class, pulling her sock back up to her knee, tucking in her blouse, her excited eyes told the girls around her that it was something much more. "I'll tell you at gym," she whispered to us.

Two hours later Anne, Bliss, Michelle, and I hung back in the locker room as the rest of the girls walked out to the gym for volleyball. We gathered around Eileen on the changing benches. She sat

with her palms pressed down in front of her and
looked at each one of us dramatically. She had been
walking on Maple Street, she said, a block from
school, when three sixth-grade boys crossed from
the other side of the street. One of them knocked
her book bag off her shoulder. Before she could run,
two of them held her against the redbrick wall and
the third one touched her through her clothes.

We all sat there, stunned.

"Touched you where?" Anne whispered.

Eileen stood up against the bank of lockers. She
motioned to Anne and me. "This is the brick wall,"
she said. She had Anne hold one of her hands
against the lockers, and she had me hold the other.
"Tighter," she told us. "So that I can't move." Then
she had us each hook her feet with one of ours.

"I was so helpless," she said. "I couldn't even
kick. They could have done anything."

"What did they do?" I whispered.

She sat back down on the changing bench. "The
third boy," she said, and then brushed her palm,
once, across her sternum, closer to her neck than to
the area of her shirt that covered her training bra.

"That's all he did?" said Bliss.

"Then he put his hand downstairs."

We gasped.

"Under your skirt?" Michelle asked, in awe.

"No. On my belt. Like *that* was the magic spot.
Then they all ran off."

We sat back and breathed. Eileen looked around
at us again. "They didn't know anything," she said.

We made her tell us again, made her go over

every moment. "They could have done anything,"
she was saying again when Miss Price, the gym
teacher, walked in.

"Girls, what are you doing?" she said sternly.
"Come out here immediately."

We jumped up and walked out to the gym,
Eileen in the middle of us, our protective hands on
her hair, rubbing her arms, making sure the other
girls could see that we'd been trusted with a secret.
They begged us to tell them. Eileen nodded, so we
told the story in fevered, whispered bits as Miss
Price demonstrated the proper way for a girl to
serve a volleyball.

The "attack" held everyone's imagination for a
week, until Karen Glass told us she had French-
kissed a delivery boy and was going to do it again
that afternoon. A few days later Debbie Rose
brought a condom to school and passed it around
in study hall. And gradually the girls at All Grace
forgot about Eileen's ordeal.

But I couldn't forget. Months later I would still
catch myself thinking about it in class. And not
only at school. At night, too, alone in bed. For almost two years I kept picturing it, and I realize now
that I saw the same image in my mind every time:
Eileen's small hands pinned tight to the redbrick
wall, her feet hooked and separated.

And now, years later, it comes back to me again,
at ten to seven on a Friday evening, as I sit in a
quiet pew at St. Mary's Cathedral on Sixty-first
Street and Fifth Avenue. The cathedral where I'll be
married two weeks from tomorrow. Mark and I

meet tonight with Father Cronin, the priest who will marry us. We need him to approve the vows we've written for each other, and we want to hear the words he's chosen to say in the last moments before he joins us as husband and wife.

I run my hands along the smooth wooden back of the pew in front of me. It's been so long since I've been to church. I'd forgotten how peaceful it can be. How quiet. None of the sounds of the rushing city. Just the whispered footsteps of the people who enter, kneel at the beginning of the deep red carpet leading to the altar, and then step quietly into one of the many pews. I look up at the high ceiling, at the exposed white columns, detailed with engravings of infants and angels. At the stained-glass windows, each depicting a different saint. It is beautiful, this church. And it has the rich smell that never leaves the memory. Wood, candles, cloth . . . and something deeper, something almost beyond words. Tradition. Faith.

I look back at the Chapel of Forgiveness, the small alcove by the entrance where Father Cronin asked us to meet him. It is empty now, so I stand and walk to it, passing again the basin of holy water just inside the front door. I step into the alcove. Upon one wall is a wooden scroll.

In your charity pray for the souls of the Paulist Fathers who have gone before us with the sign of faith.

And then the names of the departed. Irish names, all of them. Mallon. O'Hearn. Ferry. Mc-Grath. A hundred others. I think of the priests from my childhood, in the church in Greenwich. Father Ryan. Father Derry. Father Connolly. Gentle men, all of them.

"You're early, my child."

I start, and turn around.

"Father Cronin. Hi."

He is a slight man with a thin, almost gaunt face saved by the red in his cheeks, and gentle but penetrating brown eyes. His white collar is immaculate against the black of his robe.

"Mark should be here any minute," I say.

He nods kindly. On the wall across from the scroll is a crucifix. I've rarely been so close to one so large, so detailed. Beneath it, at kneeling level, are rows of candles.

"Would you like to light one?" he asks.

"Yes."

He doesn't have to know how long it's been. I light the wooden stick from the one lit candle and touch it to the wick of another. The flame sputters and holds. I put the stick down in the tray. A few seconds later Father Cronin's hand touches the small of my back.

"And now you kneel," he says gently.

"Of course," I say, flushing. I kneel and clasp my hands. The only sounds are our breathing and the rustle of his robe.

"Father Cronin?"

"Yes?"

"I have doubts."

I hear the front door of the church open, and I turn quickly and look toward it. It isn't Mark.

"Speak freely, Mimi."

"I've been tempted."

He doesn't answer for a few seconds. I watch the candle's dancing flame.

"What else?"

I don't dare lift my eyes from the candle to the crucifix.

"That's all."

Father Cronin kneels beside me. The sleeve of his robe touches my bare arm.

"We are all tempted, Mimi. Fidelity would mean nothing without temptation. Faith would mean nothing."

"How do I know, Father? If I'm strong enough? To resist."

"Do you want to resist?"

I pause.

"Yes."

"Then you will. Each one of us has strength we don't even know. It arises out of faith. When you need it, it will serve you. Now rise, my child."

I stand to see Mark in the church doorway, looking around. He sees us and waves.

"Sorry I'm late, Father Cronin," he says, walking into the alcove. He kisses my forehead. "What did I miss?"

"The lighting of a candle," says Father Cronin.

*   *   *

She wears a little black dress; her legs, beneath the table, are bare and crossed.

"You've had girlfriends," she says, her eyes on mine.

"Sure."

"Then you've had that moment when you knew."

Her black hair shines in the low light of the bar.

"I'm not sure what you mean," I say.

She has let the shawl slip off her delicate shoulders, and when she leans toward me, her breasts press against the table's edge.

"Scott was standing at the stereo last Friday night. Our third date, right? He was going through the CDs, pulling one out, putting it back in. I was watching him, and suddenly I knew. I can't tell you why, but I knew."

"That you were done with him."

"Yes. That I would get through the evening, and that would be it. And just as I was sitting there on the couch, realizing this, the doorbell rang. I went to answer it, and it was you."

Elise leans back as the old bartender comes with our drinks, a vodka and tonic for her and a pint for me. She takes the lime in her fingers, runs it along the edge of the glass, then squeezes it into the middle and drops it in. As she raises her glass, the bracelets on her arm slide down to her elbow.

"I don't believe in coincidence," she says.

I touch her glass, and we drink.

It is Friday night at 9:30 and we sit in a small booth at Lessons, on 112th Street and Broadway. We are the only customers in the place. She takes a sip, and I watch her throat shiver as it goes down.

"You said it was a long story, Jake. Why you picked that night to come back."

"It isn't, really. I was just thinking about my past."

She looks down at her hands and then back up at me, her dark eyes searching.

"Okay," I say. "It was a year to the day that my grandfather died."

She takes this in, her eyes deepening. "I like that," she says.

We sit quietly for a while. Beneath the table I let my knee drift to hers.

"You're a stewardess," I say.

Her lips part in surprise, but after a second, understanding dawns in her eyes.

"Clete the doorman," she says. "Teller of secrets. Actually, I'm a graduate student. That's why we get to live in Columbia housing. Sasha and Tracy are stewardesses. Flight attendants, to you." Her knee presses against mine now.

"Where are they tonight?" I ask.

"Sasha's in Alaska," she says, then pauses. She takes the swizzle stick, pushes the lime to the bottom of her drink, and pins it there. Her eyes look straight into mine. "And Tracy is somewhere over the Pacific."

I slide out of the booth and offer her my hand. She takes it and stands, and we walk to the door and out onto Broadway. The wind is up and she holds the shawl tight to her neck. We walk to the corner, and then I spin her and back her gently against a streetlight. I carefully loosen her fingers from her shawl, and it falls away from her throat. I kiss her, hard, feeling her breasts against my chest as she comes into me. "Again," she whispers, but I take her lean arms from my neck and walk off a few feet. I can feel it gathering inside me. All of it. I look up Broadway, into the night. In the distance I can just see the black gates of the university. I feel her hand in my back, small and warm. I close my eyes.

"Hey," she says gently.

I turn. Her eyes are electric, trusting.

"Don't worry, Jake," she says, her voice steady. "I saw it in you last Friday, and I'm not afraid. I like my princes dark."

"How dark?"

She kisses my chest, then looks up again into my eyes.

"Try me."

"Mimi?"

"Yes?"

"Did you . . . ?"

"Almost."

"Damn."

"It's okay."

We lie in the dark, just afterward, Mark on his back and me against his chest.

"I could —"

"It was wonderful, Mark." I trail my nails along his shoulder.

"I mean it, Mimi."

"Shhh . . . Really, it was wonderful." I kiss his neck.

We lie quietly, the only sound the wind through the open window playing gently with the plastic shades. And now, far off, a car horn. How was it that I used to feel, in these moments? Completely happy. At peace.

"Father Cronin was something, wasn't he?" Mark says.

"He was wonderful."

"I thought he'd go Latin on us, but those were some vows. Your mom will love them."

"She will."

"Two weeks, kid."

"I know."

My hand finds his and squeezes it. He runs his fingers softly through my hair, down to my neck and back again. And again. And again, until his strokes shorten and his breathing lengthens into sleep.

Father Cronin's words *were* beautiful. He talked about the journey of joined souls. About the power of union. Hearing them in that alcove, I'd felt so strong. And I know I'll feel strong in two weeks, when I hear them again. I breathe deeply and let it out slowly. And then again. Faintly, from the apartment below, come the sounds of opera. Verdi, I think. It's like listening to clouds.

The sharp tones of the cell phone break the silence.

"Ow!" says Mark.

"I'm sorry, I'm sorry," I say, getting up with a

start, rubbing his shoulder where I've just dug into him. "I'll get it."

I reach for the lamp and turn it on. I sit up. I take my robe from the chair and pull it around me. The ringing continues, insistent.

"Jesus," he says. "They can't be serious. It's eleven o'clock."

"They said to be ready for anything. Monday's the fifteenth."

The phone is in my purse on the desk. I take the purse and walk quickly to the living room. I sit down on the couch. I take out the phone and hit the pulsing button.

"Mimi Lessing."

"Mimi, it's Jake."

The shiver starts in the small of my back and shoots up all through me. I pull the robe closed over my knees.

"I'm here," I say.

"Do you have a pen?"

"Yes," I say, reaching for one.

"Eight two three West One hundred and twentieth Street. On the corner of Amsterdam. Apartment fifty-three."

I write it down and then quickly fold the piece of paper in two.

"We're ready, Mimi."

I hang up the phone and put it back in my purse, along with the folded address. I close my eyes.

"What's wrong, kid?"

Mark stands in front of me. His sleepy eyes are beautiful. Calm, trusting.

"They need me," I manage to say. "The Taylor account is blowing up."

"Bastards. What's the guy make, two million a year? You'll have him paying less than we do." He sits down beside me and puts a warm hand on my hair.

"Look what I've done," I say, reaching into my purse for a tissue and pressing it to the small cut on his shoulder. "I'm sorry."

"Must have been some dream, Meems. You can tell me all about it when you get back. Did they say how long?"

"No. You'll stay here, won't you?"

"Where would I go?"

"Thank you."

"Mimi, are you okay?"

"Yes. It's just . . . all catching up with me. I'd better shower," I say, standing. He pulls me to him and nuzzles his face in my robe.

"Be quick," he says. "You know what's waiting for you."

Observe the time and fly from evil.

Those are the words inscribed beneath the steeple clock of St. Mary's Cathedral. I looked up at them just four hours ago, but now I ride through the darkness toward Jake Teller. The taxi turns into Central Park and speeds through the curving park streets, the lamps giving way to blackness as we wind beneath the overpass, the rare scent of trees reaching me through the open window. We emerge onto Amsterdam at Eighty-first Street and turn north, past the Natural History Museum, up through the familiar, busy Eighties, the sidewalks dotted with cafés and bars, and now into the quiet, foreign streets of the Nineties.

I have on the dress I wore last Friday. The same one. And the same cobalt sweater. Before I took them from the closet, I walked to the bed to see if Mark was asleep. He was, his face in the crook of his arm, his breathing steady and peaceful.

We are into the Hundreds, past 110th Street now. I've never been up this far. We pass the gates and grounds of a big university. Columbia, it must be.

"Which side, miss?"

"I'm sorry?"

"Which side of the street?"

"I don't know. Either one."

At 120th Street he pulls over to the corner. He turns and looks back at me, his rough hand grabbing the divider.

"In this part of town, dressed like that, you should know where you're going. What's the street address?"

I look at the slip of paper in my lap.

"Eight twenty-three."

He looks out through the front of the cab and points at the corner building.

"I'll wait till you're inside."

"Thank you."

I pay him and step out of the cab. I stand in front of a giant prewar apartment building. The brick walkway is lit by a streetlamp shaped like an old gaslight. In the window of the lobby ahead of me I can see a uniformed doorman. I pause. If I could just get a glass of wine somewhere or sit by myself for a few minutes. But the taxi waits at the curb, its engine running, the driver watching me. I walk to the lobby.

"Good evening, miss," says the doorman as he holds the door for me. He is a black man in his sixties, flecks of white in his short dark hair. Suddenly I realize that I don't know what to say.

"I'm here to . . . ," I start.

He waits.

"I'm going to apartment fifty-three. But please don't call up."

"You must be Jake's friend," he says.

"Yes."

"Jake told me you'd be coming. Just a minute."

He steps to a small table just inside the front door. He reaches down beside it and comes up with something. "He said to give this to you," he says, and holds out a black pouch that is just a little smaller than my purse. It is made of soft felt and closed at the top by a gold drawstring.

"I don't understand," I say.

"Jake Teller, right?"

"Yes."

"Jake come by this afternoon. He told me you would come tonight, and I should give you this."

"Thank you."

I take the pouch and walk to the elevator and press the button. But I feel dizzy, and the gray elevator doors in front of me start to blur. I feel the way I felt in art class, in the ninth grade, when I posed perfectly still for twenty minutes and then stood suddenly and tried to step off the platform.

"Are you okay?" the doorman asks.

"I'm sorry. Would it be all right if I sat down for a few minutes?"

"Sure."

He takes my arm and guides me to the left, to a sitting area, a couch and chairs in front of a small fireplace. I ease down onto the brown leather couch.

"There you are," he says.

"Thank you. I'm fine," I say. "I just need a minute."

"Take as long as you want."

He steps away, and I take a deep breath and let it out slowly. A small fire burns in the fireplace, close enough that I feel its warmth on my legs. I look down at the black pouch. The felt is the softest material I've ever touched. I turn it in my hands. Through it I can feel three — no, four — hard objects.

"Miss?"

I look up to see the doorman holding out a glass of water. "You look like you need this."

"Thank you."

I take a sip. The doorman steps past me, stiff in his movements. He takes a poker from the mantel, parts the fireplace gate, and turns over the bottom log. A shower of sparks lifts and then settles. My fingers rub one of the objects through the soft felt. It is thick, with sharp corners. The others all seem to be in cases of some kind. What was it Father used to say? *We find the people we need to find.* The doorman puts the poker back in the stand and then turns and lowers himself into the chair beside me.

"How do you know Jake?" he asks.

I pause.

"We work together."

"And Elise?"

"I haven't . . . met her yet."

"A nice girl," he says. "You'll like her." He sits with his hands crossed in his lap. I can see that one is steadying the other.

"You sound like you know Jake," I say.

"I know Jake going back twenty years. He grew up in this building."

I look at him.

"He grew up here?"

"Yes, he did. When he come back the other day, after all that time, don't know who was more surprised."

"Which apartment did he grow up in?" I ask, knowing the answer before he gives it.

"One you're going to. Fifty-three."

I hold the pouch to my knee now, feeling its weight through my dress, the sharp angle of something pressing into my skin. I cover the pouch with both hands, as if the doorman might somehow see right through the felt. We are quiet a few seconds.

"What was Jake like as a boy?" I ask.

He smiles and looks into the fire for a few seconds. He seems to search the flames for an answer.

"Kind," he says.

The buzzer rings from outside, and the doorman stands quickly. "You gonna be okay?" he asks.

"Yes, thank you. I'll go upstairs now."

Memory is the cruelest sense.

I remember clearly our first evening together. The electrifying sound of her deadbolt, the soft clicks as her door opened and closed, and then through the speakers a sigh and her first words:

"What a day."

I knew early that she would not be like the others. I knew the next morning, when she awoke and did not turn on the television. I heard the sound of the tea kettle, the toaster, and the rustle of the newspaper as she brought it in from her doorstep. She read it while she ate, and if she spotted an item of interest, one that intrigued her enough to set it aside, I heard the crisp sound of scissors on paper. After breakfast she dressed to the music of the classical station, and then stepped out her door at 8:20 for the walk to the subway and the ride to midtown and work. Twenty blocks away, I closed my eyes in thanks. I had found her.

And now one year later I sit in a car in Harlem, staring at the building Miss Lessing has just walked into. She stepped from the sidewalk onto the brick walkway like a child stepping alone into a dark forest, glancing back over her shoulder at the taxi that had brought her, her eyes tense and fearful. And yet she turned and walked into the building. Compelled, drawn forward. By what force?

I will know soon.

Two mornings ago I stood behind the newsstand on Eighty-sixth and Lexington, at the mouth of the subway entrance. When Miss Lessing walked past and headed down the stairs, I fell in just behind her, invisible in the morning crush. And as she reached into her handbag for her subway pass, I dropped the tiny Øre inside.

Where it lies now, listening. Listening inside the handbag Miss Lessing carried into 823 West 120th Street. Not thirty minutes after telling her fiancé that she had been called in to the office for work.

This far uptown, this far west, the Øre in her bag cannot reach the mother unit on the windowsill of my apartment. But it can reach the one in the back- seat of this car. Which I have wired into the car stereo. And so I have listened these past few min- utes, as Miss Lessing spoke with the doorman about Jake Teller. And I listen now as the grinding elevator carries her up to him.

She is crossing from desire into need.

"Please, Jake," she says, her voice still strong, but drops of sweat have broken out on her neck, and as my climbing fingers reach the very edge of her black silk panties, only to lift away off her thighs yet again, she turns her face, for the first time, hard into the deep red covers.

Thirty minutes ago we sat on her couch, her bare leg tight against the knee of my gray corduroys. She touched my cheek, then the top of my shirt, then ran her fingers slowly down to my belt. I stopped them there, reached beside me into my jacket, took out the white silk tie, and placed it in her hand. She looked at it and up at me, and she unfolded it and laid it across her black dress.

"For me or for you?" she asked.

"For you," I said. And then I nodded toward my jacket. "Both of them."

She looked down again at the tie. She closed her fingers around each end and then rolled her wrists, once, winding the silk around them. She looked at me and smiled, her dark eyes steady.

"One strong drink first," she said.

And now those white ties bind her delicate wrists to the metal bars of the bed that stands in the room I slept in as a child. Her lean, tanned arms are spread wide, defenseless, her black, flowing hair is pinned beneath her lithe body, and her belly and legs, freshly oiled, glisten in the hot spotlight I've rigged to the foot of her bed.

She has been a playful captive. She smiled as I secured her right wrist, her shining eyes looking from my face to my hands as I then took her left arm and slid six of the seven bracelets, one by one, down to her wrist and off. The seventh I slid the other way, up to her biceps. Then I wound the silk tie around her left wrist and tied it, too, to one of the thick metal bars of the bed frame.

"I'm yours now, Jake," she murmured. "Do what you will."

I walked across the room to her desk. In one of its drawers I found a pair of heavy scissors. "You wouldn't," she said, watching me as I returned with them, but she sighed languorously at the cold touch of the blade and trembled with pleasure as I cut the straps of her black dress, pulled it down off of her, and dropped it to the floor.

"You're getting expensive," she said.

I looked down the length of her, taking her in. Her tanned skin, set off against the black lace of her bra and panties and against the scarlet blanket beneath her. Her full breasts, bigger than I'd thought, her smooth, toned belly and taut thighs. She was no trick of fashion. I touched my hand to her knee. She smiled and closed her legs demurely, her black panties forming a perfect, alluring vee. I reached into my back pants pocket and pulled out the blindfold.

Her lips parted in surprise.

"My color," she said, but with the first speck of caution in her voice. She let me slip it over her eyes, though, and moments later her caution dissolved when I took a bottle of body oil from her dresser, opened the cap, and released the exotic scent of papaya into the room. She offered me her ankle, toes pointed, sighing luxuriously as I moved up her legs, kicking her small heels in excitement as I worked her lower belly, dropping her head back in pleasure as I rubbed the warm lotion deep into her shoulders and slowly up her tethered arms.

When I finished, I walked to the desk and unscrewed the black, four-foot flexed-arm desk lamp. I brought it to the bed, clipped it to the metal frame at the foot, and then brought the arm down and toward her. I turned it on. I walked to the wall and switched off the overhead light. The effect was magical. The room lay in darkness while Elise, a trussed angel, lay in strong, hot light.

I turned and walked out of the room.

I walked through the quiet apartment to the kitchen. The refrigerator is where ours was, and the counter, too. On it stood a vase with fresh-cut roses. Twelve of them. I checked the note on the card. *To the most beautiful girl in the city. One more chance? Scott.* Working quickly, I fixed myself an Absolut and tonic. Next to the limes in the crisper I found a cluster of mint leaves and broke off a few. I looked down the narrow room to the kitchen table at the end. It is just where ours was, in the small area by the window. I walked to it and sat down. Out the window I could see the side of the next building, the same three windowsills I remember from twenty years ago. Past them, only the black night. I picked up the phone and dialed.

It rang once, twice, three times. We hadn't spoken since I left her at the river railing three days ago. Left her in her blue dress and white sweater, holding the black cell phone that I told her to throw into the river. It rang once more. And then again.

"Mimi Lessing."

I closed my eyes. I gave her the address and told her we were ready. I hung up the phone and stayed at the kitchen table for a few moments, looking out the window. Then I stood and took a small dish towel, ran it under warm water, and wrung it out. I took the towel, my drink, the mint leaves, and a rose from the vase and walked out of the kitchen and down the hall to the front door. I unlocked the deadbolt, quietly, and opened the door a few inches. It held. I walked back down the hall to the living room, to the stereo. In the CD collection I found one labeled *Spanish Strings* with a picture on its cover of two acoustic guitars crossed at the neck. I walked back to the bedroom doorway. She was a sight, shimmering in the light of the lamp, her hands relaxed, one oiled leg moving sensually up the other.

"Jake?"

"Right here."

I walked to the bed and put my hand on her knee.

"Don't leave me again," she whispered.

I put my finger to her lips, and she took it into her mouth. I touched the bottom of my glass to her forehead, and she gasped with pleasure. Then I placed the glass, the wet towel, the mint, and the rose on the nightstand. I took the chair from her desk and placed it a few feet from the bed. I moved the nightstand out from the wall, positioning it between the chair and the bed, catercorner to both. She listened as I worked, concentrating, following my movements around the room.

"What are you doing?" she asked finally.

"No questions," I said, and she smiled. I walked to the small CD player on her dresser. I took the CD from its case, loaded it, and snapped the cover closed.

"Music," she whispered dreamily.

"Soon," I said.

I walked to the bed and sat down. I put my hand

gently on her hip and looked down the shining length of her once more. She was ravishing.

"It's time, Elise," I said.

She breathed deeply, pressed her golden legs tight together, and smiled.

"I'm ready," she said.

And then I started my passes.

Long, slow passes with the backs of my fingers, starting at her feet and ending at the tight line of silk that bound each wrist. She was in heaven, sighing more deeply the higher I rose, her every nerve alive to my touch. She parted her legs for me, gasping as I trailed up the inside of her thigh, again as I curved around her panties to her tight belly, and again as I reached the base of her bra, lingered, and drifted around it. When I finished the first pass, I started again. Again she lay in rapture, luxuriating in my slow climb, the lightness of my touch inflaming her. As I eased around her panties again, she turned her hips, hoping to guide my fingers into her swell, but I skirted it and pressed her back down with my free hand. Up to her bra my fingers climbed, lingering longer than before, my nails just grazing the black silk on their way by.

By the end of the third pass, her black panties were damp and she had gathered in her fingers the two inches of white silk that I'd left between wrist and post. By the end of the fourth pass, the ache was in her, deep in the swollen places that I wouldn't touch. And now, three slow passes later, she says, "Please, Jake," and turns her face, hard, into the deep red covers.

And I move back down to the bottom of the bed and start on her feet again.

"You can't," she whispers as I rise past her calves, pressing a little harder, watching the long, graceful muscles of her thighs tense like a sprinter's. I'm a few inches from her panties when I feel it — a change in the air of the room. I stop, turn, and see Mimi Lessing in the doorway.

She holds on to the doorsill with one hand. In the other, I see it — the outline of the black felt pouch. Mimi stands in darkness, but I can see the white of her stockings. She has taken off her shoes. I can see that her hair is down, and I can see, too, despite the darkness, the shock in her beautiful eyes. I hold them with my own and raise my hand to her, warning her to wait.

And then I turn back to Elise.

One last time I trail my fingers past the soaked black silk of her panties. "You . . . ," she whispers, biting her lip now. One last time I climb to her bra and now past it, up near her shoulder, pressing down on the strap just hard enough that she feels the pressure on her nipples four inches below. I run my fingers up to her throat, up her right arm, and then slowly up her left, past the binds this time, stroking her fist until she opens it with a soft moan, then caressing her tiny palm, and finishing, finally, with the tips of her fingers. I stand and walk to the dresser.

I push the button on the CD player, and seconds later gentle guitar notes seep into the air, so low at first that Elise isn't sure she hears them. Yes, now she does. Music. She curls her fingers, then relaxes them, and settles deeper into the bed. Her wait is over, she thinks. At last. I look to Mimi, still standing in the doorway, one hand holding on to the sill. I motion to the chair, and she walks carefully to it over the hardwood floor. She sits down, smoothing her dress nervously. I pass behind her, my hands inches from her shoulders, her pure neck. I sit down again on the bed. Elise feels it give and wets her lips, expectant. I reach down, lift the heavy scissors from the floor and touch them to her belly.

"Yes," she gasps, certain of their destination. I move the cool blades up her stomach, passing them over the front of the bra and up to the straps on her shoulders. I cut through one, then the other. The straps fall away, revealing the creamy slope of her breasts, the body of the bra still covering the rest. I ease the scissors between her breasts, close them around the clasp of her bra, and lift the bra away, making sure the dangling strap brushes her nipples before I drop it to the floor. Her breasts are round and beautiful, a shade whiter than her belly, the nipples pink and crisp.

"Jake," she says. "Touch me."

I reach down next to the bed and come up with another white silk tie.

I touch it gently to her neck. "God," she whispers, thinking the silk is the bra I've just cut off her. I trail it between her breasts, down her belly, down the inside of her thigh.

"Just wait," she whispers, digging her heels into the covers.

Past her calf I take it, slowly, and then loop it suddenly around her ankle. She gasps and tries to bring her leg up, but I hold it firmly to the bed, knot the silk tight, and then take it hard to the far edge, pulling her body down toward me, snapping the silk she clutches in her fingers right out of them. Quickly I knot the new tie to the metal bar of the bed frame. She turns her left knee in toward her right leg, trying to keep them close, but I knot the final tie around her left ankle, straighten her leg, and take it hard the other way, parting her legs sharply. She gasps in shock, and then again as I yank her farther down the bed and tie the final silk tie tightly to the cold metal bar.

Just like that, Elise is spread-eagled.

She pulls hard against the new restraints, the muscles in her calves and thighs tensing, straining, beautiful. The silk doesn't give. She wets her lips twice, three times, panic starting to rise in her. She surges again. The white silk ties dip and tremble, like power lines in the wind, but they hold firm. She collapses, her breathing quick, shallow. She tries to pull out with her wrists now, but there is no more slack, and her efforts only tighten the knots. She gasps in pain. I move my hand to her thigh. Again she surges, and again the ties hold. I close my eyes and let her struggle, her thigh pulsing against my palm as she fights, then collapses, fights, then collapses, fights, then collapses yet again.

For thirty seconds she struggles, desperate, and then she starts to quiet. I open my eyes. Her ribs

still rise and fall, but her breathing slows, steadies.
She lifts her face from the covers. "Okay," she whispers to herself, almost inaudibly, the taut cords in
her neck softening, her fingers, balled into fists a
second ago, starting to uncurl. She seems to take in
the room again, to breathe in the scented oil, feel
the warmth of the lamp on her skin, hear, anew, the
soothing music. "Okay," she whispers again, testing the binds but lightly now, not fighting against
them but gauging them, measuring them, and, yes,
relaxing into them, as if the silk were caressing, not
binding, her delicate wrists and ankles. I lean in
and watch her closely.

She is surrendering.

Surrendering not just to the ties but to the idea of
them. Surrendering because the true burn isn't in
her wrists or in her ankles, but in the places that I
won't touch. "Okay," she says again, and I close my
fists and rest them for a moment on the knees of my
corduroys, because it hits me that she isn't talking
to herself but to me, and I know that she understands, for the first time, the promise in those strict,
unrelenting white ties. It is the promise of release.
Sweet, long, hard release, like none she's ever
imagined, and she knows now that fighting will
only delay it, will only stoke the fires I've built
deep inside her. And so she whispers, "Okay," one
more time, a soft plea, and takes a last deep breath
and lets it out slowly. I put my hand back on her
warm thigh, feel it flutter, flutter, and then go still.
Her wrists, her ankles, her hips — everything is
still. Still, and quiet, and completely submissive,

and it's my turn to steady myself against the tide inside me. I look down at the dark floor, and then again at her taut, shining body.

Tonight's true journey can begin.

Mimi Lessing sits only a few feet away, but in the darkness she is a silhouette. I can see, though, the black felt pouch in her lap. I lean toward her and hold out my hand. She hesitates, then lifts the pouch with both hands and holds it out to me, like an offering. I take it from her and rest it on the bed, squarely in the light of the lamp.

I look closely at the golden thread that holds the pouch closed. I can see at the base of it the tiny, distinctive knot that I tied this morning in my apartment. She hasn't looked inside. I untie the knot, then slip my fingers into the soft mouth of the pouch and force it open. I reach in and pull out a red candle. It is thick and squat, its edges sharp, and I place it on the blue cloth that is stretched tight over the top of the nightstand. Place it quietly enough that Elise doesn't hear it over the gentle, soothing guitar. I take a lighter from my pocket and strike the flint. Elise turns toward the sound and wets her lips. I light the candle.

The flame is equidistant between Mimi and me, and in its light I see that she wears the same pink dress she wore last Friday. The same deep blue sweater. I called her at home and she went to her closet and dressed the same way as last week. In the candlelight I can see, too, her beautiful, balanced face. Her soft eyes, which rise to meet mine.

I see fear in them, but beneath the fear I see excitement, the same excitement I know she sees in mine.

I take a breath, let it out, and reach into the black pouch again.

I pull out a small silver case the size of a ring box and place it on the nightstand. Mimi looks down at it, then back at me. I reach into the pouch and take out another silver case, a little larger than the first, and place it on the nightstand, too. And then I take out a third one, larger still, as wide and long as a compact disc but much thicker. I place it beside the first two and drop the empty pouch to the floor. Mimi stares, mesmerized, at the neat row of silver cases, at their sleek tops, which shimmer in the candlelight.

I lift my glass from the nightstand and take a long, steadying sip of vodka, feeling its cold, sweet bite in my throat. Elise hears the rattle of the ice and wets her lips again. I pick up the smallest silver case, place it on the bed in front of me, and lift the cover.

Mimi leans forward, and it is now her lips that part as she watches me lift, from the soft felt bed of the case, and turn slowly in the hot light, one of two inch-long metal clamps. The jaws of the clamp are coated with hard, black plastic, and they separate when I press with my thumb on the lever at the other end. If I release the lever, the jaws will close. How far they will close is determined by the small metal screw that has been inserted in a hole bored into the middle of one arm. Turn the screw to the right, the clamps are forced apart. To the left, they tighten.

I lift from the nightstand the red rose I took from the vase in the kitchen. I hold it by its rough green stem and start it up Elise's belly. She moans softly. I trace it to the slope of a breast, and then up, and then press the head of the rose over her nipple. "God, yes," she gasps, trembling at this long-awaited first touch. I twirl the rose slowly, letting its impossibly soft petals kiss and caress her. In seconds her pink nipple swells and hardens.

"Oh God," she says, trembling with gratitude.

I lean in, twirling the rose with one hand, watching the open petals transport her, while pressing down with the thumb and forefinger of my other hand on the lever that separates the black plastic jaws. I twirl the rose faster, watching her breathing accelerate, her lips whispering, "Yes, yes, yes," as her nipple hardens further. She starts to rock gently against the ties, her breathing coming faster as I twirl the rose faster, her hips thrusting, thrusting again, and once more. I lift the rose away, steady the black jaws on either side of her swollen nipple, and release the lever.

They close like a vise.

Her body jerks in shock. Her mouth forms a perfect circle, but for two, three seconds she doesn't make a sound. And then a piercing cry. And now:

"No. Jake. Oh, Jake, what —"

"Shhh."

The clamp is at its gentlest setting. It pinches no tighter than if I held her nipple firmly between my fingers. I let it go and watch it stay in place, trembling and then still, standing straight up like a clothespin on a line.

"Oh, that's tight, Jake. Jake. Please."

I put my finger to her lips. This time she doesn't take it into her mouth. I reach into the silver case and lift out the second clamp. I lower the red rose over her free nipple and start to twirl. "No," she says, biting her lip this time, shaking her head, trying to fight the soft touch of the petals. But there is no resisting them, and in seconds they've done their gentle work, swelling her pink nipple to the size of the first one. I lift the rose away, release the lever of the new clamp, and watch its jaws grab and tighten. She gasps.

"Please. You don't —"

"Shhh."

I put my hand to her damp forehead and lean in close.

"With every word," I say, "I'll tighten them."

"Jake," she whispers, panicked now.

I take the small metal screw of the first clamp between thumb and forefinger and give it a quarter turn, watching the hard black plastic bite into her pink nipple. She cries out.

"With every word," I repeat.

"No."

I turn the other clamp the same amount. She gasps in pain, and then is quiet. Out of the corner of my eye I see Mimi reach down and lift from the floor the ruined black dress I cut off Elise an hour ago. She holds it in her lap and buries her hands in it. Her eyes stay on Elise.

The clamps are tight but not punishing, and after a few seconds she begins to adjust to them, to the pain they administer. Her nails ease out of her palms, her breathing steadies. Yes, it hurts, but this much she can stand. Partner to the pain, though, is fear, and I can see it in her face now, in her mouth and throat.

I wait ten more seconds and then press my palm, hard, into the soaked black silk of her panties.

She gasps. In spite of everything, she gasps — a deep, shocked, primal gasp of pleasure. I press again, my palm tight against her flat pelvic bone. She drops her head back and a small moan escapes her. I press again, and again she moans, the clamps forgotten, their ache no match for the shocks of pleasure my palm sends all through her. I press again and hold it for five seconds. And again, this time for ten. She sighs in deep rapture and thrusts her hips. I release and she waits, lips apart, her whole body seeming to open up, to soften. I take my hand from her panties, rest each index finger carefully on top of a nipple clamp, pause, and then pull the clamps gently down toward her belly.

She cries out, betrayed. I bend them farther, her bunched, compressed nipples bending with the clamps. She cries out louder. I pull them down another half inch, a full inch, an inch and a half, the clamps parallel with her belly now, small, fast cries of pain coming from her. I hold the clamps still. Her body arches, her every muscle tensing to head off the pain. I look quickly to Mimi. One hand grips the bottom of her chair, the other holds the torn black dress to her mouth. I hold the clamps still another five seconds.

I let them go, and watch the pain rocket through her.

She cries out as if scalded, her body jerking so violently that it takes my breath away, the waves of pain, true pain now, rocking her as the clamps snap up, then bob back and forth. Another sharp cry, another, and then her cries dissolve into pained gasps that soften, soften, and finally subside as the clamps, sticking straight up again, tremble and settle still.

I reach down and press again on her black panties.

This time I use my fingers, locating, through the wet silk, the soft, swollen gateways to her center. She spasms beneath me, not quite free of the pain, but gasping even so at my touch, and again as my fingers find, and now separate, her silken, receptive folds. "Oh," she gasps, the heart of her still inflamed in spite of the cruel wait, in spite of the pain, inflamed from my earlier passes and burning now as I tend to it at last, massaging through the silk, each tiny shift of my fingers setting off deep waves of pleasure. Her hips lock and thrust. Softly I work her, then harder, then harder still, then softly again, watching her face slam from side to side, her gasps building toward a rhythm.

I take my hand away and reach again for the clamps.

Her whole body braces. I bend the clamps toward her belly again and she cries out, her neck coming off the covers, her back arching. She tries to bargain for clemency with her breaths, careful not to form words, speaking in short, pleading cries that cut off when I stop the clamps, bent almost to her belly now, and burst out again when I release them.

She jerks once, twice, her breathing shallow and fast until the clamps are still once again. I reach down to her panties, and within seconds I've taken her back across the line, my fingers finding a tender, swollen strip so sensitive that the slightest flicker sends her head back. Her thighs spasm every few seconds, not from pain now but from surges of pleasure. A long sigh from her, and four short breaths, and another long sigh, and four more short breaths. I take my hand away.

She braces again, but less urgently this time, and though she pleads with soft cries when I bend the clamps, and jerks when I release them, the pain doesn't rock her like before. It is familiar now, without terror, and before the clamps have even stopped trembling, I see her hips begin to move — small, rhythmic thrusts as she waits for, and imagines, the next warm burst of pleasure. I give it to her.

It is like pressing into a sponge. I probe deeper this time, ever deeper, her hips rising the little they can to meet me as I push the silk inside her. I find a spot that makes her sob with pleasure and I work it, granting her thirty, forty, fifty seconds of heaven, her cries intense, rising. Yes, she is starting to climb, and as she does, I can tell that she feels, deep inside, the first stirrings of a finish. Mimi Lessing can tell, too. She can't keep still. She lowers the torn dress to her lap, brings it to her chest, lowers it again. Her knees are pressed tight together. I take my hand off the black panties again.

Elise is calm now, bracing without fear, certain she can bear the clamps. Eager for them, even, because of the pleasure that waits on the other side. Pleasure like none she's known ever — deep, escalating pleasure that's taken her further and further and so must, very soon, take her the rest of the way. She draws a breath, lets it out, curls her fingers into her palms, and waits.

I reach past the clamps to the nightstand and pick up the thick red candle.

In its light I see that Mimi's forehead is damp. Her neck, too. She holds the torn black dress in her lap, and she watches me as I take the candle away, not realizing where it is headed. I bring it to my chest and then hold it out over the bare belly of Elise. Mimi looks down at her, then back at the candle, and Mimi's hands start to knead the black dress in her lap.

The broad shoulders of the candle have melted away, leaving a wide mouth that holds a pool of liquid wax. A pool as still as a lake at dawn, but heated almost to boiling by the flame rising out of it. The only sounds in the room now are Elise's breathing and, from the stereo, the gentle notes of two acoustic guitars dueling playfully. I rest the fingers of one hand lightly on her wet black panties, as if to delve into them again. She squirms in excitement, daring to think that I'm through with the clamps, that it will be pleasure from here on in. She eases her head back onto the covers.

I tilt the red candle and spill a drop of burning wax onto her belly.

Her piercing cry splits the room. She seizes so hard that I'm sure the silk ties will break. They shake, strain, but hold. The hot wax hardens in seconds, but her spasm has set the clamps in motion again, and so it is twenty, thirty more seconds of pain for her. I take the wet cloth from the nightstand and wipe the wax from her, leaving her belly clean, pure, with just a faint pink circle to mark her pain.

"Please," she says, gaining her breath. "I can't ta —"

She cries out as I turn the small metal screw of one clamp, compressing her pink nipple. She shakes her head back and forth, frantic now, but keeps silent. Above her, at the head of the bed, her fingers dig into her bound hands, the pink beneath her nails visible now through the clear, flawless polish.

I look at Mimi. She sits in darkness again, but I see that she has begun to rock. Slowly, with her legs tight together and Elise's dress clutched again to her chest. She doesn't look down at the floor, as she did last week, but keeps her beautiful eyes fixed on the red candle. And I move that candle slowly down the body of Elise. Past her panties. To her thigh. I tilt it again.

The hot wax draws another cry from her, and another hard spasm, and the clamps start to shake again. I wait until they calm, until her pain subsides and with it her gasping cries. I wipe the spot of wax from her thigh and hold the candle steady just above her. Ten, fifteen seconds I wait. And then I see it: the tremble in her hips. Not even the fresh pain of the wax has dimmed the fever, and now that she has endured it she waits, desperate, for her reward. Aren't those the rules? Pain, yes, but then pleasure? She waits, trembling, for my fingers to return to her burning center; to search out, deep inside her, another swollen, aching, magic spot.

I wait a few more seconds, and then I move the candle up and drip hot wax onto the delicate slope of her breast.

She almost comes off the bed. This time I don't wipe the wax away or wait for the clamps to settle. I take the candle to her bound ankle and tilt it again. And then to the smooth, freckled skin of her shoulder. The soft well of her elbow. Each drop hits her like the point of a whip, and so close together that her pain is continuous now, fierce spikes of it from the wax and always, beneath it, the constant, grinding bite of the clamps. Her cries are continuous now, too, filling the room as I splash one trim calf, then the other, and then climbing a full octave as I pour the last of the burning wax in a slow, punishing, six-inch line from just below her breasts down to, and into, her tender belly button.

I straighten the candle, place it on the nightstand and sit back, shaking. I look at Mimi and see that she is shaking, too. Rocking slowly and shaking and staring at the floor, unable to look at Elise.

I can look at her. I watch closely as the pain controls her for a full minute, until the clamps are finally still and her hard spasms give way to a steady trembling, as if she were shivering from cold. I take the cloth and clean her, wiping away the small circles of wax. She moans softly, in gratitude, but as I clean away the final mark on her, the line of hot wax down her belly, she starts to shake her head, and I see that her lips are whispering, soundlessly, two words, over and over.

"No more. No more."

I reach to the nightstand and I pick up another silver case.

Mimi looks at it, and then at me, and I can see in her eyes the war going on inside her. I wait for her to shake her head or turn away, but she simply looks back at the silver case, entranced.

I place the case on the covers, between Elise's open legs. I'm careful to lift the lid with a loud *click*, but she continues to whisper silently to herself. I close the lid quickly and take the sprig of mint from the nightstand. I crush it between my fingers, releasing its aroma, and hold it just under her nose. She lets out a soft cry, a cry of wonder, as the pungent mint fills her senses, triggering in her some memory, some innocent kitchen memory that frees her for just a second from the bed and the binds and the clamps. I rub the mint over her lips and then take it away, and Elise returns to the moment, revived, testing the ties gingerly again, first with her wrists, then with her ankles, breathing softly to keep the clamps from moving. Yes, she is with me again. And when I open the silver case, she hears it and listens, alert.

It is called a Contour.

It is pink and shaped like a heart, and it is cov-ered with tiny, jelly-like nodes. Mimi, leaning for-ward, the sweat shining like dew on her forehead, looks at it without a trace of understanding. I move down the bed and sit at Elise's hip. She feels this, sensing my preparation, and as I look down at her, the Contour snug in my right hand, she braces, her tongue searching her lips for a final, calming taste of mint, her every muscle tensed again. I put my left hand on her belly, then look at Mimi.

I slide it inside of Elise's black silk panties, and then inside of Elise.

She convulses.

Instinctively her legs spasm, trying to close, but the binds hold them beautifully still. Her head comes up off the covers, her throat straining in ter-ror. She was braced for pain but not there, any-where but there, and her terror keeps her from trusting her own sensations. She only knows that she is helpless and that something is inside her, and so she surges again and again, crying out with each surge, setting the clamps in motion, and it is twenty seconds before she starts to quiet and twenty more before the clamps are still and thirty more before she starts to believe, *dares* to believe, what her body is telling her — that this is reward, not punishment. Because inside her I'm turning the Contour gently, allowing the beauty of its design to go to work, and as I turn it again, she lets out a gasping cry, and as I ease it in a little deeper, sweet, stunning realization breaks over her, and she sighs the purest sigh I've ever heard.

In seconds I have her fitted.

I take my right hand out from inside her and rest it on her belly, and when she feels it there, next to my left, and still feels, inside her, the dense, insistent presence, she nearly collapses. Minutes ago my fingers could work only one spot at a time. Now the Contour works many, and though she can't roll her hips but the tiniest amount or lift them more than two inches, even these small motions widen its rippling reach, and her only challenge now is to keep the nipple clamps still as the pleasure starts to build inside her.

Mimi holds one arm tight to her breast now, her eyes on my empty right hand. And she looks again into the open silver case. And I reach back into it and take out the source of her fascination.

The black remote.

I lay it on the covers, hit the ON switch, and ease the power setting up to 1. And together we watch her.

She feels it right away, her lips parting in joy, but these first swells are so subtle, so delicate, that she thinks they are natural, the response of her swollen folds to the probing touch of the Contour. She sighs and lays her head back slowly onto the covers. I roll the power setting up to 2.

And I can almost see, through the blindfold, her dark eyes snap open.

She gasps and turns her head, as if to listen. She gasps again. Ten seconds pass, fifteen, and then her mouth opens in wonder, because inside her the jolts are still coming, and they are stronger, yes, stronger than moments ago, and aren't they . . . could they be . . . yes — they come at *perfect intervals*. And so the truth sinks into her, and just as it does the last Spanish guitar notes fade from the stereo, leaving the room to her cries.

Cries that make Mimi reach out and press her fingers into the tight blue cloth of the nightstand. That make me take my hands from Elise's belly and press on the knees of my corduroys. I watch her hips rise with each jolt she receives. Every three seconds they rise, and just as she had no defense earlier against the pain, the burning wax and biting clamps, she has none now against this pleasure, and so she cries out, and cries out, and cries out as the patient Contour, deep inside her, metes out wave after wave.

I roll the power switch to 3. And then to 4.

"Oh!" she cries, jarred, the shocks intense now. She bites her lip to keep still, to keep silent, to keep from coming apart. "God!" she cries out finally, tensing instantly in fear, bracing for the turn of the screw. But I leave the clamps alone. I move up the bed, dip my shirt into my cold drink, and touch it to her forehead.

"Jake," she gasps. I wipe her fevered brow. "Thank you." I dab her damp, burning cheeks, letting her talk now. "Oh God, thank you. Thank you. You can't know." She reaches for my fingers with her mouth, wanting to take me inside her, to share with me a portion of the killing joy coursing through her, but seconds later she turns her face into the covers, overcome, my fingers forgotten, the cooling cloth forgotten, everything forgotten but the relentless, saving bursts inside of her.

5. 6.

"Oh Jesus."

Mimi drops the torn black dress and rocks, both arms hugged to her chest. She rocks and watches Elise fight to stay whole, the jolts so strong now that she braces for each one as she used to brace for the pain, trying to absorb them in her hips, to channel them down into her legs, away from the clamps. It's no use. Each burst rocks her whole body, jolting the clamps again and again. But she doesn't cry out in pain or even wince. She is beyond the clamps now, and though they shake with each blast she receives, her cries remain cries of pure, stunned pleasure.

7.

We can hear it now, Mimi and I. Beneath her cries, we can hear it. Deep and rhythmic, like the beating of a heart. Dispensing, dispensing, dispensing. Merciless. And we can hear, too, the timeless, unmistakable edge seeping into her cries. She is closing in. Mimi twists her hands in her lap, agitated — not because Elise is minutes away but because Mimi knows there is one silver case left on the nightstand, and she knows its time has come. I start to reach for it, but she picks it up and turns it in her hands. The hard silver sparkles in the light of the candle. Elise's cries come sharper, ever sharper. Mimi lifts the lid and looks down into the case, and I see the surprise in her eyes. She lifts out a thick metal chain, gold, sixteen inches long. She is struck by its weight, but she handles it like a necklace, even touches it to her flushed cheek. I hold my hand out, and it isn't until she hands it over that she sees the small clips at each end of the chain, and as I take it and move back down to the center of the bed, she looks to Elise, to the tight clamps that pinch her nipples, and sees for the first time the tiny metal rings on the levered ends of each clamp. And fear rises in her beautiful eyes.

I touch the chain to Elise's thigh. She starts once at its cold touch but not again, not even as I trail it up her leg, and over her panties and up her belly. She is deep inside herself now, gone to wherever women go in the last seconds. She doesn't hear the soft click as I hook one end of the chain to the ring of one clamp, and then the other end to the ring of the other. I hold the chain in my hand, careful to preserve its slack. And then I break her golden reverie by hitting the OFF switch on the black remote, opening my hand and letting the chain slide from my palm down onto her belly.

She cries out in pain, her trance shattered. The chain lies coiled below her breasts, just enough slack in it to save her, but not enough to protect her from its brutal pull. She feels the sudden, fierce burn in her nipples as the clamps dip, and deeper down, in the breastbone, she feels heavy, wrenching pressure.

"No," she gasps.

I edge the chain back up, relieving her torment, and restore the waves inside her.

8.

Pleasure reclaims her within seconds. She's felt nothing, ever, like this, the bursts so strong now that each one lifts her black panties away from her mound. Twenty seconds I give her, then cut her off again. And pull the chain down her belly. A little farther this time.

Her piercing cry drives Mimi out of her chair. She stands over the bed, helpless, smoothing her dress desperately, enduring Elise's sobs of pain until I rescue her by edging the chain up, and then transport her with the touch of a button.

9.

Mimi sits down, shaking.

Thirty seconds of current. Five seconds of pain. Forty seconds of current. Five seconds of pain. Fifty seconds of current. Five seconds of pain.

She climbs and climbs on the current, the pleasure so concentrated now, so pure, without any way to dilute it. Shock after shock deep inside her, and yet the strong white ties hold her spread and bound, and perfectly still. And just as she starts to crest — betrayal. I stop the current. And moments later, agony as I tug the chain down a fraction farther than the time before, hold it for five searing seconds, until the veins stand out on her arms, and then inch it back up her oiled belly and hit the button again.

Mimi can't watch the punishment. She shuts her eyes when I kill the current and doesn't open them until she hears cries of pleasure again. And so she doesn't see what I see — that the punishment has become part of her pleasure. A strong tug on the chain nearly breaks her in two, but she needs it. It takes the breath from her lungs, but she needs it. Because the punishment alone keeps her from finishing, and there is no moment more magical, more transporting, than the moment I release her from the throes of the chain and deliver her back to the Contour. I do it again now. A cathartic gasp comes from her, and her head lolls on the red covers as if she were drugged. And then the deep, sighing, euphoric tremble all through her as she surrenders anew to the rhythmic bolts of pleasure that take her in seconds from agony to the brink of deliverance.

I ease the power setting to its maximum. 10. Mimi turns in her chair, toward the head of the bed. She can't watch the center of Elise anymore. Can't watch the jolts she is taking there. So she watches her hands. Her bound, delicate hands, which betray her pleasure as clearly as her rising cries, her fingers diving into her palms with each burst, then fluttering open as the wave recedes. And diving in again. And fluttering open. And I see, on the knees of her dress, that Mimi's fingers are doing the same.

A full minute of current, a minute twenty, a minute thirty, and then, instead of cutting it off and reaching for the heavy chain, I lean down and press hard on her soaked black panties, doubling the explosions inside her and bringing her, instantly, to the edge.

I lift my palm, and then press again. It's too much for her. And almost for me. I feel her hit the edge hard and start along it. I lean in. "You're free," I whisper, and she surges, possessed, her cries coming from deep in her throat, from even deeper, from some private place no one will ever reach again. I press and release, press and release, press and release, and I see tears now, rolling down from under her blindfold as she slams her face from side to side. I've read her body all night and I read it now — she is one hard press away. I give it to her, and I hold it, and I brace for her finish. But she hangs on, fighting off the first set of spasms, and then the next. She won't give in yet. She's waited too long, endured too much. Somehow she coaxes a few more seconds from her burning center, precious seconds that let her catch one last, killing wave. She arches, and cries out, and rides and rides and rides.

And I hear from across the room a sound from twenty years ago.

I look to the window. Beneath it. A drawn out hiss, two knocks, another long hiss. The radiator. This was my room for five years, and every two hours for five years I heard that sound. I stare at the old gray radiator. Hiss. Knock, knock. Hiss. Mom used to say it was God checking up on me. She said that when I heard it I should whisper his name and knock twice on the bed frame to let him know I was safe. The sound comes again. And again.

Elise's cries bring me back to her. I look hard at her bound, shining body, rocking in ecstasy, outside of herself in my old room. I pick up the black remote and switch off the Contour. I lean over her and give the screw on one clamp a full turn, and before her cry of pain can fade, I do the same with the other, watching the pink nipple disappear beneath the black plastic jaws. And then I tug on the chain, slowly, ignoring her desperate gasps of pain, taking it farther, farther, taking it as far down her belly as it will go. The clamps come with it, bent dangerously now, like fishing lines just before they snap.

I stand and walk to the window. And I sit down on the radiator.

Mimi is out of her chair again, stunned, standing over the gasping Elise, and now looking to me, her pleading eyes more beautiful than ever. She sits down again, to be closer to her, but she can only watch helplessly as Elise struggles to catch her breath through the pain. And I turn and look out the window.

I look up the street to the heavy trees that guard the entrance to the park. And down at the green mailbox on the sidewalk in front of the building. This was her view. All those days, as she watched me from this window. A hundred sidewalk football games. A thousand walks to school.

The radiator makes its noise again. And from Elise, sobs of agony as she tries to summon the breath to form words.

A cooling breeze comes through the window, as if from long ago. And I don't see the street anymore, or the old green mailbox, or the trees that guard the magic entrance to Morningside Park. I see the deep bows of the Japanese doctors as the hearse pulled away from the hospital.

"Please," Elise manages, her voice breaking. "Jake."

The doctors all bowed as one, holding their bows until the hearse was out of sight, until we were driving through the crowded Tokyo streets to the crematorium.

Silence from Elise now. Not a sound in the room.

I signed for the ashes. At sixteen, I signed for the ashes and then stood in the lobby with two heavy ceramic urns, waiting for the taxi that would take us home.

Her cries start up again, but with a new tenor to them. Familiar. Rising. I turn and see Mimi on the bed, sitting where I was. She has rescued Elise from the clamps, and is just now laying the black remote back on the covers. She stands and looks at me, her cheeks streaked with tears, her sweater held to her neck, and she walks to the door and out of the room. I stare at the empty doorway. The radiator is quiet now, and Elise's cries fill the room again. Deep cries, every three seconds. She isn't fighting the waves anymore. She has surrendered to them, and they are leading her home.

I pull my belt hard through its loops and walk quickly to the bed. I pull my shirt over my head and toss it to the floor, kick off my shoes and step out of my corduroys. I take the scissors from the floor and I cut her panties away from her. I turn off the remote, steady her with one hand, and ease the Contour out of her. "No," she whispers, but she feels my bare skin on her and knows what's coming, and her head drops back to the covers in rapture, in sweet, exhausted anticipation. She trusts me still, despite everything, and as I line her up, she braces one final time, to receive me. I grab the candle from the nightstand and take a sliver of ice from my drink.

"Your dark prince," I whisper, and I move the flame toward her thigh. Three inches away, two inches, and suddenly she feels it, and now, at an inch away, she really feels it, and I move it still closer and in one motion lift the candle and press the ice hard to her thigh, and she screams in imagined pain, convinced there is flame against her skin, and now as I surge into her, she screams again, and again, and I'm four, five, six thrusts into her before she realizes that it was ice, that she is free. I pound her, knowing that her screams found Mimi. In the hallway, maybe, her face in her hands, or at the front door, reaching for the knob. They found her and pierced her and finished everything between us. So I pound Elise harder, groping on the covers and finding the scissors and reaching behind me and cutting the tie to one ankle, and then the other. She can kick and thrust and come at me now, and does she ever, fucking like the freed tigress she is, like no girl ever has, all fury and desperate need. Quickly to the brink and then over it,

spending herself against me once, twice, three
times, and still I pound her. Harder, ever harder,
feeling her beneath me, hot, tight, feeling her but
not seeing her, and barely hearing her cries of
"Jake" and "God" and "Yes," even as I pound her
harder, hooking her under one knee and pulling
her up into me with each thrust. Barely hearing her
but hearing very clearly, from out in the hallway,
the click of the front door, and then another click as
Mimi Lessing closes it behind her and walks crying
down the long hallway of my childhood, down to
the end and then right, to the elevator, where she
stands alone in the quiet hallway while I gather it
all inside me, in my old room, set myself, give Elise
a second to say her prayers, and finish us both off.

CHAPTER THIRTEEN

It took me forty-eight years to find the first one.

I glimpsed her through the window of a Park Avenue florist late one spring afternoon. It was the simplest gesture that caught my notice — the way she wiped her hands on her apron. I stepped into the crowded shop, breathing in the fragrance of fresh-cut flowers. She was blond, petite, about twenty-two, and she worked behind the counter preparing the arrangements that an older man, clearly the owner, would call out to her. I watched her as I waited in line, enamored by the grace and quiet concentration with which she assembled each bouquet, gingerly selecting flowers from the refrigerated vases, trimming them, artfully mixing in soft ferns and baby's breath, then tearing a sheet of heavy plastic from the cutter and wrapping her creation with care. Once finished, she would step shyly to the counter, her eyes rising to meet the customer's as she held out the bouquet, then lowering demurely once again.

I ordered a dozen red roses from the owner. He nodded to her, and as I paid him, I watched her open the glass door and choose twelve of the finest from a vase inside. As she laid them on the arranging table, a quiet "oh!" escaped her. A thorn had cut her palm. I saw two drops of blood fall onto the green stems. She put her palm to her mouth and glanced quickly at the owner, whose back was to her, and then at me, smiling in a way that both asked my pardon and secured the secret between us. She pulled a leaf from a vase of flowers and pressed it deftly to her palm, holding it there with her thumb as she completed the arrangement, then glanced at the owner again as she stepped to the counter and extended to me the stunning bouquet. Her eyes, filled with innocent thanks, rose to mine and held them, and then she looked down at the counter once more.

I had found her. The woman who would close the wound.

Within a month I had gained access to her apartment and prepared it. And within a week she had betrayed me.

"Her latest," she called them.

I listened through my speakers as she spoke on the phone to a friend of "her latest." She described their actions together, sparing no detail. I turned off the stereo and stood for a few minutes in my quiet living room. I thought of everything I had risked. When I turned on the stereo again, she was saying that she missed a man she had met a month ago. Missed what it was that he could do to her.

"There'll be others," said her friend, and then they laughed. Schoolgirl laughs, grotesque.

Three nights later the young florist brought home a man she had met that evening at a rock music concert. That night he became her "latest."

Her last.

CHAPTER FOURTEEN

"*Tout est prêt.*"

Madame Brodeur's words, two hours ago. We met at La Boheme, the coffee shop around the corner, and over espressos she took me line by line through ten single-spaced pages. A wedding and reception for 180 guests, and there isn't a detail she hasn't attended to. The order of the receiving line, the length of the gift table, the tip envelopes for the Boathouse valets. Two hundred other details, at least, and it wasn't until she'd checked off the last one that we rose from the table.

"*Tout est prêt, Mimi,*" she said. "Everything is set." She smiled and took my hand in hers. "All you have to do is come."

I lift my wineglass off the coffee table, lean back into the pillows of my couch, and take a long sip.

It is nine o'clock on Tuesday night, and I am alone in my apartment. Alone on April 16 — V-Day, as we call it at the office. There's still the corporate filing deadline a month from now, but the worst is over. I've survived another tax season.

I take a slow sip of chardonnay. It is wonderful, calming. Ferrari-Carano. I remember the sculpted roses that lined the walk from the vineyards to the tasting room. And inside, on the wall, the place cards from White House dinners. Most of all, I remember the gaps in the vintages. On harvest day the winemaker tastes the grapes, and if he shakes his head, they don't make chardonnay at all that year. I told this to Mr. Stein when I brought him a bottle, and he said that's why we don't have any wineries on our client list.

I pour a second glass, close my eyes, and listen to the music. Kreisler's violin concertos, performed by the prodigy Joshua Bell. It came in the mail one day last year, a giveaway from a classical music station. This song is my favorite. "Caprice Viennois." It makes me sad and happy at the same time, like the black-and-white photo of Kreisler himself on the CD liner notes, standing on the deck of a boat in 1935, his hat raised toward the shore as he leaves for America.

Mark went home an hour ago. I won't see him again until the rehearsal dinner at The Palm a week from Friday. There's a tradition in his family for the groom to spend the final ten days of bachelorhood apart from the woman he will marry. His father says it goes back to the last century. I'm not sure I believe him, but both of Mark's brothers did it, too. So an hour ago I kissed him good-bye in the doorway. I'll see him at The Palm, and then at the altar.

I walk with my glass to the stereo. I wait out the last peaceful notes of the song and turn it off, then stand for a moment in the quiet apartment. I pick up a wedding invitation from the credenza. The card is thick and heavy, the color of cream. I run my fingers over the raised black lettering. *Joe and Dorothy Lessing request your presence at Saint Mary's Cathedral in New York City at six o'clock on the evening of Saturday, April 27, for the union of their daughter, Mimi, with Mark Alan Guidry.* I lay the card back on the credenza. *The union.*

I walk into the bedroom and slide open the mirrored closet door. We made love this morning, Mark and I. He kept me with him every second, his eyes open and on mine. "Forever," he said at the end. I take a white Deer Bay sweater from the shelf and put it on, the soft cotton luxurious against my arms. Beneath it I wear a lavender boat-neck top and matching capri pants. I slip my bare feet into white mesh shoes. I walk back into the living room, look around at the still apartment, and turn off the light. I step into the hallway and close the door behind me, then walk down the five flights of apartment stairs and out the front door into the spring night.

The streets are crowded, alive. I step past a humming line of people outside of Tremblay's, drinking wine on the sidewalk as they wait for tables. I reach Second Avenue just as a young man is stepping out of a taxi on the corner. I wave to him, and he holds the door for me. "Thank you," I say, and slide inside. He closes the door for me.

"Sixty-fourth and First," I tell the driver. I sit back, lulled by the motion, by the spring breeze through the window. A recorded voice welcomes me to New York and tells me to buckle up for safety. "Right here is fine," I say minutes later, and the driver pulls to the corner. The voice reminds me not to forget anything. I pay the driver and step out into the night. I walk one long block east, away from the lights, the noise, and then cross the street to the stairs of the skyway. I climb them and stand at the top.

I can see the river now, fifty yards away. I can see half a mile up and down the walkway. I see runners with flashing night patches, people walking their dogs, couples arm in arm. And I see Jake Teller alone at the railing, standing where we met seven days ago, looking out at the black water.

I start toward him across the skyway.

In my bed as a girl, during storms, I would say the names of Connecticut towns. Through each terrifying burst of thunder, I would recite them as fast as I could. Darien, Storrs, Old Saybrook, New Canaan. As long as I didn't run out of towns, the thunder couldn't hurt me. I reach the curving ramp that leads down to the river walkway.

Last Friday in Elise's apartment, I opened the front door and closed it again, so that Jake Teller would think I had walked out. I closed it and sat on my knees in the foyer, whispering the names of Connecticut towns. I whispered them until the end, until she was finally quiet. And then I let myself out.

I reach the river walkway. He is a good person, I know it. I can't explain why, but I know it. He turns from the railing and sees me. He wears slacks and a short-sleeve blue shirt. His eyes take me in, and then he looks away. I walk to the railing and stand a few feet from him.

"Finish all your accounts?" he asks.

"Yes."

It's too hard to look at each other, so we look out at the water. To the south, just before the river curves from sight, I can see the lights of a single boat moving toward us. At least a minute passes in silence.

"Your parents were killed when you were sixteen," I say.

Jake looks at me, hard, then back out at the water.

"Who told you?"

"I read your file, at work."

"My file," he says quietly. "They don't just leave those lying around."

"Mr. Stein once told me where they keep them."

"He trusted you."

I watch the water.

"How did it happen?" I ask. "Your parents."

He is quiet a long time.

"They went off a mountain road in the rain."

"You weren't in the car."

"No."

"How did you find out?"

Jake rubs the black railing. The boat grows bigger as it glides toward us up the river.

"Tell me something that isn't in your file, Mimi."

Even at night, outside, his blue eyes are charged, bottomless.

"Mark's been the only one, ever," I say. I grip the railing. The wind, stronger now, stirs the waves.

"I got home late at night," he says. "A family friend was in the living room."

"Where had you been?"

"On the team bus, coming back from a basketball tournament."

An old couple, elegantly dressed, pauses close to us on an evening walk. The woman tends to the man's scarf as he catches his breath. "Okay," he says. She smiles and takes his arm again, and they continue up the walkway.

"Tell me something else," Jake says.

"The other night, at home, I put ice to my wrist."

"You couldn't take it."

"Just seconds."

On the river, the boat is closer now. It is a twenty-foot cabin cruiser. *Serenity* is written across its bow.

"Your grandfather raised you," I say. "He died a year ago."

"He had a heart attack."

"The girl you followed to the theater. That was a year ago."

His eyes flash.

"Why did you ask me here, Mimi?"

"I want to understand. You take everything from them. Why?"

He looks at me, and for just a second his eyes are naked, desperate. He looks away.

"When you watch," he says. "What excites you the most?"

I close my eyes.

"The girl in the theater, Jake. It was after your grandfather died, wasn't it?"

He doesn't answer.

I see Nina Torring again, as Jake takes her leg to the post. Elise, as the first drop hits her.

"Their struggle," I whisper.

"What else?"

I feel the flush in my face. All through me. I look at him again.

"The way you take away every defense — one by one. The first girl, Jake. The one in the theater."

"It was a week after he died."

The boat is even with us now, moving quietly. A man stands alone at the helm, his hands resting casually on the bottom of the wheel. At peace. Gliding past Manhattan in the dark.

"One more, Mimi," Jake says. "Friday night."

I close my eyes tightly.

"The Century Motel on Tenth Avenue. Ten o'clock."

I can feel my engagement ring against the railing.

"Who is she?" I ask.

Jake doesn't say anything. *Serenity* is past us now, heading toward open water, her rippling wake disappearing as she moves away. All along I've told myself I could walk away. It was never true.

"We could set rules," I say.

"No rules."

"Limits."

"No."

I look straight down into the black water. And now up into Jake Teller's blue eyes.

"Room twenty," he says. "The last one. It won't be locked."

CHAPTER FIFTEEN

I wasn't on the team bus the night my parents were killed.

It was the night our small American high school played for the championship of the Far East Basketball Tournament. We'd never reached the title game before, and though we'd torn through the Kanto Plain League that season and had four starters who would go on to play small-college ball, no one imagined as the tournament began that we'd be any match for the best military high schools in Asia. They had one resource we didn't — black players — and it usually made all the difference.

Sixteen teams would be whittled down to one over four nights of games at Yokota Air Force Base, a two-hour bus ride from our school. For the opening round, we drew a break — Hong Kong International. They were a private school, like us, and we took them apart. The next night it got tougher — a base team from Seoul. They were heavy favorites,

but we came out firing; before they knew what hit
them, we were up by fifteen. We hung on to win by
three, and just like that, we were through to the
Final Four.

In homeroom the next morning, the principal's
voice came over the intercom. "In honor of our
Mustangs," he announced, pausing for effect,
"there will be no tests tomorrow." You could hear
the cheers out by the highway. All day long Mus-
tang fever built in the classrooms and hallways,
and that night 250 of our 300 students piled into
two yellow school buses and made the trek to
Yokota to cheer us on.

Coach knew we couldn't handle the Guam
Raiders in the paint, so his game plan was simple.
"Get every loose ball," he told us. "And fire away."
We did, answering their dunks with three-point
shots, hustling, scratching, keeping it close. We
trailed by four after one quarter, by three after two,
by two after three, and by two, still, when I stepped
to the free-throw line with three seconds left. I
made them both, sending the game into overtime;
and minutes later, when our senior captain, Bud
Jenks, hit a floater in the lane to win it, our fans
rocked the wooden bleachers of that old base gym
as if they were the back-row faithful at Lambeau
Field. We were in the finals, and the only thing
standing between us and school history was the
best high-school basketball team in the Far East —
the Wagner Falcons.

The Falcons were the pride of Clark Air Force
Base in the Philippines. They'd won three straight

Far East tournaments, and in the opening minute of the first game of this one, with fourteen teams watching from the stands, their *point guard* drove baseline and dunked, serving notice to all that they played a different brand of ball than the rest of us. They won their first tournament game by thirty-five points, their second by thirty, and their semifinal game by twenty-two. Still, as our team rode the bus back to Tokyo Thursday night, fresh off our last-second win, there wasn't a guy among us who didn't think we could take them.

Coach started his pep talk twenty hours early. Some coaches, he said, would look at a team like Wagner and see reasons to lose. But looking around this bus, he saw reasons to win. Twelve of them. Twelve kids who knew the value of sweat, who knew what it could earn you if you gave enough of it. Twelve kids who weren't afraid, who were glad for the chance to play the best team out there because the trophy would mean that much more when we beat them. Twelve kids who weren't alone but were a part of something larger — a special community, and here Coach pointed out the back window at the two yellow buses just behind us. It was midnight on a school night, and they carried 80 percent of our student body.

He was quiet for a moment, and then he looked around at all of us again. He saw twelve pretty good basketball players on this bus, he said, and one damn good basketball *team*, and if for thirty-two more minutes this damn good basketball team would do the things that had gotten us here — box

out, take charges, set screens, rotate on defense — if
for thirty-two more minutes we would stick together and play without fear, then, well, he didn't
care who took the court against us — he liked our
chances. Coach finished his talk just as the bus
pulled into the school parking lot, and as I walked
to my bike in the dark and then rode the ten minutes home through the cold March night, I had all
the reasons I needed to beat Wagner. Eight hours
later I would be given one more.

On game days, each player would find a gold
crepe-paper *M* taped to his locker, with a message
of luck from one of the cheerleaders. *You can do it!*
it might read, or *Win tonight, Jake!* The morning of
the championship game, I eased the front wheel of
my bike into the bike rack and walked to my locker,
blowing on my hands in the morning cold. I turned
the dial on the combination lock and glanced at my
gold *M*.

Jake — Win tonight and I'll kiss you! — Naomi

I stopped turning the dial.

Six years before, on my first day at the American
School, Naomi Kenn had seen me sitting alone at
recess and had held out a piece of soft red candy
wrapped in transparent paper. She laughed as I
tried to unwrap it. "You can eat it," she said. "It's
rice paper." I put it into my mouth, and to my wonder the paper melted onto my tongue.

She was the daughter of an American missionary
and his Japanese wife. A nice, quiet girl who lived,

as I did, out near the school. In junior high, on the weekends, I would shoot baskets for hours on the outdoor court, and Naomi would come by after church, in shorts and a T-shirt, and hit tennis balls against the practice wall nearby. At four o'clock or so, we'd walk to the *yakitori* truck that was forever parked across the street from the school, and we'd watch the old man cook skewered chicken on his grill, the dripping *tare* sauce sending the flames right up to his dancing fingers as he turned the sticks.

Missionary families were allowed a summer in the States every five years. Two weeks after ninth grade ended, Naomi Kenn left for California. Three months later, on the first day of tenth grade, I stared across the school lobby at a lithe Amerasian beauty with big almond eyes, skin of light caramel, and a tight, packed body that retained, despite its new enticements, its essential innocence and grace. Naomi Kenn. The sweet mix of her genes had exploded into bloom that summer, and they'd transformed the thin, pretty missionary's daughter into, in the words of the guys in gym class that first day, "one tight little package."

That fall she was the only sophomore to make the cheerleading squad, and I was the only sophomore to make the varsity hoop team. I averaged fourteen points a game, a school sophomore record, but neither my rainbow threes nor my slashes to the basket triggered the same buzz in the stands, or even on the team bench, as Naomi Kenn did each time she bounded onto the court during a timeout.

She was the middle cheerleader of seven, the centerpiece, and she executed the faux hip-hop moves with a joy and innocence ten times as alluring as the studied cool of the older girls. Even the coaches would break the huddle a second early to catch the finish of their signature routine, which ended with Jessie Case and Teri Evans, seniors both, launching Naomi skyward, where sweet gravity lifted her skirt up and out, exposing the tight black vee of her cheerleading panties as she reached out for her small white shoes, then went limp and plummeted back into the linked arms of her spotters, only to spring out of them into a cartwheel, and then another, and a third, her taut thighs flashing, and then a graceful turn and back the other way, her final cartwheel taking her back to the pyramid that Jessie and Teri had retreated into, where she closed the routine, for good and all, with a deep, thrilling split.

Jake — Win tonight and I'll kiss you! — Naomi

I opened my locker and taped the gold *M* to the inside. I'd never kissed a girl before, and the thought that Naomi might be my first, and *that night*, took my mind off the Wagner Falcons for the first time since the buzzer had sounded on our semifinal win. I stared into my locker, then smiled and shook my head. She meant it innocently, of course. As she meant everything. If we were to pull off the upset and I held her to it, she would smile and brush her cheek against mine. Still, I felt a burn at the base of my spine as I walked through the halls to homeroom, nodding at the fists of support from other students and trying to visualize, again, the precise spots on the court where I could get off my jumper.

The mood on the ride out to the base was taut and determined. Coach took a scuffed leather basketball from the team bag, and as he turned it in his hands, he told us that his father had once told him that a man, if he's lucky, gets five special days in his life. This was one of his five, Coach said, and he thanked us for it, and then handed the ball to Bud Jenks and walked to his seat at the front of the bus. Bud held the ball a little while, and then he asked each of us to take it and to think about what we, personally, were going to do to win this game, and he started the ball around the team. Everyone had their time with it, and when the last guy handed it back to Bud, he walked to the front of the bus and gave it back to Coach.

Man for man, we didn't belong on the same court with the Falcons. But as a team, that one night in March of 1990, we were their equal. We played a tight zone and collapsed on everything inside, daring their guards to beat us over the top. They would have, they were that good, but at the other end of the court the hot shooting that had carried us through the tournament held true. We knew they were quicker and stronger than we were, so we set screen after screen, and knocked down jumper after jumper, and when they adjusted in the second half, fighting over them, we went back door, sending the screener to the basket for a layup.

The crowd spurred us on. Not just our own legions, a raucous sea of black and gold, but the base crowd, too, which rooted politely for us at the start, to keep from sitting through a blowout, but grew louder and more committed the longer we hung in. And we hung in and hung in and hung in, and when our point guard drew a charge from theirs with the score tied and sixteen seconds to play, suddenly it was our game to win.

Coach's call was to take the clock down to eight seconds and then to run Bud through a double screen that would free him for a shot from the corner. They were ready for it. Bud's defender fought over the first screen and under the second, the one I set, and he was right on him as Bud caught the pass and squared to the basket. As Bud left his feet, my man ran at him, too, so I leaked out to the wing, just in case. Sure enough, Bud — double-teamed in the air — dropped the ball off to me as the clock hit four, and I set my feet as the clock hit three, then left them, and it was as if I was back on the outdoor court at school, just me and the rim, shooting one of ten thousand shots, and I let it fly as the clock hit two, and I held my follow-through, and held it, and held it, and I was still holding it as the ball split the net, and the buzzer sounded, and a swarm of black and gold swallowed me up.

The trophy was ours.

I walked out of the locker room twenty minutes later to see Naomi Kenn standing against the far wall. She wore jeans and a powder blue sweater, and her shining black hair, still wet from the shower, was pulled back in a tight ponytail. I crossed to her, and she stepped toward me and gave me a hug.

"I knew you would make it," she said, releasing me but staying close.

"It felt pure," I said.

Over her shoulder I could see my parents, talking with other parents by the door of the gym lobby. It was my mother's fortieth birthday, and we had agreed that, win or lose, we'd all drive back together to Goemon, her favorite restaurant, for a late-night dinner.

"I owe you something," Naomi said, smiling shyly. "But not here." She looked down, then back up at me, and a look came into her eyes that I'd never seen. "Jake," she said, in a whisper that spiked my blood. "Don't take the bus back."

"My parents are driving me."

"Can you lie to them?"

I looked at her, not sure I'd heard.

"Because if you can lie to them, I know a place we can go."

Beyond her, down the hall, I saw my mother look up and see me. She waved, her eyes brimming. I waved back.

"Where?" I asked.

"It's a secret. Will you meet me out by the base gate in ten minutes?"

I nodded, and she walked away. She walked away, and I walked down the hall to my parents and told them that there was going to be a party on the team bus and that none of the other players would be missing it.

"You might have told us earlier, Jake," my father said, "and saved us twenty minutes." But his tone was gentle, his heart full. He put his hand on my shoulder. "I thought you'd have to bank it," he said.

"I had the angle."

He squeezed my shoulder and stepped aside, and Mom hugged me close.

"We're so proud, Jake," she said. "We always knew . . ." She stopped and swallowed, her hands smoothing my shirt, straightening the top button. "We'll see you at home."

I told Coach at the door to the team bus that I would be riding back with my parents. "My mom's birthday," I explained. Then I walked to the gate of the base, where Naomi stood in the door of the guardhouse, talking to two MPs. She smiled good-bye to them, and we stepped through the spotlit gates and walked through the quiet streets to the nearest train station. We reached it just before the rains came. Sudden and hard, streaming down the train windows as we rode, blowing into the car when the doors slid open at deserted country stops.

We'd been friends for six years, easy and natural, but we rode in silence, the air between us charged, electric. Every few minutes the rocking of the train would bring her knee against mine. At Tokyo Station we changed to the Chuo line, and when we passed Shinjuku I knew where we were headed.

The rain eased, and eased some more, and by the time we walked through the wicket at Tamabochi Station, it had stopped completely. The night was clear, the streets fresh and sparkling, as we walked the ten minutes to school.

We passed the *yakitori* truck, dark and shuttered, and stepped onto the school grounds. The buses had come and gone. From the bushes beyond the tennis court came the trill of a lone cicada.

"Do you still have your key?" she asked. I looked at her a moment.

"Yes," I said.

She meant the key to the gym. Coach gave one to every player so that we could come in early to shoot. I slipped it into one of the big double doors, which opened in with a sigh. I'd never seen the gym so dark and silent. Cavernous. The roll-down bleachers were still in place from the pep rally that afternoon, the walls still draped with banners and streamers. Naomi took my hand and led me under the silent scoreboard and across the wooden court, the dead spot by the free-throw line creaking as we passed, our way lit only by the little moonlight that seeped down through the rafters. Her hand was impossibly warm. She led me to the far corner, to the thick gold wrestling mats rolled up like enormous carpets, the largest one high enough that I could lean back against it. I did, and she stepped between my legs and kissed me.

Nothing will ever be softer than her lips that night. Nothing will ever taste better. Her first kiss was sweeter than the candy she handed me the day we met, her breath more delicate than the rice paper that first stirred my sense of wonder.

"My first one," I said, just afterward, and she bit her lip, her eyes pure and wide. She reached up and took down her hair, shaking it loose. We kissed again, and then again, her hands on my chest, mine on her shoulders, and then down the back of her blue sweater.

Kisses were all I'd hoped for, ever, but she moved in tighter between my legs, tight enough that she could feel me through her jeans. I braced for her to back away, but she stayed, and then to my shock she began to move. Gently, slowly, but unmistakably, the whisper of her jeans filling my senses. I put my hand to her cheek, fighting to keep steady. She took two of my fingers in her tiny hand and pressed them to her open neck. Then she pressed them to the tight swell of her powder blue sweater. And to her belly. And onto the button of her jeans.

Can you lie to them? she had said. Sweet Naomi Kenn.

Neither of us moved. I could hear, just behind us, the back door of the gym rattle once in the wind. Her dark, beautiful eyes held mine. And then she took her hand away and nodded, and I opened the button on her jeans. She nodded again, her eyes deep and trusting. I took the zipper in my fingers and pulled it down. When it reached the bottom, she drew in her hips and let her jeans slide down her. Down past her panties — white, stunning. Down past her perfect thighs.

We were both trembling now. I didn't know where to touch her, or how, so I took the bottom of her blue sweater between my fingers. She pulled it out, gently, took my fingers in hers again and pressed them to the lace band of her panties. I ran my finger along it, mesmerized. "Yes," she whispered. I ran it back. "Yes," she whispered again, breathless, expectant. I couldn't do it. "Jake," she said, urgent now, but I still couldn't, so she slid her own fingers inside the band of her panties and lifted them away from her skin, giving me a glimpse of dark heaven, and when I still didn't move, she took my fingers again, and Naomi Kenn, the sweet, pure missionary daughter, guided them inside her panties and pressed them into her wet pussy.

Instinct told me to spread them wide, and her sudden cry pierced me to the bone. I tried to ease them back out, certain I'd hurt her. "No!" she said, pressing a hand to her panties, pinning my fingers in place. One, two, three seconds, her eyes on mine again, steadying me. "Okay?" she whispered, and I nodded, and she took her hand away and put both her hands on my shoulders. I stayed dead still, not quite believing that I was inside her. And then slowly, ever so slowly, Naomi Kenn eased forward, taking my fingers deeper into her.

Her first gasp sent a thousand volts right through me. She gasped again, her fingers digging into my shoulders as she eased forward a little more, then a little more, moving up onto her toes, her shoes barely touching the gym floor, and then not touching it, her strong legs circling mine, then closing around them, all her weight now transferred on to me. I put my left arm around her waist. I had her. And her eyes found mine again.

"Okay," she whispered.

I moved my fingers, gently, and the first shocks of pleasure broke over her sweet face. I moved them again and sent her head back. She put her arms around my neck and brought her face to my shoulder, and then, as I worked my fingers inside her, she put her lips to my ear and treated me to her every sound.

Sounds I hadn't imagined in all my dreams, sounds that rose and deepened as I slipped a third finger into her, and then a fourth, her shoes kicking the backs of my knees as the waves hit her. And they hit her and hit her and hit her, and she rode them, passively at first, in thrall to my fingers, controlled by them, "Jake!" and "Yes!" and "God!" in my ear as the sensations inside her built and built. Within minutes they were too much for her. Within minutes she felt the first stirrings of release, and her soft cries of wonder gave way to gasps of joy, then, as the shocks kept coming, to grunts of pure want. And Naomi Kenn, the sweetest soul in a school of three hundred, began to surge against my fingers.

She was ninety pounds to my one-seventy, but I had to brace against the hard, rolled mat as she drove herself against me. With an athlete's power she drove, her thighs tight on my hips, driving, driving, her hands in my brush cut, on my ears, then pounding my shoulders as she lost control, her eyes closing, her head thrown back, her cries rising up into the rafters of the gym I grew up in. The gym where I first learned to sweat, to work, to sacrifice, where I first learned, that night, the truth of sex — its fury, its isolation. Learned it all in the split second when Naomi Kenn opened her eyes and I searched them in vain for a trace of the girl I knew. She shut them again and threw her head back, and I could only hold her against me as she bucked and bucked, and no harem whore ever fucked her king any harder than sweet, pure Naomi Kenn raged against me in her final seconds. Raged and raged and finally collapsed, her pounding heart against mine, her cheek on my chest, her ninety pounds limp, broken as I turned her, gently, and set her on the wrestling mat, then knelt into her and held her tight. I held her and held her, until I could feel her shoulders begin to shake, until I could feel on my skin, like the water of life, the hot tears that rolled from her eyes.

I must have biked the two miles from the school to my house in five minutes, oblivious to the night around me. I didn't notice the rain start up again, didn't see the police car parked at the end of the block, didn't wonder at the lights in the living room, when my parents should still have been away at dinner. It all registered at once, as I opened the front door and saw, in the *genkan*, the three pair of black, polished, hard-tip shoes. I took my own sneakers off slowly, untying the laces, and then walked down the dark hall and into the living room. Coach — ashen, old — sat on the edge of my father's favorite chair, and behind him, their hands crossed formally at their belts, stood three policemen. Two, actually, and one interpreter.

I knew enough Japanese to understand the key words. *Jiko*. Accident. *Torakku*. Truck. *Yudachi*. Mountain storm. I heard them from the policeman and then again, surreally, from the interpreter. I stared at the white gloves of the policemen. Immaculate. Ludicrous. Did they have to wear them? *Furyo Jiken*. Freak. I looked at the interpreter. "It was not their fault," he was saying, his pronunciation precise. "Even thirty seconds sooner. Even ten seconds . . ."

You might have told us earlier, Jake, and saved us twenty minutes.

I step from the fire escape back through the open window into my apartment. I walk to the kitchen and sit down at the table. I dip my fingers into my drink, flick them, and watch the drops sizzle and vanish against the face of the iron. I hold it by the handle and press it, hard, to the white silk tie on the table, watching the steam escape into the air. I take the iron slowly up the length of the silk, flattening every crease, every wrinkle, shrinking the fibers, strengthening them. I finish the first tie and iron the second one the same way. And now the third. I look at the clock. Six o'clock. I iron the fourth tie, then fold each of them and slip them into the wide pocket of my blue Guayabera shirt.

I carry my drink to the window and step out onto the fire escape again. I lean on the railing, take a long sip of vodka, and look down on the city. Manhattan at dusk, quiet, coiled. I watch the lights in the windows come on one by one.

I went years without thinking of Naomi Kenn. And then I shook Mimi Lessing's hand in Mr. Stein's office and looked into her face and I saw it. In her eyes. The same purity, the same killing innocence, but in a woman this time, not a girl. And beneath that purity — something else.

I take another long sip of Absolut. She understands. In some way I can't fathom, Mimi understands. If things were different — but they never are. I close my hand around the black railing, remembering hers along the river. Her tiny fist on the river railing. The glint of her ring. In my pocket, against my chest, I can feel the warm ties.

She dreams of them, I know. She has listened and she has watched, and it hasn't cured her. She still dreams of the silk, so soft and ruthless. Dreams and then wakes, and she can almost feel it against her skin.

I finish my drink and look west, out over the roofs of the buildings.

Two hours, I'll make it last. Longer.

Tonight, Mimi Lessing will learn the worth of dreams.

And their cost.

CHAPTER SIXTEEN

Her name was Sister Grace.

Thirty-seven years ago, on a warm March afternoon, I sat in the last row of the eighth-grade classroom at West Side Catholic. The scent of spring came through the open window behind me, mingling with the fresh shavings of the pencil I was sharpening onto the floor. I looked up at the sound of the door, expecting to see the stern face of our Latin teacher, Father Keegan. Instead, I saw the beautiful substitute.

The nun's habit she wore could not contain her radiance. No, the strict black cloth only set off the pale blue of her eyes, the warm color in her cheeks, the ivory of her neck beneath the high collar. And most of all, the quiet, stunning swell of her bosom. Sister Grace spent the hour administering an exam, her soft footsteps filling my senses as she walked slowly down the ordered rows of desks, from the blackboard to the windows and back again. I wondered how the boys around me could concentrate on their tests. Each time she neared, I grew flushed and dizzy, the black text of my exam swimming on the page in front of me. She would reach me, turn, and then start back the other way, and I would lean low over my paper and breathe in. She smelled of rainwater and salvation.

That night in bed I gave into the fever for the first time. The priests on Sunday, the Fathers at school had been clear: when boys felt the fever coming on, they were to clasp their hands and pray. I had always done so, but not that night. Nor the next. Nor the next. Even now I remember the intensity of those first visions, and their innocence. I imagined her by a waterfall, her back to me. Lowering her habit inch by inch. It took her a full week to reveal her neck, another to bare her shoulders, a third to uncover her smooth back. I awoke each morning filled with shame, but each night I returned to her. I would go only so far, I told myself. So far and no further.

When she appeared in class again, I drank in every delicate detail. The white of her fingertips as she pressed a piece of chalk to the board; the curving outline of her legs as she moved. And as before, the swell of her bosom beneath the saintly black cloth. My nighttime visions grew bolder. Soon she had stepped clear of the habit and walked naked into the calm blue water. I wouldn't allow her to turn toward me. Not until I saw her again.

I waited desperately for her to return to our class, but April passed without her presence. And then May. And then early June, and the final week of classes. I thought I had lost her, but when I took my report card home to my father and he saw that my Latin scores had fallen below ninety, he grew angry and called me into his study. My punishment, he said, would be to endure a summer tutor. Which of my teachers should he approach?

She came each Saturday afternoon, and for one hour we sat across from each other at the mahogany table in our living room.

"*Malus*," she would say.

"*Male, malum, mali*," I would answer, struggling to keep my eyes on her hands.

"*Amor.*"

"*Amorem, amoris, amori.*"

Our lessons were from two to three, and when they finished, my mother would take me to the reading room at the Alcott Hotel, where I would read the international papers to her as she sipped a double martini. As soon as we returned home, I would excuse myself to my room, soak a washcloth in hot water, and lie down on my bed, the cloth over my eyes.

My visions grew ever bolder. Sister Grace naked in the water, turned toward me now. Her face, then her neck, then her shoulders rising into view. I pressed the warm cloth hard to my eyes, torn between her purity and my unspeakable desire, keeping her breasts below the waterline, yes, but allowing my free hand to drift down and do the devil's work. Afterward I would rush to the sink and scrub my hands with coarse soap, then kneel on the cold tiles and pray.

All through the summer this continued, until the last Saturday in August. The day of our final lesson.

At the end of it, Sister Grace put her hands on my shoulders. "You've been a fine student," she said, her mesmerizing swell just inches away from me. "I hope to see you in the fall."

My mother and I walked to the Alcott, as usual, but we found the front doors barred and the worried concierge on the sidewalk. A waiter had been felled by tuberculosis, he explained. The hotel would reopen on Monday.

And so we returned home.

As my mother removed her gloves in the foyer, I walked ahead of her down the hallway. A few feet from my father's study I stopped still, not comprehending the sounds that came through the door. I looked back at my mother. For just an instant she stood with her head tilted, as if she might be listening to a bird. "Go to your room," she said quietly. I didn't move. She walked toward me, her eyes no longer on mine but on the closed door of the study. In those eyes, already, were the first glints of madness. "Yes," she said as she reached me, and then again, dreamily, "yes, you had better stay."

She opened the door and I saw the black habit strewn over the back of my father's armchair. I heard his gasping roar and, much softer, her startled cries. And across the room I saw the end of everything. My father's strong forearm in the small of her back. Her delicate fingers, curled and gripping. Her blue eyes, wide in shock. And her breasts, the breasts that had haunted me, that I hadn't dared to imagine, pressed hard into the desktop.

I open my eyes. The white plaster of the windowsill is stained with sweat, and chipped where my fingers have dug into it. I relax them and close my eyes again. I stand still in the quiet apartment. For several minutes I stand, until the visions subside and the storm inside me passes. When I open my eyes again, my mind is clear. Clear of the images of thirty-seven years ago, and clear of all doubt. All weakness.

I cross the living room to the far wall and walk slowly along it, running my hand across the cassettes that fill the mounted oak case. Cassettes that rise from just short of the floor to eye level and stretch to the window. A full year of Miss Lessing's evenings and mornings. These past few days I have listened obsessively. Pulled tapes at random and listened, as if somewhere among them I might find the moment when I lost her. Instead, I found treasures.

October 14. Miss Lessing in the kitchen, listening to the classical music station as she prepares dinner. "Minuet," she says, and then a few minutes later: "Finale." Teaching herself to recognize the separate movements in an orchestral piece. The next day I sent her the Kreisler that is now her favorite.

June 2. Miss Lessing in the living room, listening to National Public Radio. A commentator mentions that Michelangelo was seventy when he began work on St. Peter's Cathedral. "Wow," she says softly, and then I read her thoughts. The remark would put her in mind of the elderly. She would think of her father. I waited, and she walked to the kitchen and phoned him.

May 10. I take the cassette from its slot and turn it in my hands. I hold it to the light, as if I might see into it. May 10. The first time I heard her with her fiancé.

Her sounds were beautifully simple and quiet. The sounds of a woman who turns to sex for the deeper communion it offers. What thrilled me most in listening was to hear the . . . catch in her soft cries, the restraint. Even in love she *withheld*.

I replace the cassette in its slot and walk along the wall to the last row. I kneel down and take from near the floor the final cassette in my collection. April 16. I recorded it three nights ago, from my car. I take the tape out of its case, walk to the stereo, and slide it into the tape player. I hit PLAY and listen again to its final seconds.

"We could set rules."

"No rules."

"Limits."

"No. Room twenty. The last one. The door won't be locked."

I walk to the window again and look down at the street below. A line of drivers in their parked cars wait for the six o'clock chimes that will make them legal. Across the street the gilded awnings sparkle in the fading light.

At thirteen I was sent to a military school in Virginia. One hundred and forty-seven boys in my class, and I was the weakest. When I had been there a month, my father wrote to say that he had put my mother in an institution. "It is what she needs," he wrote. "Pray for her."

From the speakers behind me, above the low hiss of the tape, come the sounds of the river. The rustle of the wind on the waves. Jake Teller must have walked away without waiting for her to answer. I close my eyes again.

It is their struggle that excites her. The stripping of their defenses, one by one.

I turn and look at the long wall of tapes. There are more than a thousand of them. Tomorrow I will box them all up and put them away, just as I did with the others. But the collection is not yet complete. I have one more cassette to make.

Four hours from now Miss Lessing is due at the Century Motel. An Øre lies beneath the bed in room twenty. Another beneath the front desk.

I walk to the stereo and turn it off. The apartment is quiet again.

Tonight I will give her one final chance to refuse him. Fate is character. Character, fate. Four hours from now Miss Lessing will choose hers.

And I will listen.

CHAPTER SEVENTEEN

I wear low heels, and a trace of Maige Noire.

The same pink dress and my cobalt sweater. It is five minutes to ten o'clock, and I sit on a wooden bench outside the ice room of the Century Motel. A few feet from the door of room twenty.

It is the last motel room, as he said. Past it is only the ice room, and then a chain-link fence at the end of the motel property. I look at the door, blue and bare. Almost the way I imagined it. Lying in bed last night, and tonight as I dressed, and in the taxi on the way over, I pictured the door and nothing else. As if I might walk to it and then turn and walk away.

The night air is cool and soothing. From this bench I can see across the parking lot into the window of the motel office. An old man sits at the front desk, reading by the light of a lamp. Every few minutes he turns the page.

I look down at my watch. 9:58. I close my eyes and rub my hands over the knees of my dress.

I called my mother thirty minutes ago. Just before I left the apartment. I thought she would be in bed, reading, but she was in the garden. "What's wrong?" were her first words. I was fine, I told her. I just needed to talk.

She saw my wedding dress today. She was downtown, passing by the shop, and couldn't resist. It was ravishing. The final alterations were done, the beads — seven thousand of them — sewn on by hand. "You'll cry when you see it," she said.

I open my eyes. 10:03. I stand and walk to the door of room twenty. I try the handle, and it turns easily. I pause. I look back, past the parking lot and the office, out to the lights of Tenth Avenue. Up into the dark city sky.

One night, in a lifetime, without rules. Without limits.

I open the door, step inside, and lean back against it. And I stare, transfixed.

In front of me is everything I didn't let myself imagine. The white silk ties on the posts. The black blindfold on the pillow. A cassette player on the nightstand. A lamp clipped to the headboard. The curtains by the lone window are drawn tight, and the heat is on high. I stand a full minute with my back to the hard door.

I walk slowly to the bed and sit down on the edge. Just as I did three weeks ago, at the Roosevelt Hotel. Was it only three weeks ago?

He takes everything from you, Mimi. Everything.

The two white silks at the head of the bed are

tied low on the posts and lie across the red covers. They end in graceful, knotted loops that wait patiently for my wrists. The loops are impossibly far apart. At the foot of the bed, the other two ties hang straight down from the posts. He won't use those until he's ready. I reach out and touch the white silk, careful not to disturb the knot. It is so soft. I close my eyes, trembling. This room has been waiting for me my whole life. The soft ties, the blindfold, the heat. Waiting. I only had to come to them.

I slip off my shoes, walk to the chair by the window, and place them beneath it, with my purse. I hang my sweater over the straight back of the chair. I look to the door, then undo the buttons on my dress and slip out of it. I fold it carefully and lay it on the chair. I place my watch on top.

I'm down to bra and lace, grateful now for the heat. I walk to the bed again. I look down at the careful arrangements, at the desk lamp pointed down the center of the bed, the delicate knots in the looped ties. I sit down. I take the black blindfold from the pillow and slip it on, its smooth felt soft on my forehead. I pull it close to my eyes but leave it just above them. I lie down on my back on the covers.

I reach up with my right wrist and slip it through the loop of silk. I turn my body, reach up with my left hand, and pull on the loose end of the tie encircling my right wrist. I watch the knot constrict, watch the silk close around my wrist, feel its thrilling bite. I pull it tight, then turn onto my back again and press my legs together.

I lie still for a minute.

That first night, in the bar, I saw cruelty in his eyes. And the blood rose in my face.

I reach up with my free left hand and pull the blindfold over my eyes. Darkness. I slide it up again and stare at the ceiling, my heart racing. I breathe deeply, twice, three times, then pull it down over my eyes again, easing into the darkness this time, letting my other senses take over. I feel the coolness of the covers beneath my legs, hear for the first time the sounds of the room, of the night. The deep, subliminal hum of the heater. A car engine, starting.

Soon it will be music instead. I dig my heels into the covers.

The room is so hot. I feel the first beads of sweat in the well of my neck. In the darkness and quiet, there is nothing to slow my imagination, so I see the sweat on the faces of the others. On the forehead of Nina Torring. The throat of Elise. I press my legs together again.

I reach with my left hand for the other silk tie. It is too high, too far. No, I can reach it. I touch the silk with the tips of my fingers. He will do the rest. He will guide my wrist through the loop and then pull it tight. I can see his hands, his concentration. I feel the first stirrings inside me.

Clear your mind, Mimi.

I think of the garden in Greenwich. The winding path of stones from the patio, the roses by the far wall. My mother, gardening at night in her old clothes. Earth on her knees. Tonight she released the ladybugs. She sprayed them with sugar water, to weight their wings. If you can keep them in the garden for twenty-four hours, they become territorial and will stay.

Footsteps.

Outside on the concrete walk. Coming quickly. Reaching the door. Passing it. I wet my lips and exhale. But now — rattling. The scrape of a bucket. The ice room. I cross my ankles and press my knees tight together. The footsteps start back. To the door . . . past it . . . fading . . . gone. I ease one ankle off the other and breathe out again.

Fifteen minutes ago I called Mark. From the bench outside the ice room. I knew he wouldn't answer, because he screens his calls. I called to hear his voice on the machine. To see if maybe . . . I don't know. As I listened to his voice, clear and strong, a taxi pulled into the parking lot. Its passengers stepped out, and the driver looked over at me. All I had to do was raise my hand. I closed the cell phone and put it back into my purse, and watched the taxi turn and pull out onto Tenth Avenue.

A soft click, a breath of wind, another soft click. The door.

I turn toward it and listen. Nothing. Wait. The rustle of clothing? No. But a sound. A sound that I've heard — the give of the door. The soft sigh I heard when I leaned back against it.

He is in the room.

Jake Teller is in the room, and he is standing where I stood. Watching me.

I cover my bra with my left arm. The room is still

and silent. I can feel his presence, the way the others could. He is appraising me. Slowly, I take my arm away. I take it away, and I reach and find the silk loop again. I can just slip my wrist through it. I lay my head back on the pillow.

Thirty seconds pass. I will keep still. Thirty more seconds pass. I feel the bed give beneath him. He is beside me. He is leaning in close. I'm trembling now. He doesn't touch me. Ten more seconds pass. Ten more. Please. Anywhere.

Click.

The lamp. I feel its brightness through the blindfold, its heat on my neck. I wet my lips. And now I feel it — butterfly wings against my left wrist. Not his fingers — the silk. Gossamer soft, closing slowly, and now tightening, tightening, tight now, tighter, and now pulling my wrist a few more inches toward the post.

I'm bound.

I feel the soft burn in my shoulders and across my breastbone. Bound. I pull gently against the ties. They give an inch, no more. I pull harder and gasp as the knots tighten into my wrists. I reach back with my fingers and take up a few inches of silk. I twist them and try to pull out. I can't. Panic rises through me. I pull harder, harder, but the silk is too strong. It is like steel, and the harder I pull, the tighter it closes. I try to slip my wrists out from the loops, but they are too tight. I kick my heels on the covers.

"Please."

Silence.

I won't be like the others. My breathing is fast and loud in the quiet room. I calm it. My struggle will excite him. As theirs excited me. I bring my legs together and somehow, against everything inside me, I keep them still. The lamp is trained on my throat, and I can feel the sweat trickling down into it, gathering. I try to concentrate on the cool of the covers beneath me. If he would just touch me. If I could hear a sound from him. A whisper. My name.

Thirty seconds pass. A minute.

To imagine it was nothing. To listen, to watch — no. To lie here in the pitch dark, helpless, waiting for him to begin . . . is beyond everything. I close my legs tighter, but already I feel the wetness between them. He will see it, as he saw it in the others. I cross my ankles. The thought of silk, closing around each one, pulling them apart . . .

Click.

The lamp again. No. I can still feel its heat.

The tape player.

Music. The last preparation. Piano notes now, filling the quiet room. Patient. Haunting. "Convento Di Sant'Anna." I drop my head back and pull against the ties again. This time I don't feel the burn in my wrists, but in the center of me. "Convento Di Sant'Anna." I see Nina Torring's bedroom. His discipline, her cries, the ice. I bring my legs up and then slowly back down, but inside I feel the spreading wave.

I see the bed I lie on as if from above. The red covers, the white silk. I see myself as Jake Teller must see me. Spread and bound, the tendons standing out in my arms, in my throat. I see the lace that protects me and the scissors that will cut it loose.

I see all this, but I am still.

Still, though I know now that he will break me. I will plead, like the others, and cry out. Already I can feel the cries building. Cries Mark has never heard, could not imagine. In the deep dark of the blindfold I see it now — the church in the fading light. Empty.

I'm bound. God, it is so simple. So pure. Submission.

The piano plays softly, beautifully. For so long I've wanted this. Since I could dream. I hear the twist of a bottle cap. The strong scent of oil fills the room. He will touch me now. In seconds.

Please let me last. Let him do anything, but let me last and last.

He touches me. The backs of his fingers on my face. Stroking me gently, gently. I am slipping into ether. Weightless. Free. And now he is touching the blindfold. Lifting it. I blink in the blinding light of the lamp. What's wrong? Why is —

I can't breathe.

CHAPTER EIGHTEEN

I couldn't do it.

I sat on the bed at the Century Motel, the white silk ties laid out in front of me on the red covers. It was seven o'clock, and the last light of dusk came through the window and fell across them. I reached for the solid wooden post at the head of the bed, and ran my hand down along it. Then I gathered up the ties, folded them, put them in my shirt pocket, stood, and walked out of the room. Ten feet away, outside the door to the ice room, was a wooden bench. I sat down on it and stared across the parking lot. I took my cell phone from my pocket, then put it away again. Better that she come and find the door locked, the room canceled. Better that she come and leave betrayed. I looked again at the door to room twenty, then walked across the parking lot to the motel office, where I told the old man at the desk that I had to cancel my reservation.

"We still got to charge you," he said, his eyes sour and challenging.

I didn't argue. I stepped out the door and stood on the sidewalk of Tenth Avenue. A breeze came up from the west, from the water. Between the buildings I could see the sun sinking into the Hudson. I started to walk.

South to Forty-second Street I headed, then east. Out of the gray, gritty clamor of Hell's Kitchen, through the neon corridor of Times Square, past the majestic white library at Fifth Avenue. I kept walking, past the quiet office towers of midtown, through the Friday night chaos outside Grand Central. I walked to Third Avenue, the sidewalk crowds thinning, and then on to Second.

I walked the width of the island, until I was finally cut off by the gates of the United Nations. I turned south and walked down to Thirty-fourth Street, then cut up across the car ramp, wound down past the heliport, stepped through the open fence, and stood, alone, at the beginning of the river walkway. It was full night by then. I crossed to the river railing.

There was still time to go back. To reclaim the room, prepare the bed, and wait. I looked across the water at the lights of Roosevelt Island. I reached into my shirt pocket, took out the white silk ties, and threw them over the railing. Three fell folded into the water, but the last one unfurled and was lifted by the wind, out and away, toward the far shore. As if changing its mind, it fluttered back toward me. Then it swirled a last time and dropped into the black water.

I stood at the railing, watching the slow progress

of the ties, white lines wreathed in black water, as they drifted toward the sea. I looked at my watch. 8:20. I'd have to hurry.

I walked back to First Avenue, moving faster now. Down to Twentieth Street, then west to Third Avenue. To the green common and across it, to the path through the garden, and then to the door of the Columbarium.

Where I stand now, at a quarter to nine. I have fifteen minutes.

I step into the deserted lobby and walk across the marble floor to the stairs. Soft classical music plays, seemingly from out of the air. I climb to the second floor and then to the third. Grandpa's niche is on this floor, but I keep climbing, up to the fourth-floor landing, where I step out into the circular walkway. I start around. The rooms on this floor are all named for trees. The Cypress Room. The Sequoia Room. Here it is. The Cedar Room. I pause in the entrance, then step inside.

I am all alone, but it is thirty seconds before I can look at the niches that surround me. I move along the west wall. Names, dates, keepsakes. Gladys Stoppard, 1920–1982. A small watercolor. Jerome Henderson, 1941–1990. A cross. Ryan Glasson, 1972–1989. A varsity letter. I keep moving. William Jennings, 1931–1996. A service badge, leaning against the urn.

I come to the end of the west wall, and now start along the north one. I walk ten feet and then stop. Their wedding photo looks back at me. And behind it, the two urns. Two gray, Oriental urns. The urns

I held in my lap ten years ago, on the flight from Tokyo to New York.

It's been ten years since I've seen them. The day of their inurnment, I waited in the lobby until Grandpa came to tell me that the director was through. I wanted to be alone with them, I said. He nodded, but I walked to the top floor, the fifth, and looked out the window at the city for five minutes, then walked back down to the lobby. Every year, on the anniversary of the accident, I've done the same thing.

I look now at the picture. Dad at twenty-five, cocksure, grinning. Holding Mom's hand to his vest. Her veil is lifted, and though she looks into the camera, the laughter in her eyes is for him. She is twenty-three.

I clean the glass. It is peaceful in this room. Serene. The air is scented with flowers, and the music plays softly, eternally. The two urns touch at the shoulders, like shy lovers. I'll bring something next time. A rose. I'll bring it soon.

I stand in silence, looking into the niche, until I hear the chime of the closing bell. I touch the glass with my fingers, turn, and walk out to the walkway, then back to the marble steps, down them, and to the lobby. A custodian stands patiently at the door, holding it open. "Thanks," I say. He nods kindly, his eyes on the floor. He closes the door behind me, and I step down the walk and into the garden. I sit down on a stone bench at the garden entrance and swipe the sleeve of my jacket across my eyes.

The cell phone is heavy in my pocket. I take it out. I have both her numbers, home and cell. I pick up a stone from the ground. All the ways I've thought of her, and what I want most now is to show her the Columbarium. To show her the way their urns touch at the shoulders. Then I want to walk with her along the river walkway. The whole way along it, from the heliport at Thirty-fourth Street up to Gracie Mansion. Walk with her and explain. Her hand in mine. I toss the stone away, shake my head, and stand up.

She has her man for that.

I put the cell phone away and start down Third Avenue. I walk to Sixth Street, then head west, the street life thickening here in the Village, the sidewalks a riot of vendors and walkers. The smell of Indian food mingles with the scent of flowers from an outdoor stand, and then both give way to the smell of pot. I continue west, drawn now, realizing for the first time where I'm headed. At the hoop court on West Third Street I pause, my fingers in the fence. Five-on-five, full-court, under the lights. One dribble and then launch a thirty-footer, then turn and cock an ear to the crowd, letting their roar tell you you've split the metal nets again.

I cross the street, and suddenly I'm standing in front of the Waverly Theater. Where all this began.

I stand just where she stood, the woman I followed. Where she stood waiting for a stranger who had touched her, unbidden, in the dark. I remember the fear in her eyes. Terror. In her apartment I brought it out again.

I brought it out in all of them. In Melissa Clay. In Diane Silio. In Nina Torring. In Elise. Fear and, finally, pain.

I close my eyes, here in the middle of the busy sidewalk. It wasn't enough. I went further every time, and still it wasn't enough. It never would've been.

It is 9:30. Mimi Lessing is at home, dressing quietly. Thinking of the ties. Wondering if she will have the courage to open the door and walk inside. I touch the cell phone in my pocket, then take my hand away. If I were to call her, I'd tell her not to marry him.

I open my eyes. I turn away from the theater and walk slowly along West Fourth Street. Nina Torring's art gallery should be right around here. West Fourth, she said. I look out for it, remembering again her body under the lamps. Her stillness. The gleaming ring in her nightstand drawer. I walk past a tobacconist, a clothes store. Here it is. Tucked between a drugstore and a florist. White Swan Galleries. I walk to the glass.

She's had a break-in. The front door and windows are covered in yellow police tape. DO NOT CROSS is repeated all along it in thick black lettering. I start away but then turn back. I walk to the glass again. The gallery lights are out, but there's enough light from the street that I can see inside. The pictures hang on the wall undisturbed. The room is immaculate.

I walk into the drugstore next door. The Asian man behind the counter looks up, then back at the video he's watching on a small TV perched on a crate on the floor. I pick up a lighter from the stand in front of the register and hand him a five.

"What happened next door?" I ask.

He rings up the sale and makes change from the register. "Lady missing."

"Missing?"

He nods. "Missing."

"How long?" I ask.

He shrugs. "Store close one week."

I take the change and the lighter and step back outside. I walk back to the gallery glass. What could he mean, "missing"? I cross the street and start down West Fourth, passing the hoop court again, then the Blue Note jazz club. I walk to Bleecker, then to Sullivan, and turn right, the murmur of the Village dying quickly as I walk down the tree-lined block.

Three sixty-four Sullivan Street. Nina Torring's apartment. I look at the black gate, at the heavy mahogany door. At the flowerpots, filled with rich earth and roses. "My New York garden," she had said as she took out her keys. Across the street is an outdoor café. The Caffe Lune. I walk over and take a seat at a sidewalk table. A young waitress comes from inside and sets a coaster in front of me.

"Hi," she says.

"Hi. Absolut and tonic, please."

"Sure. Lime?"

"Yes."

She walks back inside.

I stare across the street at Nina Torring's apartment. The waitress returns with my drink and sets it in front of me. I take a long sip.

Missing.

CHAPTER NINETEEN

We have left the city behind us, and the river as well, and now in the darkness the suburbs slip away. I watch the white lines of the Thruway vanish beneath the car, and I listen to the smooth murmur of its engine. And to the only other sound — the soft breathing I know so well.

Soon the chloroform will wear off. It pained me to use it, to see her beautiful eyes dilate in terror as I pressed the soaked cloth to her face. But I had no choice. The work we have before us tonight requires privacy, and space. And so I cut loose from the posts the silk ties that bound her hands, and dressed her on the bed in the clothes she had folded neatly and laid on the chair by the window. I gathered together the items that had seduced her — the tape player, the lamp, the blindfold, and last of all the four ties — and slipped out the door and walked across the parking lot to the car. I drove the car into the space in front of room twenty, then surveyed the lot around me. It held only other cars.

Thirty yards away, through the window of the motel office, I could see the desk clerk sitting with his back to me, the phone to his ear. I activated the front-desk Øre, and his casual voice came through the car speakers. A personal call. I stepped from the car and opened the far back door, the one that faced only the ice room and the fence. I slipped back into room twenty.

It took only seconds to carry Miss Lessing to the car door and ease her into the backseat. She slept there beneath a quilted blanket until we had passed safely through the toll plaza and onto the Thruway we travel now. A short while ago, in the far corner of the John Jay Memorial Rest Area, beside a thick bank of trees, I watched the last of the few cars disappear back onto the open road. Working carefully in the dark, I moved Miss Lessing to where she rests now. Beside me.

Her hands are tied behind the passenger seat with one silk tie, her ankles bound in front of her with another. She is more delicate than I have ever imagined. Her complexion is pure, her body light and graceful. Looking at her slender neck, at her face tucked into her chest in sleep, I see again the innocent young woman of a year ago. And I can almost convince myself that there has been some mistake.

I grip the wheel tighter and look back at the road.

Just hours ago I sat three blocks from the Century Motel, listening through the car stereo as Jake Teller canceled the reservation to room twenty. I closed my eyes in gratitude and touched my head gently to the top of the steering column. She had refused him. I drove to her block and parked in front of La Boheme, from whose window I had watched her on so many evenings. I lowered the car window to let in the cool night air, and I activated her apartment Øres.

And heard, twenty minutes later, Miss Lessing ask the operator for the street address of the Century Motel.

I stared into the car speakers. And as I sat there, the truth sinking in like slow poison, Kreisler began to play. "Caprice Viennois." I looked out the window at the block I had learned to see through her eyes. At the delicate stonework of the prewar building, the watercolors in the window of the art gallery. At the slate of wines on the chalkboard at Vine. Kreisler played on, her favorite violin refrain approaching. I turned off the car stereo and sat for a few minutes in the nighttime quiet. Then I started the car and pulled away.

I had just enough time to rent and prepare the room. And then to park again a few blocks from the Century Motel. I sat in the driver's seat, my eyes closed, listening to the silence of room twenty. Ten o'clock came. Silence. 10:01. 10:02. 10:03. Could it be? Through the car speakers came the soft, damning click of the motel-room door. She had come.

She stirs. I look over quickly. She lifts her face from her chest, whispers something, then gives in again to the soft pull of unconsciousness. I reach with a gloved hand and touch her cheek. She stirs

again, her light perfume reaching me. Now she is
still. I look back at the black road.

The others were never pure. Not the young
florist and not the waitress who succeeded her.
Claire was her name; she poured espressos and
lattes at a First Avenue café. A young woman who
wore light colors, even in winter, and kept a place
in her heart for the older customers. "Go sit," she
would say. "I'll bring it to you." A young woman
who spent her breaks curled in the café corner,
reading Kerouac and Burroughs.

A young woman whose boyfriend, I soon discovered, brought cocaine to her each Friday night. Cocaine she could not afford on a countergirl's salary,
so she paid him another way. As I listened.

We drive now past dark, forgotten commuter
towns. Ardonia. Port Ewen. Saugerties. We are
sixty miles from our destination. An hour, no more.
I look again from the road to her clear, smooth face.

The others were never pure. Miss Lessing was.
She stirs again, with more authority now, wetting
her lips, shaking her head once, slowly. I look back
at the dark Thruway.

She will soon be again.

CHAPTER TWENTY

"Another?"

"No, thanks."

The waitress smiles and walks back inside. I leave a five for her in the bill tray, step through the gate and out onto the sidewalk. I look across the street again, at the dark mahogany door of Nina Torring's apartment building. I wonder if her husband is in there, waiting by the phone. My old teammate, Nick Simms. Maybe that's it. Maybe she left him and won't call. I start up Sullivan Street, toward Bleecker. Just before the corner I turn around and look back, but I see only the empty sidewalk and the dark trees that have been planted every twenty feet.

I turn onto Bleecker, glad for the lights of the Village again. A breeze brings the scent of pesto out the open door of an Italian restaurant. In its window are loaves of bread, arranged like flowers. I step to the curb and wave down a cab.

"Eighty-first and Amsterdam," I tell the driver.

We make our slow way west through the crowded Village, then up the West Side Highway, and now across again. "Right here is fine," I tell him at the corner of Eighty-first Street, and step out into the cool spring night and walk the half block to my apartment. On the front steps I look at my watch. 10:30. Mimi is home by now, or else with her fiancé. If she ever went to the Century Motel at all.

I let myself into my building and climb the three flights to my floor. I walk down the short hallway to my apartment door and slip my key into the lock.

"Jake Teller?"

I turn to see a man step down into the hallway from the stairs between the fifth and sixth floors. He looks about fifty, and he is wearing a gray suit jacket, neatly cut. He stretches his legs, as though he's been sitting there for some time; as he walks toward me, he reaches into his jacket and in one quick, easy motion comes out with a police badge. I've never seen one up close.

"Yes, I'm Jake Teller," I say.

"I'm Detective Crusin. Can I ask you a few questions? Five minutes, tops."

"About what?"

"A missing woman."

I look at him. Beneath his glasses, his dark eyes are sharp. "Let's go inside," I say.

We step into the small kitchen, and I close the door behind us. We stand facing each other.

"You want something to drink?" I ask him.

"Yes. Water, please."

I step past him, take a glass from the cupboard and some ice cubes from the freezer. *Nick Simms. Nina told him.* As I fill the glass at the sink, I can feel the detective taking in the place. The messy living room, the open door to the bedroom. I turn to see him pulling out one of the low-back chairs from the kitchen table. I hand him his glass of water, and he sets it on the table, next to the iron, which still stands upright. He sits down, and I sit across from him.

"Did her husband give you my name?" I ask him.

"Husband?" he says, a hard edge to his voice. "Her doorman gave me your name."

I feel a touch like cold steel in my spine.

"Doorman?"

"Clete Reynolds." He watches me closely. "Your old friend."

"Elise?" I say. "Elise is missing?"

He sits quietly for a few seconds, his hands resting on his legs.

"Not legally. Not yet. But she missed her mother's fiftieth-birthday party last night, a party that she helped plan. She missed class this morning. No one can reach her."

"If she's not miss —"

"I went to school with her father." His voice is tight. He takes a pen and a small notebook from his suit jacket. He pages through the notebook, then looks back at me. "The doorman thought Elise might be with you."

I shake my head. "I saw her last Friday night. That's it."

"You're not her boyfriend?"

"No."

"She told the doorman you are."

"We had one date."

"Last Friday."

I nod.

"What did you do?"

"We went to a bar."

"And then?"

The speed of his questions is disarming. I almost reach for his glass of water, which sits untouched on the table. Instead, I stand and walk to the refrigerator. I take out a can of Coke and open it. "After the bar, we went to her place," I say, my back to him. I walk to the chair and sit down again.

"Just the two of you?"

I pause. "Her roommates were away."

"The two of you were alone?"

I look at the table, then at the iron. On its metal face I can see threads of white silk. *This guy knows whatever Clete knows.* I meet his eyes again.

"A friend of mine came up for a little while."

"What's your friend's name?"

I look away again, then back at him.

"I can't tell you her name, Detective."

"Why not?"

"Because she wasn't supposed to be there."

He lowers the notebook to his leg and looks hard at me.

"A girl is missing," he says.

"Not legally."

His eyes flash, and then he smiles grimly.

"She probably went away for the weekend," I say.

"Probably. That's what I told her parents." He runs a hand through his slick hair, then reaches for the glass of water and turns it slowly. Then he clips his pen onto the notebook and slides the notebook back into his suit jacket. "Do you have a business card?" he asks quietly.

"Yeah."

I take out my wallet, find one, and hand it to him. He turns it in his fingers, and then he looks out into the living room for a few seconds, and finally back at me.

"Last Friday night, Mr. Teller, Elise's neighbors . . . *heard things.*"

Somehow I hold his eyes. He waits for me to say something. I'm quiet.

"What do you think they heard?" he asks.

Again I'm quiet. Ten seconds, he waits. I can hear the soda fizzing softly in the can. Finally, he takes out a card of his own from his jacket pocket and lays it on the kitchen table.

"When you figure it out, I suggest you call me. Because if Elise isn't in class Monday morning, I'm going to come by" — he looks down at the card I gave him — "Hyson, Levay, and I'm going to take you into your boss's office and ask you some pretty hard questions."

He lets his words sink in, then stands up and slides the chair carefully back under the kitchen table. He walks to the front door and unlocks the deadbolt. He turns around.

"Who did you think was missing, Jake?"

"No one."

"No one," he says. He nods, then opens the door and leaves.

I listen to his footsteps reach the stairs, start down them, fade, and disappear. I sit still for a few minutes, then stand and walk slowly to the sink. I dump out the Coke and rinse the can carefully with hot water. I set it on the counter. I walk into my bedroom and sit down on the bed.

Elise Verren is missing. And Nina Torring.

I go to the dresser and find on top of it the phone number for Anne Keltner. Mimi Lessing's maid of honor. The first seduction I let her witness. I lift the cordless phone from its wall mount and dial her number. Two rings, and then her voice.

"Hi. I'm not here. Say the right things, and I'll call you back. Bye."

Her voice is playful, assured, as it was at the Roosevelt Hotel in the first moments. The *beep* of her answering machine sounds and I cut the call. I walk out into the living room to the far window. I push it open and step out onto the fire escape. The night air is a relief. I lean on the black railing and look down at the street below. I watch the flowing lights of the taxis, listen to the rising nighttime murmur of the city.

Mimi witnessed the seduction of three women. Two of them are missing and the third isn't home. I shake my head. No. *One* of them is missing —

Nina Torring. Elise Verren has high-strung parents.
She could have met somebody last night, the way
she met me a week ago, and she could have blown
off her mother's birthday, and her class today.
Anne Keltner could be anywhere — it's Friday
night.

I run my hands over the rough black railing and
breathe in the hard, mineral smell of the night. I
look at the windows of the building across the
street. Most of the blinds are drawn, but a few are
open, and through one I can see a young woman,
standing at the counter in her lit kitchen. She is
mixing something in a bowl.

But what if Elise really is missing? What does it
mean? The only connection in this world between
Nina Torring and Elise Verren is that I seduced
them and Mimi watched. But no one could possibly
have known. I've told no one. Mimi . . . there's no
way she's told a soul.

The young woman across the way looks up suddenly from her mixing bowl, wipes her hands on
her apron, and answers the phone. She smiles,
leaves the counter, and sits down at her kitchen
table. She twists the phone cord in her fingers as
she talks.

Only one person has ever seen Mimi and me together. Anne Keltner.

The young woman looks out her window. She
looks away, and then out her window again. She
stands, lays the phone on the table, and walks to
the window, her smile gone. She looks straight

across, at this building, this fire escape, at me. She lowers the blinds.

I stare at the closed blinds, and it hits me — someone is watching. If Elise Verren really is missing, then someone has been watching us. Nick Simms? No way. If he had found out, he would have come straight at me. Who else? No one on my side. Mimi then. Her fiancé? Not likely. He doesn't strike me as a fighter. Who, then? Anne Keltner is the only one who's ever seen us together. I close my eyes. No, that's not quite true. Mr. Stein saw us together. Brought us together, the morning he assigned us to the Brice account. And then again the day we prepped him for their lunch. But Mr. Stein, our senior partner, a voyeur? Violent?

I open my eyes and stare now into the rusted, peeling metal of the black railing. *Andrew Brice requested her.* That's what Mr. Stein said. Twenty years without even one question for the firm, and then one morning he calls and requests Mimi Lessing. What was it she said? She had met him a year earlier, at the elevators. *For thirty seconds.* I look down into the street again, at the lit doorways of the apartment buildings, the dark walkers making their way toward Amsterdam. I shake my head. It's too crazy. But why does an old man request a young woman that he met for thirty seconds a year before? Because she's beautiful, that's why. Okay. But why does a cop, who could've gotten my number a hundred ways, wait in my hallway to talk to me if he's just doing a favor for a friend? If he doesn't think in his gut that Elise is missing?

I breathe in the night air a last time, then step back through the window and close it behind me. I latch it, walk to the bedroom, and pick up the phone.

CHAPTER TWENTY-ONE

"Please answer me. Please."

Even in terror she is beautiful. Even with the high red of her cheeks gone white.

She woke gradually, and then all at once she began kicking her bound ankles off the car floor and twisting her body in an effort to see what held her wrists. Then she looked suddenly at me and was still. I had imagined this moment in so many ways, but never like this. Shock, then recognition, then terror flooded her brown eyes.

"Andrew Brice," she whispered, and I was riven by the sound of my name from her lips. I kept the wheel steady and looked back at the dark road ahead of us.

"Where are we going?" she asked, her voice trembling. I didn't answer. "Why?" she asked a minute later.

She has courage. For five miles she sat without speaking. She tested the strength of the silk, quietly twisting her bound hands behind the seat back. She searched the darkness outside her window. She tried, somehow, to imagine what had brought her here and what might see her through. But now, as we pass the sign for Medway and she sees how far from the city we have come, the silence and the darkness and the strict ties overwhelm her.

"Please answer me," she says. "Please."

I reach with one hand for the storage compartment between our seats. She leans away from me, toward the car door. I lift the top and remove a plastic case. I take a cassette tape from the case and slip it into the stereo. Silence for a few seconds, and now, filling the car, soft, plaintive piano.

"Convento Di Sant'Anna."

I watch the shock register in her eyes. Her wrists are suddenly still.

"Nina," she whispers, almost too low for me to hear.

Yes, Nina.

I spread Nina Torring as Jake Teller had spread her, leaving her eyes free so that she might see the metal instruments laid out beside her on the black felt. She remembered everything. The length of the binds. The position of the lamps. The order of the music. When she had given me every detail I needed, I asked her why she had allowed it. I told her that if she could make me understand, truly understand, she would be released.

No one can be introspective under torture. But under the threat of it, yes. Such concentration. She had grown up in a strict household. She was sure that was part of it. She had learned to value control.

I took a cloth from the stand beside me, and her eyes followed my hands as I selected a sharp length of metal from the felt and began to polish it. Please. Control. She had learned to value control. Above all else. And so to surrender that control . . . to have it taken away . . . Did I see? And it was only once. Would only ever have been once. Please. The perspiration poured down her Nordic face, and still she strained for precision. For truth. It hadn't just been surrender. No, it had been something else. Something more. Release. That had been it. Yes, release. She had wanted release. Please. Could I understand that? Please.

"And what of your vows?" I asked her, and laid the polishing cloth aside and raised the shining metal to the light.

Now we pass the sign for Ravena as the last piano notes fade. In the silence before the next song begins, Miss Lessing tries to meet my eyes. She cannot, so she is looking down into her dress when the twin acoustic guitars begin to play. Peaceful, meandering. Her slender legs shake now, as if she has stepped from cold water. They shake because she recognizes the music again. The song that played as I sat in my car, across the street from the Harlem apartment, listening not only to these gentle Spanish guitars but to the gasps and the cries of Elise Verren.

Elise, too, was given to understand that her lies would be punished. That the truth might set her free. And she, too, remembered everything. From her I learned of his toys. She described each in detail — its attributes, its purpose. And when I needed no more, I showed her that I, too, had toys. Harder ones.

A new sound intrudes, and Miss Lessing turns her face toward the backseat. Her purse lies back there, on the floor, and coming from inside it are the tones of a cell phone. Two rings. Three rings. Four. She looks at me desperately, and again toward her purse. Five rings. Six. And now silence. She closes her eyes, and I see tears start down her cheek.

She is quiet as we drive on. The Spanish guitars build, build, and now finish, leaving us in deep, intimate silence. Lines of perspiration have broken on her forehead. She waits, tensed, for the next song. And as the violin starts up, she gives a soft sigh of shock.

"No one could know," she whispers, biting her lip in anguish.

Kreisler. "Caprice Viennois."

She fights to control her breathing. "Please," she says, but as the magic refrain approaches, I hold up a hand for silence, and this gesture and then the notes themselves make her turn her face into the leather seat. These seventeen pure notes were *her* notes. She had confided their beauty to no one, not even her fiancé, and yet here they are, chosen by the man who drives her, bound, into the night.

The notes end, giving way to the body of the piece again, and I engage the turn signal, its steady click cutting through the music for a few seconds as I ease into the right lane and then onto the exit ramp. Miss Lessing looks back, back toward the relative safety of the Thruway, and now ahead through the windshield at the empty, desolate rest stop before us.

I pull in behind the low brick restrooms to a spot hidden from the rest of the lot but with a view of the exit ramp behind us. I turn off the engine, then turn the ignition key to auxiliary, so that Kreisler can continue to play. I release the trunk latch. "Please," she whispers, meeting my eyes now, trying to measure my intentions, my limits. I use the button beside me to lower her window. The touch of the night wind on her face makes her gasp and close her eyes and breathe in deeply what must to her be the smell of freedom.

I step out my door and walk to the trunk. I open the stout black bag and take from it the cloth I used at the Century Motel. It still reeks of chloroform, but I hold it over the mouth of the heavy glass bottle and douse it again, and then, holding it out and away from me, I step to her window.

"Please," she says, "you have to —" but her words are lost as I hold the cloth with one hand over her nose and mouth. She struggles, and now is still. I take the cloth away, and her face falls softly to her breast and rests there. I remove my gloves. I touch her hair. I look down at her bosom, at her dress, at the two inches of smooth leg above her socks. I touch my fingers to her cheek.

Something in the wind reaches me, and I turn.

In the distance a set of headlights break the darkness, just beginning their slow approach down the exit ramp. I must work quickly. I open the back door and untie her hands, then ease her into the backseat, as I did at the motel, covering her with the same quilt. I return the soaked cloth and gloves to the black bag, close the trunk, and step to my door. The twin headlights are just now reaching the rest area proper.

I slide behind the wheel. I pull out from behind the brick restroom and start across the lot, our refrain playing for its final time now. Music from another age — measured, graceful. I accelerate onto the ramp and gain the Thruway again, merging into the well-spaced, northbound lights. In five minutes we will be safely through the toll plaza.

In fifteen we will be home.

CHAPTER TWENTY-TWO

The cowbell over the door chimes as I walk into Aquarius, an old-time sixties bar on Seventy-eighth and Broadway. Acoustic guitar pours from speakers mounted in the ceiling corners. Any song that played at Woodstock is on the jukebox in here. I look to the back and see that the wooden booths are all filled, so I take a window seat along the rustic bar. The bartender, his hair pulled into a graying sixties ponytail, makes his way down to me. I order two Guinnesses and watch as he pours them the right way, in stages, taking other orders as the dark ale settles.

Jeremy will be here any minute with the copy of the Brice file that I took to his place a month ago, the night he prepped me on financial instruments.

"What's going on?" he asked me on the phone.

"Just meet me," I told him.

The bartender returns and puts two pints of Guinness in front of me. I watch the heads settle, the foam cascade in layers to the bottom. At the

Knicks game, Jeremy said something about the Brice file. He said something about it not being clean. I didn't want to hear it at the time. The cowbell rings again, and I look up to see him walk in the front door. Even in Armani, and with a sharp leather briefcase under his arm, he still looks like a high-school senior. He takes the barstool beside me and lifts his pint of Guinness to mine.

"Cheers," he says, his eyes sparkling the way they used to on the morning of a big exam. He pulls a manila folder out of his briefcase and lays it on the bar. "I wondered when this would pique your interest, Jake. Is he in trouble?"

"I don't know. What did you mean at the Garden, Jeremy, when you said his file wasn't clean?"

He taps it with the bottom of his pint glass.

"You've read it, right?" he asks.

"We aren't at TDX anymore. I do some of my own work now."

He puts up a hand. "Just asking." He pauses. "You remember it?"

"Brice inherits a pile from his dad. Liquidates everything, except for a . . . farm upstate somewhere."

"A winery. In Albany."

"Right. Which he sells a year ago." Jeremy watches me, nodding intently. He waits for me to go on. "That's pretty much it," I say.

He shakes his head sadly. "You missed it, Jake," he says softly. "The red flag." He opens the folder and hands me a sheet of paper. I squint to read it in the low light. It is the deed of sale, transferring ownership of the winery from Andrew Brice to the Iliad Corporation. I look it over, then back at Jeremy.

"See anything wrong with that?" he asks.

I examine it again. "The price," I say finally.

"What about it?"

"Too low."

"Bingo." Jeremy takes off his glasses and hooks them into his shirt pocket. "Thirty acres outside Albany," he says, "with a winery on the grounds. Worth fifty grand when he inherited it in 1970. Thirty years later, he sells it for two hundred."

"A third of what he could have gotten. A quarter."

Jeremy nods.

"So he's a bad businessman," I say. "Where's the crime in that?"

Jeremy sits quietly for a few seconds, as if with a little time it might all become clear to me.

"You've seen his portfolio," he says finally. "What there is of it. Don't you think Brice is too cheap to be that bad a businessman?"

"Yeah."

"I thought so, too. So I did some digging." Jeremy puts his glasses back on and leafs through the papers in the folder. "Brice sold the winery to the Iliad Corporation. Six months later the Iliad Corporation sold it to Seine, Incorporated. Six months later they sold it." He holds up copies of the three sales deeds. "It's amazing what you can find on the Internet." He lays them back on the bar and looks at me again, expectant.

"You lost me," I say.

Jeremy sips his pint again, then rests it carefully on the bar.

"Have you ever heard of a nesting scheme, Jake?"

"No."

"It's named after those Russian nesting dolls. You know the ones — you take the head off, there's another one just like it inside. You take that one off, there's another one. Then another one."

"Sure."

"Here's how it works. You have a piece of property, right? You sell it to a dummy corporation that you've set up. A short time later, that dummy corporation sells it to another dummy corporation. That one then sells it to another. And so on. We studied this in b school. It was all the rage in South America in the eighties among the drug lords. Anyplace they had something big going on, they'd pull a nesting scheme. That way, if the drug lab blew up, they've got a piece of paper saying they sold the property years ago."

"And the paper trail back to them is a wild goose chase."

"Right."

"Okay, I get it. What's it have to do with Brice?"

Jeremy takes off his glasses again and holds them against his leg.

"I think Brice has a nesting scheme going."

"Meaning what?"

"Meaning the companies that bought the winery

are dummy corps that he made up. He never really sold it at all, Jake. The winery is still his."

I reach for the manila folder, slide it in front of me on the bar, and page through it until I find the piece of paper I'm looking for. "Only one problem with that theory, Jeremy." I hold up the paper. "Canceled check. Seventy grand to the IRS. And right here, on the memo line: *Sales tax on winery*."

Jeremy doesn't even look at the canceled check. He looks at me. Patiently, until he sees in my eyes that it's starting to sink in.

"That's why a nesting scheme works, Jake," he says quietly. "Because you pay the IRS. Who would ever think to question it? Remember, it's not money you're trying to hide. It's ownership. And you pay to hide it."

"That's why the sale price was so low."

He nods. "Brice made it as low as he thought he could get away with."

"But he's out seventy grand," I say.

"Yes."

"Why?"

Jeremy sighs. "I have to admit, the 'why' got me." He looks at me. "I had Pardo swing by the place last week."

I laugh. "You bulldog. Pardo?"

"He's in Albany half the time, right? Ten minutes away. Well, every nesting scheme I've ever seen, it's because the owner's up to something on the property. So I had Pardo drive over and take a look."

"What did he find?"

"Nothing. The place is overgrown, abandoned. The winery itself is crumbling."

"So there goes your theory."

"Down in flames. Still, Jake, it's strange. Three different companies own the property in one year. What are the chances that none of them would do anything with it? But that's what happened. Iliad buys it — does nothing. Seine buys it — does nothing. Lessing Winery buys it — again, nothing."

I look at him.

"What winery?" I ask.

"Lessing Winery. The last dummy corp. The one who owns it now."

I pick up the three sales deeds from the bar and shuffle through to the last one. There it is, under buyer:

LESSING WINERY

I look for the sale date.

MAY 1, 1999

"Jesus."

"What is it, Jake?"

I stare at the deed again. LESSING WINERY. *Mimi Lessing*. I stare at the type until it starts to blur. In my head I hear again Mr. Stein's words to Mimi. *You made a stronger impression on our legacy than he did on you.*

"Jake?"

"One second." I open my wallet and take from behind my license the scrap of paper with Mimi's phone numbers on it. I take my cell phone from my jacket. I hesitate, then dial her home number. Three rings, and then her machine. I dial her cell phone. It rings. Twice. Three times. Four, five, six. I cut the call.

"I need one more favor, Jeremy."

"What's that?"

"Your car."

CHAPTER TWENTY-THREE

The Spanish town of Cagaya once served the Crown by providing interrogators for the Inquisition. It was a profession passed down within families through generations, and there is still an alley off Cagaya's main square that the residents call Torturer's Lane. At the end of it is a redbrick building that pays grim homage to the town's place in history. It is a leather-goods store, but on its walls hang working replicas of the devices that wrung confessions from the damned three centuries ago. None are offered for sale to the public, but if a passionate collector should make his way to the store, he would find the proprietor to be a man of business.

I stand inside the front door of the winery my father purchased in 1968. It lies in ruins. In one corner stand the rusted press and crusher, in another the collapsed bottling machine. Beside the weathered front door is a gnarled pile filled with woven picking baskets, steel trellises, and field boots.

Nothing in it has been touched in three decades. Along the side wall are two 500-gallon stainless-steel tanks, meant to ferment the wines my father would craft in his retirement. They have stood empty for thirty years now, casualties of the cancer that struck him down.

I lean my shoulder against the heavy, rusted front door and push it closed, sealing out the moonlight and the intermittent sounds of the country night. The 5,000-square-foot winery is quiet now, and most of its expanse lies in darkness. But not all of it. Ten yards in front of me is a large circle of light. I start toward it across the packed earth floor. The light emanates from within a ring of barrels. Forty-four barrels of white French oak, double-stacked to a height of five feet and arrayed in what would be a perfect circle except for the opening in front of me. Each barrel is filled with cabernet sauvignon, and together they give off the damp aroma of wood and wine that permeates the air of the winery.

I stop in the opening and touch one of the rough, stained barrels with my fingers. Within this ring of barrels, facing one another in two rows of three, are six standing heaters, each sending its heat down and toward the center. Within these rows of heaters, across from each other, are two 300-watt lamps, each again training its bright light into the center of the circle. And in that center is Miss Lessing.

Three hours ago I found her spread wide and stripped to her barest lace. She is again. I enter the

ring of barrels and walk to her side. She is starting
to stir, starting to break free of the narcotic pull of
the chloroform. Her brow is clear and relaxed, and
now she wets her lips, imagining maybe that she is
as before, bound lightly on a motel-room bed,
awaiting the soft touches of Jake Teller.

As her senses return, she will realize that she is
not lying on a bed at all, but on a table of hard canvas. And when she tests the binds that secure her,
she'll find that instead of the soft silk that inflamed
her imagination, her hands are fitted now into
gloves of coarse, strong, old-world leather. And
closed tight around each ankle is a heavy strap of
the same hide.

The black blindfold covering her eyes will keep
her from seeing that each glove, and each anklet,
forms the end of a thick coil of leather, the other
end of which is stitched to the spoke of a receiving
wheel. These four receiving wheels, one beside
each corner of the canvas table, are in turn con-
nected to a master wheel just past the head. The
master wheel is made of heavy wood and stands
five feet high, as tall as the helm of a ship. Turning
it requires strength; but when turned, it moves each
of the receiving wheels as well, winding the leather
coils around their spokes and thus pulling each
glove, and each anklet, toward its corner. Along
with the limbs they hold.

I watch her fingers flex in surprise, and I see the
muscles in her thighs tense as she tries in vain to
bring them together. "No," she whispers, waking
now. "Where . . . please."

I step closer to her.

"Who's there?" she asks, trembling. She turns her face toward me.

I don't answer, but step to a small stand a few feet away. On it is a cassette player. I press the PLAY button. And now I step back to her and place my hands for the first time onto the smooth white canvas table. The table that forms the base of the device that the old torturers of Cagaya called the *revealer*.

Its true name is the Spanish rack.

CHAPTER TWENTY-FOUR

I'm not ready to let her go.

That's all it is. So I'm headed up the New York State Thruway at one in the morning. Headed for an abandoned winery where I expect to find . . . what? I'll look around in the dark, and then I'll drive to Pardo's place and do what I should have done with Jeremy in the city — get drunk.

Pardo couldn't believe I was coming up. I asked him if he knew any place we could get a beer after 2:00 A.M. He knows five that don't start serving until 3:00. When you work for the governor, apparently everyone in town wants to make you happy. "We'll end up at Nirvana, Jake," he said, his voice exultant. "A bar for the ages. It's where the dancers go when the strip clubs close."

I pass the sign for West Point, keeping Jeremy's Grand Am at a steady seventy-two. Only a few scattered lights break the darkness of the road ahead.

Brice met Mimi one time by the elevator. He

made certain that she worked his account. And he named a winery after her. A winery he doesn't want anyone to know he owns.

That's it. That's all I have. And Nina Torring. And Elise Verren.

I inch up to seventy-five. Ahead of me, shining in the headlights, is the first road sign for Albany.

Fifty miles.

CHAPTER TWENTY-FIVE

Her skin shimmers in the strong light, oiled not by crude hands but by the perspiration drawn out of her by the heaters, her fear, and now her pain. Thirty minutes ago her wrists were two feet apart. Now they are five. Her ankles, too, each pulled toward a canvas corner as the receiving wheels — turning in sync with the master — wind the leather coils around their spokes. I step away from the heavy master wheel and move to her side.

She lies in quiet, pained concentration, fighting to keep her breathing deep and even. She has a runner's frame and great courage. The others by this stage were crying out in wrenching sobs. She has spoken just three times, once after each turn of the wheel. "Mr. Brice," she said, "please stop." More urgently each time, but this simple plea and nothing more.

I look from her to the tray that stands beside the rack. The tray is covered by a black felt cloth, and on it lie three shining metal instruments. I pick up the middle one, a four-inch fork with two sharp prongs at either end. Attached to its center is a leather collar, as thin as a necklace. I hold the fork up to the light and then turn back to her.

Perspiration has soaked her brassiere and the other piece of bare lace that covers her. I lift my eyes back to her face. In the set of her mouth, in the soft movements of her head, I can see that she is trying through strength of will to escape her pain. I lay my hand on her forehead and bring her back. She gasps. I press my fingers to her crimson cheek, which burns as though with fever, and then I slip my hands beneath her neck, and secure the thin leather collar around it. She gasps again as I tighten it, and again at the cold touch of metal, though I am careful to lay the fork lengthwise across her throat, facing its sharp prongs away from her skin.

"Please," she whispers.

I rest my hands on the edge of the canvas, watching as she wets her lips in desperation.

"Mr. Brice. Are you there?"

Rivulets of perspiration run down her face, but as my silence sinks into her, she finds her courage again. She sets her mouth and, almost imperceptibly, turns her head. I follow it and realize for the first time that she is escaping into the music.

Beethoven's *Eroica* has played softly through her increasing pain. It plays still, and she is concentrating her mind on it. Intently she listens, secretly, lifting her chin the barest amount to follow the rising notes of a flute as it flutters through the scherzo.

"Listen for the center of gravity," I say. "It pulls him back, no matter how far out he dares to go."

She turns her face sharply toward my voice.

"Thank you," she says. "Thank you for speaking."

I reach down and slide off the black blindfold and lay it beside her on the white canvas. She blinks in the strong light, struggling to make sense of what she sees. She looks quickly to her right hand, staring in fascinated horror at the leather glove that secures it. She looks down at her legs, and then around her, at the receiving wheels and at the tall heaters lining each side of the canvas rack. And now at me.

"You're here," she says, her voice almost a whisper. "You're here with me." Her eyes find mine and hold them. "Please, Mr. Brice. Whatever has happened. Whatever you think —"

"No words," I say. I lean toward her.

"Please," she says. "I'm sorry, but I must talk. To make you see —"

I touch her face and she turns it into the canvas, away from me. I turn it back, lifting her chin so that she faces me again, and take in my fingers the metal fork that rests on her throat. "God, please," she says frantically. "If you would just tell me why —"

I turn the fork, and she is silent.

It is called the Heretic's Fork, and it was another of Cagaya's tools of truth. Two sharp points rest beneath her chin now, two more on the bone of her sternum. The slightest movement of her head will drive the four points through her skin. The strap between the fork and the collar keeps it from slipping.

I look down at her. She is silent, barely able to part her lips to breathe. I turn and walk past the row of heaters to the barrels, where I stand in the sudden chill, my back to her. I breathe in the fragrant oak beside me and look up at the stainless-steel tanks, and beyond them at the dark rafters. Where the roof tiles have rotted away I can see up into the black country sky.

I close my eyes and see her again by the elevators that first morning. Unguarded innocence in her eyes. I turn to look at her. Within the leather gloves her hands are balled into fists. Her toes are pointed in pain. She lies perfectly still.

As *Eroica* starts into its finale, I walk back to her. I rest my fingers again on the edge of the canvas rack. The white lace of her brassiere is mesmerizing. It too has been stretched, and the swell of her bosom now presses against it. I glance down at the lace between her hips. It just barely conceals her. I look back to her face. Her pained eyes plead for mercy.

Their struggle.

The way you take away every defense. One by one.

I walk to the master wheel and grasp it firmly with both hands. I give it a half turn, and watch as the receiving wheels follow.

The pain sears her, but she can't cry out. She can only breathe sighs of agony. I step back to her. Perspiration pours down her face now, pooling in the well of her sternum, just below the sharp points of the fork. She tries to close her eyes in concentration, but they open again in fear and pain.

The pain is not in her wrists but in her shoulders, not in her bound ankles but above her slender thighs. Deep in the stretching ligaments it starts, soon to move through into the bone. She is lithe, limber, but already I can see the blades of her shoulders starting to rotate inward, and each muscle from wrist to shoulder, from calf to thigh, shines now in taut, desperate relief against her skin.

I walk back to the wheel and give it another quarter turn.

Another exhalation of pain from her. Deeper this time. Too deep. Returning to her side, I see the tiny dots of blood in the soft skin below her chin. Her back arches dangerously now, and though the points of the fork keep her silent, her shoulders have turned farther inward. The next turn of the wheel will pull them free of their sockets, and begin the deep, final hemorrhaging.

Eroica gathers for its finish. Beethoven wrote it for Napoleon, and within it is all the grandeur of conquest. She is beyond its solace now. All of the night's pain is concentrated in her eyes, and beneath that pain is understanding. She knows she can't endure another turn of the wheel, and so she watches me desperately.

I wait for the final notes to sound and fade, then lay my hand on her burning forehead.

"It's time," I tell her.

She closes her eyes in anguish as I step away

from her. I walk to the master wheel, take hold of the smooth wood, and brace myself. And now I give it a full, hard turn — back the other way. I step to her side again.

"To the brink and then back. Isn't that how he does it?"

I reach down and brush her damp hair from her forehead. Her wrists and ankles have been returned to the canvas, and her back and shoulders are level again. Tears of pain and relief stream down her crimson cheeks. She is still spread wide, brutally wide, but she is out of danger.

It is time I let her speak.

I take the Heretic's Fork carefully in my fingers. Engraved on its side is ABIURO. *I recant.* Those four soft syllables, requiring so little movement of the tongue, were all the fitted sinner could murmur before being led to the stake. I start to turn the fork away from her, but then raise my head suddenly. Above her low, pained breathing and the steady hum of the heaters is a new sound. I look quickly into her eyes. She closes them, but too late. She has heard it, too. I listen again, and the sound is louder, unmistakable now — churning gravel. A car is ascending the quarter-mile grade that leads from the service road to the winery clearing.

He has come.

I leave the sharp fork in its place. She opens her eyes and watches desperately, helplessly, as I pick up the black bag from the floor beside the rack and leave her. I walk quickly out of the ring of barrels and to the winery door. I kneel beside it. From inside the bag I take the bottle of chloroform and two fresh sets of gloves. The car is closer now, no more than fifty feet from the clearing. I pull on one set of gloves, and over them a second, industrial pair, and then take a rusted pail from the pile of forgotten refuse by the door. I stand the pail upright and empty the bottle of chloroform into it, careful to turn my face into my shirt and breathe in short breaths. I reach back into the black bag and take from it a heavy leather mask. I drop the mask into the chloroform and, using a steel trellis from the pile beside the door, force the mask below the surface and pin it to the bottom of the pail. I hold it there, listening as the grinding of gravel reaches the clearing, then ceases. A car engine cuts off.

I lift the mask from the chloroform, take it in my gloved hands, and wring it out. I keep my face turned into my shirt, but still the fumes are toxic, suffocating. My eyes burn fiercely. A car door slams, and in the quiet night footsteps approach across the gravel clearing. I rise to my feet, holding the soaked mask at my side.

I keep behind the heavy front door of the winery as it opens in with a rusted creak. A strip of moonlight falls across the dark earth floor. Jake Teller steps inside. He is larger than I imagined, an athlete. I cannot afford to miss. He takes one, two, three steps into the winery, and stops still. Straight ahead of him is the opening to the ring of barrels. Through it he can see the rack, and on that rack, lit brilliantly, lies Miss Lessing. Stripped just as he strips them. Spread as he spreads them.

"Jesus."

I am only a step from him when he senses me. I pull the bottom of the mask open wide, and just as he starts to turn, I bring it down over his head. He swings sharply, his elbow crashing into my temple, and I fall hard to the winery floor. But even as I fall, I see him take, instinctively, the deep breath that dooms him. He falls to one knee, the chloroform flooding his lungs, and now to both; as he reaches in slow motion for the mask, he painfully takes his last free breath of the night and falls onto his side.

I put my hand to my mouth. I can taste blood, but I hurry to Jake Teller and press in on the nose of the mask. He jerks once and is still. I pull the mask off him and fling it into the pile by the door. I rise slowly to one knee, coughing and struggling to breathe, tears streaming from my burning eyes. I pull off my gloves and toss them onto the pile, too. I rise to my feet and stand above him, breathing deeply for almost a full minute. And I kneel again. I turn him, and look for the first time into the face of Miss Lessing's corrupter.

His strong jaw is slack now, and one of his cheeks brown with earth. I stand, grasp him beneath his arms, and begin to pull. I drag him ten feet at a time, stopping to rest on my knees. He is dead weight, exhausting, his heels catching again and again in the dirt. Finally, I reach the first of the two huge stainless-steel tanks. I lean Jake Teller against it. His head slumps onto his chest, and I rest for a few seconds, breathing heavily.

At the bottom of each steel tank is a small door

through which the wine is transferred to the oak barrels. I unlock the steel clasp and pull the door open. I turn my face away, gasping. From inside comes the acrid, hollow smell of death eternal. I rest again and then, marshaling the last of my strength, grab Jake Teller behind the knees and lift his feet into the low door, then ease his hips over its rim and, with a final shove, send him into the tank.

I close the door and seal the clasp. Inside, there is no handle of any kind. No break in the smooth steel. When he awakens, to grope in darkness, he will find only the walls of his tomb. And he will have perhaps an hour of air.

I walk slowly back to the ring of barrels. I pull a handkerchief from my shirt pocket and press it to my mouth. A cut lip, nothing more. I stop in the opening and look at Miss Lessing. She lies as before, still and silent in pure light. She can see only straight above her, and a few feet to either side, so she listens anxiously to my footsteps as I walk toward her. I step into her vision, and she closes her eyes in desolation.

I lean down and carefully turn the Heretic's Fork to its side, easing her torment. She swallows, and breathes deeply again and again. I take a cloth from the tray beside her and gently wipe the spots of blood from beneath her chin.

"Please," she says, her voice hoarse.

I take a bottle of water from the tray and put it to her lips, tilting it gently, now wiping away the spill.

"Jake," she says, her voice breaking for the first time. "Jake Teller. What —"

I press a finger into her taut biceps and she cries out in pain. I lift my finger away.

"We are alone again," I say.

"Please," she says, gasping, pain reducing her voice to a whisper. "Please."

I press the cloth to her forehead and then lay it on the tray. Two metal instruments remain on the black felt cloth. From a lower shelf of the tray I take two silver rulers and a deep ceramic bowl. Mounted on a spike in the bottom of the bowl is a wide-mouthed candle. I light the candle, place the bowl beside the black felt cloth, and lay the rulers across the mouth of it, one on either side of the flame.

She looks up into the darkness, then at me.

"Anne," she whispers, her eyes pleading for an answer.

Yes. She knows the fate of all the others. Of Nina Torring, Elise Verren, and now of Jake Teller.

"Anne Keltner," I say. "The Roosevelt Hotel. You were there, weren't you?"

She closes her eyes.

"Anne Keltner escaped to Spain," I tell her, and watch as she bites her lip in pained relief. "She returns tomorrow night at ten-twelve, on United Airlines flight six-seventeen."

"No," she whispers, shaking her head.

I look back at the tray. One of the remaining instruments is a thin scalpel. The other was my last purchase in Cagaya, and to look upon it is to feel in your bones the full, merciless, medieval weight of the Middle Ages. It is a single heavy piece of metal, black as plague, built like a pair of tongs but ending in four curling, jagged points that curve in toward each other but do not quite meet. Its purpose was to tear apart the breasts of women condemned of libidinous acts. I lift it from the felt cloth and set it carefully atop the silver rulers, so that the tips of its curved claws lie directly over the strong blue flame.

The *clink* of metal on steel breaks her anguished reverie, and she turns her face toward the tray. She begins to shake.

"God," she whispers, looking up into the darkness again, then shutting her eyes tightly. "God, please." I lay my hand on her forehead. "Please," she begs, her pained eyes opening and finding mine. "What have I done? Please tell me."

I don't answer.

"Please. Whatever —"

I lay a finger on the Heretic's Fork, and she falls silent.

The smell of burning rust is in the air now, and she cannot keep from turning to look again at the black pincers. She stares in mesmerized terror at the blue flame that heats the tips of their claws, then turns her face away into the white canvas. Her forehead still burns with fever, but she shakes as though from frost; now her breathing quickens and quickens until she is gasping for air. I press on her forehead to calm her, but her eyes are wild, unseeing, and she turns her face from side to side. I take her chin and hold it still.

"The truth can still save you," I say.

She fights, but I keep her still; now I meet her eyes. "It can save you," I say, and watch my words sink in and light in the back of her eyes the faintest spark of hope. I take my hand from her, and she remains still. I step back and see in her face that she is summoning from inside the last of her will. My eyes drift to the scant lace that covers her. I close them. My mind steadies, my concentration returns. I open my eyes and look into hers.

"I'll punish the slightest lie," I say.

She looks at the jagged pincers, then quickly away from them and up into the dark ceiling. I place my hands gently on the canvas rack.

"Elise Verren's pain," I say. "Did it excite you?"

Perspiration streams down her cheeks. She is quiet for ten seconds. Fifteen.

"Yes," she says.

She sees me close my eyes in disappointment.

"Please," she says. "I didn't know what would happen. What he would do."

I turn and look away from her. I look out beyond the circle of light into the dark reaches of the crumbling winery.

"You went to the Century Motel," I say.

She is quiet.

"Even your corrupter had limits. Even he turned back. You went to the Century. One week from marriage."

"Please." I hear the anguished catch in her breathing. I turn back to her. Her eyes look to the pincers, then back at me.

"On the bed at the Century, Mimi. When the second silk tie closed on your wrist and you were helpless. What did you feel?"

She closes her eyes and bites her trembling lip. I watch her temples pulse in concentration. This last year, as I listened, I learned to read her so well that I could tell her mood by the pitch of her breathing. And now looking down at her, I read her again, and though her eyes are shut tightly, I can see the lie forming behind them. She is searching for words, yes, but not for the truth. She searches only for the words that might free her.

Her eyes open. She's chosen them. But before she can speak, she sees me look at the pincers. The tips of their four claws glow orange now. She looks at them, too, then back at me, and starts to shake. And now to cry quietly. I've broken her will to lie.

"What did you feel?" I ask her.

The soft night wind stirs the rafters, and the receiving wheels creak quietly against the burden of the taut leather coils.

"Free," she whispers, her voice breaking.

CHAPTER TWENTY-SIX

I kill the engine.

I step out of the Grand Am and look up the hill at the winery. It is an old stone building standing in a moonlit clearing. Also in the clearing is a black car; beside the car is a pickup truck. Even from here, in the moon's light I can see, painted on the back gate of the pickup, a huge, grinning red skull. Pardo. I should have known. If he'd waited for me to get to his place, we might've missed out on half an hour of drinking.

I lean against the warm hood of the Grand Am. The gravel road in front of me leads up to the clearing but winds back and around the property. It would be a noisy drive. If I climb the hill in front of me, it's no more than a hundred yards. And no one would hear me.

Listen to me. Who's going to hear me? Pardo is up there drinking longnecks with a buddy. I shake my head and step back to the car door. I pause, my hand on the handle. The quiet out here is eerie, absolute. I listen for their voices, for the clink of a bottle. Nothing. I step away from the car to gain a better sight line, and look up to the clearing again. I can see the black car better now. On its hood, glinting in the moonlight, is the familiar silver orb. A Mercedes. I walk slowly back to the Grand Am. I squat on my heels in front of it, scooping up a handful of gravel and letting some fall through my fingers. The governor makes all his staffers buy American. Pardo told me that once. And I know Pardo's taste in late-night drinking buddies, and I can't picture any of them driving a Benz. I look up at the clearing again.

I toss the rocks to the ground, stand, and start up the hill. The night air is cold and bracing. There's enough of a moon that I can see my way, but it's slow going through high grass. Thick brush grabs at my legs as I climb. I jump at a sound in front of me, looking up to see the wide eyes of an owl in the branches of a tree. Christ. Give me the city and its terrors any night.

I keep climbing, using my hands for the last, steep ten yards, and then squeeze between two bushes and step out into the clearing. I wipe my hands on my slacks. I don't see Pardo, or anyone else. Twenty yards in front of me is the stone winery. The ground is gravel again, so I walk carefully to Pardo's pickup. There's no sign of him. A six-pack of Coors lies untouched on the front seat.

I walk to the black Mercedes. A strange smell seems to come from inside it, or beneath it. Some strong chemical. I look through the window. The

front seats are bare. I peer into the back. Nothing. A
sprawled blanket. Wait. I look again. I walk to the
other side of the car, getting the moonlight behind
me. I cup my hands against the glass. Jesus. I look
quickly around me, then back into the window, my
mouth as dry as the gravel beneath me.

The blanket in the back doesn't quite reach all
the way across the seat. Sticking out beneath it, just
barely visible, are the ends of two pieces of cloth.
Two white pieces of cloth.

Ties.

Her brassiere shines like white fire. I look hard at it
now. Beneath it her breasts are the same tone as the
rest of her — a soft cream, between milk and
caramel. I see the edge of a rose nipple. I reach
down and lay a finger on the strap of her brassiere.
She gasps in pain, but I keep it there, then run it
down the strap to the curved lace of the cup.

I listened for a full year, dreaming of a true communion between us. She has only ever had one form
of communion to offer.

I slide my finger under the strap and ease it up a
fraction of an inch, until I see her full red nipple.

"Please," she says.

My eyes move down to her hips. Viewed from
above, the triangle of lace covers her completely,
but from the side I can see the shadow of her hidden beauty. I take my hand away from her brassiere
and touch with the tips of my fingers the quarter
inch of taut lace that guards the skin of her hip. It is
damp and hot. I run my finger along it.

"The key to you is in here, is it?"

"Please."

I turn to the tray, pass my hand over the pincers, and lift from the black felt cloth the thin, shining scalpel.

I can see light through the front door of the winery.

I couldn't see it from across the clearing, but I am moving along the winery wall now and can see that the heavy front door is open. It is open a few feet, and from beyond it comes a strange, muted light. It might be moonlight, streaming through a gap in the roof. I'll know in seconds. I reach the door and pause beside it, standing with my back against the stone wall, feeling its cold through my jacket and shirt. I let out a quiet breath and look inside.

It isn't moonlight, and it's coming from straight ahead of me. Jesus. Coming from inside a circle of wine barrels. High-powered lamps, pointed in and down. Standing in the light is a man. It isn't Pardo. A man standing at some kind of table, like an operating table. Looking down at someone. Jesus Christ. A woman is on the table. Tied to the table. Stripped. Wheels and pulleys.

I drop to a knee. He'll see me if he turns, but I can only kneel here, frozen in the doorway, and stare at the table under the lights. Stare at the man who has to be Andrew Brice. And the woman — Mimi. *Move, Jake.* I move, low to the ground, to the only cover in the room — the circle of stacked barrels in front of me. I crouch down behind one, pressing my cheek against the wood.

No sounds. I stand and look carefully over the double stack. Brice stands at the middle of the table. Mimi's eyes are shut, her face turned away into the table. He is touching her. Jesus Christ, she is . . . spread, her hands and ankles held in some kind of cuffs. I duck behind the barrels again. Where the hell is Pardo?

My hands are slick with sweat. I check my pants pocket, quietly. Car keys, nothing else. And as I stare down at the dirt floor, it hits me. Brice would have heard Pardo coming.

Think, Jake.

Two barrels down from the one I hide behind is a gap in the circle. It's the only way in. From the gap to the table might be twenty feet. I stand and look again over the stack. Brice is touching her again. Lower now.

"The key to you is in here, is it?" he says.

"Please," says Mimi.

Brice reaches to a tray beside the table. He takes from it a shining blade.

I ease the scalpel between lace and hip, and I cut. I reach across her and cut again.

Her hips are bare now, and I am trembling. I stare down at the tiny triangle of lace that covers her. I lay my hand on her belly, an inch from the top of the lace. She gasps in pain, stretched so tightly that even this small pressure pierces her. I rub her skin gently. Never could I have imagined such softness. Such warmth. My fingers find the edge of the lace. I can feel her heat beneath it.

I close my eyes. So this is the dance that so entranced her. The slow, brutal seduction. The final
unveiling. And then . . .

No.

I release the lace and take my hand away. I open
my eyes.

I tremble still, but from anger now. Pure, saving
anger. I stare at the white lace. All that is left of her
purity lies beneath it, and in her final moments she
would lure me into removing it. No.

I look at the tray. The pincers are ready now,
their ends glowing red. Ancient, implacable. I reach
for them.

"Wait," she says, a pleading whisper.

The others begged, too. To the last.

She whispers again, so low that I cannot make it
out. I step to the head of the rack and lean down to
her. I will hear her final words.

"Touch me," she says.

I rush low and hard.

Mimi saw me. I stood in the opening and she
saw me, and she drew him to her. "Touch me," she
says, and Brice stares down at her. I need two more
seconds. One.

He whirls.

I can't stop in time. I get my arm up and feel the
blade slash through my jacket, my shirt, my skin.
I'm off balance, right in front of him, and he slashes
again, a full, hard uppercut. I feel the breeze from
the blade as it just misses my jugular, and I fall hard
to a knee, one hand on the ground, the other

clutched to my throat. I rasp as if cut and look down at the floor as if stunned.

My eyes watch his feet. Slowly, awkwardly, they square up to me. He'll bring the blade straight down now, like an ice pick. With all of his weight committed.

I pivot, roll, and rise.

He misses and falls to his knees, crying out, somehow keeping hold of the scalpel. He's welcome to it. I stand by the tray now, with a full second to lift from it one mother of a black iron claw, its sharp ends glowing with fire. I grip it tightly, and as Brice comes up with the scalpel in a clumsy, desperate swipe, I stop his elbow with one hand and drive the claw, with all I have behind it, up into his chest, feeling the crack of bone as the force of the blow lifts him to his feet.

He stands in front of me, gasping for air. He drops the scalpel and presses one of his hands, both of his hands, to the claw, holding it to him, pressing it into his broken chest as the blood seeps down around it. He staggers forward, past me, past the table.

"The wheel," Mimi says. "Jake."

I look at her, not comprehending, still stunned at the sight of Brice holding the claw in his chest as he moves. "Jake," Mimi screams now, and I see where Brice is going, to the tall wooden wheel ten feet past the head of the table, and I see that the wheel connects to the whole device, that it binds her, that it pulls her apart.

I start toward him, but it's too late.

Brice has reached the wheel now and leans against it, swaying, one hand on a spoke, the other holding the claw to his crushed, bleeding chest. He looks back at us, no, at Mimi, tries to speak, but blood spills from his mouth. I close in on him, but he lets go of the claw and grabs the wheel with both hands.

It won't turn.

He's too weak, and as I reach him, he slides down to the floor, clutching at the wood as he falls, landing facedown now at the base of the wheel with a strangled cry. I step back as he rolls over, his shattered chest heaving, heaving again, and then still, his hands seeming to cradle the claw into him, his wide eyes staring blindly into mine.

EPILOGUE

It's just the two of us now.

We've left everyone else behind. Pardo in the hospital, overnight for observation. The police in the winery and in the fields behind it. Brice in the morgue.

We've driven almost fifty miles in silence. Since Cementon, when I pulled into a gas station to get her a bottle of water. She drinks it now, curled up in the passenger seat, her legs tucked beneath her, my blue jacket around her shoulders.

The police tried to insist that she go to the hospital. They would call an ambulance for her. Mimi said no. They told us they would need to see us again tomorrow. I assured them we would stay local and gave them Pardo's address. But when we got into the car, we both knew, without having to say anything, that we would drive home to the city.

We pass the sign for Newburgh. It is almost six in the morning. Mimi looks out the window at the trees along the Thruway. She holds the Evian bottle in her lap in one hand. Her other hand rests on her neck, rubbing it gently.

The sharp tones of a cell phone break the air. We both start, and now look at each other. The tones come from the black purse at her feet.

"My fiancé," she says.

The phone rings three times, four. I watch the road ahead of me. Five, six, seven. The car is quiet again. Rain starts to fall as we pass the exit for Salisbury, the traffic gathering around us now as we near the city. Ahead of us on the right is a motel billboard.

"Pull off," Mimi says softly.

I keep driving. Another ten miles, only the sound of the wipers and the wet road beneath us. Highland Mills. Harriman. Arden. We're into Rockland County now. Almost home. Just ahead of us is another motel sign.

"Pull off, Jake."

I stay in the center lane until we're almost to the exit, then put on my signal, cross to the exit lane, and leave the Thruway. I pay the toll, bend around onto the short access road, and turn into the motel parking lot. I pull into a space in front of the motel office. I turn off the engine.

We sit together in the quiet car in the soft, spreading gray of dawn, both of us looking through the windshield at the motel. The rain has lessened but still it falls, streaking the windshield, and after a few minutes we can't see anything outside. Still we sit, in the warmth and peace of the car, listening to the muted whoosh and rumble of the big rigs on the Thruway behind us.

Her cell phone rings again. Mimi reaches into her purse and takes it out. It rings a second time, and she opens her door and throws the phone onto the wet pavement. It bounces, the ringer cuts off, and the phone disappears under a parked car. She shuts the door, closing out the rain and wind.

Mimi holds her hand out to me. I take my hand off the wheel and close it around hers. She looks into my eyes for the first time since we left the winery.

"A few more minutes, Jake," she says. "Then you can drive me home."

ACKNOWLEDGMENTS

Thanks to Michael Pietsch, Ryan Harbage, Stephen Lamont, and Audrey LaFehr. Thanks to my agent, Jillian Manus. Thanks to the reading group: Camille, Cyril, Jacob, Joe, Kay, Lora, Merrill, and Marcy. Thanks to David Gibson. Special thanks to my mother and father.